The Truth About Vampires

by

M L Martin

DORRANCE PUBLISHING CO
EST. 1920
PITTSBURGH, PENNSYLVANIA 15238

Dorrance Publishing Co
585 Alpha Drive
Pittsburgh, PA 15238
Visit our website at *www.dorrancebookstore.com*

ISBN: 978-1-6491-3324-3
EISBN: 978-1-6491-3291-8

Prologue

My father was a wonderful story-teller, well-versed in all the myths and legends of our culture, and my brother and I grew up on those stories that supplemented our more traditional education. All children were taught the creation myth, how the Known World with its five kingdoms was sung into existence by the Earth Mother. A lesser known extension of that myth concerned the birth of the Earth Mother's first children. The Terrans as they were called controlled the elements in nature. They contoured the land at their Mother's direction and manipulated the winds and the rain. They were a peaceful people dedicated to understanding how to maintain the balance between humans and the natural order. Unfortunately, part of their understanding was that they must sacrifice one of their own each year to maintain the favor of their creator. Other cultures found this practice barbaric and vowed to wipe the Terrans from the face of the earth. We were led to believe they succeeded, but the myth persisted in this part of the world. Many people of the North Kingdom believed we were descended from this race, so we cherished the story and kept it alive.

But my favorite stories my father told involved the beautiful and terrifying creatures which inhabited the shadows and preyed on unsuspecting mortals who were foolish or arrogant enough to venture out in the darkness. These creatures were everything we were not. They were strong and fast, intelligent, rich, and above all else, they were immortal. As a child, I was enthralled by these stories and welcomed that little shiver of fear I felt when Father told them. I was particularly starry-eyed with tales of unsuspecting human females who were swept off their feet by handsome vampire lovers. As I got older, I realized that these romantic tales often did not end well for the women involved and were more cautionary than romantic.

There were many other stories as well, most of which fell into the deep well of irrelevant fantasy and were forgotten. Others I discarded as I got older and my fascination waned. I realized the tales, which were really fables, were told to modify behavior and had no basis in fact. I was disappointed. The little girl in me still fantasized about meeting one of those beautiful beings who would change my life forever.

In retrospect, I wonder how many of the legends my father believed. Was he keeping a long-forgotten memory alive by passing on the oral history to his progeny? Was there some agenda behind our unusual education in things unseen or at the least unrecognized? What if the stories were true, and everything we were, every step in our evolution toward a civilized society, was engineered by those immortal creatures? It was unthinkable. After all we controlled our own destiny, didn't we? As a female in this society, I wasn't so sure. In reality, there were not many options for a woman outside marriage. As the "weaker sex," we required the protection of a male. We went from the house of our father to that of a husband or some male relative. It had always been that way. I was supposed to be grateful that my path was clear. I should enjoy my life of abundant resources and the love of a father who indulged my unrealistic ideals, even if they would eventually come to an end, and I would be compelled to submit to the role assigned to my gender from birth. I had no illusions about having control over my own destiny, but I could still wish things were different.

The Truth About Vampires

by

M L Martin

Oakridge – North Kingdom

Chapter 1

Oakridge Estate was situated in a sparsely populated area of the North Kingdom. It was early spring and time for the landowner, William Pryce, and his overseer to ride the estate and assess the damage a particularly harsh winter had left in its wake. Master Pryce had already saddled his favorite horse and was waiting impatiently. The overseer was dragging his feet. He did not share his employer's love of horses and as a result hated these excursions however necessary they might be. But it would be up to him to help William remember the many repairs which would need to be made. It was a two-man job. They rode to the far end of the pasture, which bordered on the river separating Oakridge from the nearest neighbor. The rains had been heavy and the ground was a sea of mud.

The overseer moaned, "Did we have to do this so soon? I'm already covered in mud, and we just started the rounds. A couple more days would not have made a bit of difference, and the ground would be drier."

"You're probably right," Master Pryce conceded. "I'm afraid I let my impatience to get out of the house get the better of me. Let's follow the river a ways and then cut over at the drive. We can at least see if the path remains stable."

The two men made their way carefully along the river's edge and made note of where the rocks supporting the path had begun to shift. It was worse than expected. Just as they decided to abandon the path for a later inspection, the ground gave way beneath William's frantic horse. William shifted his weight away from the river side of the path hoping to give the horse a fighting chance to find firmer footing, but it was too late, and the horse and rider plunged several feet onto the rocks at the bottom of the ravine and into the cold water. The overseer looked over the side horrified to see that his employer was pinned under the unmoving horse. He knew there was nothing he could do but go for help, and that would take time.

Chapter 2
Grace

My name is Grace Pryce. I am the only daughter of the man whose broken body now lies in the bed before me. It was still difficult for me to believe. Father loved his horses and was an excellent rider. That one of them would be the cause of his death was an irony to everyone who knew him. It was a mystery why a path we had all had taken hundreds of times would this day disintegrate and throw Father and his horse into the riverbed below. The fall proved fatal for both, immediate death for the horse and a lingering one for my father. After lying in the cold water while the overseer went for help, Father was finally carried back to the house in excruciating pain. He confessed to me that he considered the horse the lucky one. Father knew his injuries were extensive, and he suspected that he would not survive the night.

I finally sent away the men who had pulled my father from the river. They had already done everything they could by bringing him home. The healer had given his opinion that it was just a matter of time before Father succumbed to his internal injuries. Since there was nothing more he could do either, I also sent him away. There was nothing anyone could do, and I refused to share what little time he and I would have. The only person who was welcome was my younger brother Ethan, but it was doubtful he would arrive in time and decisions needed to be made, things needed to be said. So I sat by Father's bed and waited. Even though the end was near, every now and then, he would rouse and speak with me. Those moments were precious, and I didn't want to miss the opportunity to say good bye one more time.

My brother Ethan and I grew up knowing little of what existed outside our secluded estate in the North Kingdom. My mother died when we were young, and Father was determined to make up for the loss by providing everything his children desired. The result of his indulgence was that we grew up believing we were somehow better than our neighbors. Father made certain that we were schooled in all the classics and could read and write in several languages. He encouraged my love of books, and I spent much of my free time absorbed in some heroic, and often, romantic tale. Of course, I was also encouraged to develop my domestic skills, as I would be expected to marry well. After my mother died, I ran my father's household like a good girl, all the while resenting the implied expectations.

During the bedside vigil, my attention had wandered as I considered the cruel irony of the situation. Finally, Father stirred in the bed and looked at me sadly.

"Grace, I have done you a grave injustice," he said softly. "I was arrogant enough to believe that I still had plenty of time to provide for you. You should have married long ago."

I had recently given a great deal of thought as to why in my twenties I had not yet married. My devotion to my father was only part of it. I recalled the years when my mother was alive. They entertained frequently, and the guests always included a mix of retainers and neighbors regardless of their wealth. There was usually at least one boy my age who attended along with his parents and paid me special attention. After all, I would be a good match someday. The attention made me feel special. We would sneak off when our parents were otherwise occupied and steal a kiss or two. I enjoyed their sloppy kisses and inept but insistent groping. The excitement it produced made me feel alive. Later, several of these same young men had even approached my father requesting permission to court me, but he refused on the grounds that they could not provide the life to which I was entitled. I accepted his refusals with a degree of relief. Although the admiration of those young men was enjoyable, I couldn't imagine spending a lifetime with any of them. They just didn't measure up to the heroes in my books. It was reading which nurtured my expectations as to the kind of marriage I wanted. I intended to marry someone exceptional, someone I could love.

"I couldn't leave you alone," I replied, returning my attention to my father. "Besides, I never met anyone with whom I thought I could fall in love."

My father raised his hand to stop any further comment on my part. We'd had this discussion before. It was one of the reasons he had not insisted...until now.

"It's not about love!" he asserted. "You need someone who will provide for you, protect you. Love might result, but it is not the purpose of a good marriage."

4

I chose not to respond. I did not want to waste the little time we still had arguing. I knew that the arranged marriage between my parents had resulted in a very close, loving relationship. When my mother died, Father was devastated. So much so that although Ethan and I were still young, our father vowed he would never remarry. He could not face that kind of pain again. Based on his own experience my father could see no reason why I refused to accept an arranged marriage. On the other hand, he wasn't all that anxious to see me go either. It was so much easier to maintain the status quo.

While my parents' relationship filled me with hope that love in marriage might be possible, my brother's marriage was another matter altogether. Ethan was several years younger than me, and like many wealthy young men he enjoyed the advantages of having a father who was able to provide him with a generous income. Having no real responsibilities as yet, he enjoyed the company of others like him and indulged in a variety of excesses. Because of their obvious affluence, his group of friends tended to attract women who had questionable motives. Lilith was one of those women. She was beautiful and elegant and very charming. She was also calculating, cunning, and cruel – traits very few saw until it was too late. She accurately determined that the young and naïve, not to mention rich, Ethan Pryce would make any easy mark. Several months later, Father reluctantly agreed to Ethan's marriage.

Father continued in a tired voice, "I have sent for the solicitor, but I doubt he will arrive in time to change my will, so it will be up to your brother to make sure you are settled," he continued. "He will want to do right by you, but I doubt that his wife Lilith will want you around once he inherits and Oakridge is his. Be wary of her. I don't trust her."

I knew Lilith was greedy and would resent having to provide a dowry for me. I still didn't understand why Ethan found it necessary to marry the older woman. She would have made an acceptable mistress. There were rumors she had enjoyed that position several times before marrying my brother.

Again, my father insisted, "Be wary of her, Grace. She could become a formidable enemy if she thinks you threaten her in any way." Father sighed and held out his hand to me. There was so much more to say, but he lacked the necessary energy. I sensed that this was the last conversation we would have, and I tried unsuccessfully to hold back the tears.

"I love you, Father," I told him tenderly. "I don't blame you, and I have no regrets. If necessary, I will make my own future. Please don't worry about me."

His hand went limp, and I knew my father and quite possibly the future I envisioned were gone.

Chapter 3

"Are you a fool?" Lilith raged. "Two grown women cannot share the same house. You need to get rid of her. This is no longer her house to run!"

Ethan shook his head.

"As soon as we find her a husband, she will be gone. If you would spend as much time looking for suitable matches as complaining, Grace would be married by now."

"She has already turned down most of the eligible men around here. No one seems to be good enough for her. I doubt her previously rejected suitors are now willing to reconsider just because Grace's circumstances have changed," Lilith replied. "The only way they might swallow their pride is if you offer a larger dowry than I want to provide. After all, why should we sacrifice our inheritance, so she can do something she should have done long ago? If it meant so much to your father, why didn't he force her?"

"Lilith, you're being unreasonable. Besides it is not 'our' inheritance. It is mine, and I want to see my sister happy. None of us could have foreseen the accident. I know Father meant to see Grace well settled. Please, stop this! I just lost my father, and I don't intend to argue with you over promises I made to him concerning my sister."

"Fine," she huffed and stormed out of the room. Lilith was not accustomed to Ethan standing up to her, so she was especially upset that Ethan was taking his sister's side. It did not bode well for Lilith if Ethan started meddling in her affairs. He had not questioned how she spent her generous allowance. He might decide to do so if he wanted to come up with some kind of support for Grace. It was even possible that Grace might try to exert some influence over her brother now that his father was gone. Lilith could not let that happen. She had promises to keep also. "If he thinks I'm letting this go, he has a surprise coming. They both do."

Ethan knew she would not give up. She was right about one thing, it was obvious two grown women could not peacefully coexist in the same house. Although Grace made every effort to defer to her sister-in-law about managing Oakridge, Lilith was still defensive – feeling as if Grace was silently criticizing her every decision. Sooner or later, things would blow up, and Ethan was determined to prevent all-out war. Lilith was his wife, and although he did not agree with her, he wanted to maintain peace in his own home. He was frustrated with Grace's refusal to accept their suggestions for suitors. Most would provide a good living for her even if they lacked (in her opinion) romantic potential. Perhaps, marriage was not the solution. Grace was well educated and would make a fine governess. Even well-bred single women without generous dowries often chose that path. It might be easier to find a position for her in a large, prosperous house than it would be to find an agreeable husband. Who knew, it could even lead to a marriage. It had been known to happen. This option deserved serious consideration.

Grace

Although the house at Oakridge was large, it was impossible for me to ignore the argument between my brother and sister-in-law. Was I being unreasonable, I wondered. After all, most marriages were arranged. My parents didn't meet until the day of their wedding, and they grew to love one another. As a result, my father was so devastated by my mother's death, he refused to remarry. Instead, he depended on me to manage his household. Now, I was an unwelcome guest in my own home with no prospects. It hardly seemed fair.

I sought out Ethan. We needed to discuss this. I was determined to have some say in my future without causing a major conflict. I found him in his office writing letters.

"Ethan, can we talk about this? I know you are not trying to throw me out on the street, although I suspect that is exactly what Lilith wants."

Ethan stood and hugged me.

"You have to see things from my point of view. Lilith has been used to handling our affairs, and now she has to share the house with you. It was always Father's intent that I would inherit Oakridge. You know that. It is just bad luck that it happened before you married."

"Bad luck indeed," I sniffed. "Yes. I accepted that this would not be my home forever. I just wish Lilith was not in such a hurry to get me out of her way. Do you really agree with her?"

Ethan hung his head.

"You know I have never possessed our father's strong personality or skills. Lilith came along at a time in my life when I was certain I could never live up to his expectations. She made me feel like I had potential as a man. Nothing else in my life did. I owe her a lot. I hope you can understand why I need to take her side."

"I know that you are married to her for better or for worse, so I accept your need to keep peace in your house. As such, my decision should make you both very happy. I would like to take a position. That was never Father's plan for me, but I rather like the idea, and it is not all that unusual for an unwed woman in my position. You know better than anyone that I have unrealistic ideas about marriage. I also know that you had more than one fight defending the honor of your 'old maid sister.'"

Ethan looked startled.

"You knew about that? Father and I tried to keep it from you. We didn't want you to get your feelings hurt by some of the things which were said. They were unkind."

"Even if they were true?" I said with a rueful smile. "I was not able to thank you then, so I will do so now by making your life a little easier. As soon as a position can be found, I will accept. Since I like children, the idea of working as a governess is appealing."

If I would never have children of my own, I knew I could do a good job looking after someone else's. I couldn't imagine Lilith producing nieces or nephews for me to look after. There were no families nearby who might need or could afford the services of a live-in governess, so I would have to go far afield to find a position, and I wondered how it would feel to leave the only place I knew. It might be exciting to travel if I could just embrace a sense of adventure.

Chapter 4

A cloaked figure walked through the dark alley, searching for the right place. She was a little apprehensive, but she carried a knife and knew how to use it. She had not always been "a lady." Few knew of her past or her activities of late, especially her current husband, and she was determined to keep it that way. Inquiries made too far afield might turn up an inconvenient shared acquaintance. That was not a risk she could take. This situation had to be resolved before it became a problem without an easy solution.

She located the lamp covered with a red scarf and headed that way, looking in all directions before ducking in the door of a seedy brothel. She couldn't imagine how anyone could live or work in such deplorable conditions. *Just what I was looking for,* she thought with a smirk.

A large brute blocked the entrance, looking the woman over with a leer.

"She don't take older whores," he sneered. "But I might give you a try for a discount."

"I'm not looking for a job, you dolt!" Lilith replied angrily. "I need to talk to the madam. A mutual friend told me she might have information I need, so do your job and tell her I'm here."

"Ain't nothing free here," he replied, noticing the quality of her cloak. "It'll cost ya just to see her." He held out his grimy hand and waited until she dug a coin out of her purse. He looked askance at the small bribe and kept his hand out until she added another coin of greater value.

"That's all I can afford," she said. "My allowance is small, and I'm sure your mistress will require some persuasion also."

He examined the coins again and finally agreed.

"Wait here. It's a slow night. I think she might be encouraged to give you some of her valuable time," he said with a lewd wink.

Lilith entered the establishment and found a chair in a dark corner where she sat impatiently. It had been a long time since she had been left waiting for anyone. She was deeply insulted, and became more so, the longer she had to wait. She was beginning to think that this was a horrible mistake and rose to leave. As she turned to go, the thug returned and motioned to her. She followed him up the narrow stairway to an open door.

The man bowed at the waist and said sarcastically, "Madam will see you now." He chuckled at his perceived wit as he returned the way they had come.

Lilith swallowed her irate retort and poured on the charm as she entered the room.

"Thank you for seeing me. I won't take up much of your time."

At least the madam's room wasn't as smarmy as the rest of the house. Some care had been taken to make the receiving area comfortable, even welcoming. The furnishings were in better repair, and everything was clean and orderly. What little the madam spent on the rest of the house, she saved for her own lodgings.

The madam looked up as Lilith entered.

"I hope my man told you, I don't take women your age. You might be well qualified, but there's just not much demand for experience here," she laughed as she looked Lilith over. Lilith was still a handsome woman and not without her charms, and the madam seemed to reconsider. "On the other hand…"

"I hope your man told *you* that I'm not looking for a job. What I need is someone to do a job for me. I was told you knew people who could make problems go away – for a price."

"Information doesn't come cheap," the madam said. "What's it worth to you?"

"It could be worth quite a lot if it helps rid me of a particular problem."

The women took the measure of each other for a few moments before deciding that they could do business. It didn't cost nearly as much as Lilith was willing to pay, and she left with the name of a man who just happened to be in the area looking for work.

Chapter 5
Grace

I had not seen Lilith since I overheard the argument with Ethan, so I was not sure of my welcome at the table for breakfast. Lilith, however, was in high spirits. Ethan had eaten early and retired to his study to write more letters of inquiry on my behalf. Since the two of us were free for the morning, Lilith suggested a trip to the village. I couldn't imagine why my sister-in-law would want my company. Maybe Ethan had shared our conversation, and she was happy that I had finally agreed to see reason. Regardless, she was making an effort to be pleasant, and it would be rude for me to refuse the invitation. Besides, it was a lovely morning, and it would be good to get out for a while. If Ethan's efforts were successful, I wouldn't have many more opportunities.

It turned out to be a surprisingly amiable outing, even if I couldn't shake the feeling that there was something else going on. Since I couldn't figure out what it might be, I decided to just enjoy the day. There would be plenty of time to reflect on the reason for the unexpected overture later. We walked arm in arm down the narrow streets until we arrived at the apothecary. In our part of the country, the apothecary was more like a general store. With so few people, there was no need for many different stores, so the apothecary carried not only herbs and ointments but other necessary items which could not be produced locally. It was also the location of the post office.

Lilith said, "I need to pick up something for Ethan. I'll be right out." Before entering she gave an almost imperceptible nod to a rough looking man waiting across the street. It was so slight, I thought I imagined it, until I saw the man return her gesture and walk away.

"Can you think of anything else? Anything you need for your trip?" Lilith asked me. "If not, I think it's about time we were going back. Ethan will be waiting for his lunch."

It seemed like an odd question. My trip? What did she know that I didn't? Her mention of lunch with Ethan troubled me as well. Ethan rarely required our presence at the noon meal, but I was reluctant to spoil the mood of the day by pointing that out. Perhaps Lilith knew of some reply to the mountains of correspondence Ethan was generating on my behalf. After all, she had collected several letters from the apothecary, and one of them might reveal my future. At this point, I didn't really care what that might be. I just wanted to get on with it. I realized that this no longer felt like my home. It was time for me to go.

Ethan was sitting at his desk with his head in his hands when Lilith walked in carrying the day's mail. She smiled as she presented the letters to him. She had already read them all, so it was no surprise to her that the responses were negative – all but one. That one was no surprise either since she had written it herself. It was doubtful he would recognize her writing. She had carefully disguised it. Besides, he never paid any attention to her correspondence, so he probably wouldn't even know what her writing looked like. The solution of a governess position was a perfect way to dispose of Grace. No wedding. No dowry. She could just go away. It was, indeed, perfect, and this letter would guarantee the desired outcome.

Ethan opened the first three responses which Lilith had carefully resealed and after reading threw all of them into the fire in frustration. *Why is this so hard?* he wondered. Lilith handed him the last and smiled sweetly.

"This one looked promising, so I opened it. I hope you don't mind. I think we have a solution," she said.

He breathed a sigh of relief as he read it then replied, "Yes. I think we do."

"Will you tell her at lunch? There seems to be some urgency to the request."

Grace

Lilith and I were already seated at the table when Ethan walked in waving a letter in the air. The smile and lack of worry lines on his face hinted at the good news he carried.

"I've something for you to read, Grace. I'm sure you will be pleased," he announced.

"Perhaps you can read it to both of us," Lilith suggested with an innocent smile. "I would like to hear it also."

"My dear Ethan," he began.

I have learned, through a mutual acquaintance, of your sister's interest in a position as governess. This news is well met. As it turns out, my neighbor has just lost his wife. She leaves him with three young daughters in need of care. His grief has left him totally incapable of seeing to their welfare, and there are no immediate relatives nearby.

As you might imagine, the situation is in need of an immediate remedy. Your sister appears to have the necessary skills and breeding to mentor these poor young ladies, at least until their father is capable of seeking a more permanent solution. However, he has indicated that he might consider a marriage if she is acceptable.

If your sister is still available, please put her on the next available coach. I will settle her fare when she arrives.

Most sincerely,
Robert

"This is incredibly good news" Lilith exclaimed. "Don't you agree, Grace? It might even solve two problems at once."

I sat, stunned. This was exactly what I told myself I wanted, but now that it was a reality, I was not so sure. It had all happened so quickly and had that air of "too good to be true." In addition, Lilith was glowing, and that gave me pause.

"Is it settled then, Grace? After all the decision is yours," asked Ethan expectantly. He, also, had noticed Lilith's satisfied expression. I could tell from his puzzled expression, he didn't remember writing to his friend Robert and suspected Lilith's hand in this. However, he didn't see anything sinister in her involvement and thanked her for pursuing leads which had not occurred to him.

Still at a loss for words, I nodded my assent, and it was decided. I would leave within the week.

Chapter 6
Grace

The next few days flew by in a flurry of activity. I was overwhelmed by all the preparations for my departure. Lilith was certain my destination in the mountains had a much colder climate, which meant finding and packing clothing that was stored away in trunks in the attic. There was only so much I could take with me, and the heavy clothing took up more room than expected. Lilith helped to pack the travel bags, and together, we set aside items to be sent on after I was settled in.

I still couldn't shake the feeling that there was something not quite right about the offer. Lilith was almost gleeful as the day came for me to leave. Ethan had made the necessary travel arrangements and, surprisingly, Lilith had not complained about the cost of first class coach fare. Ethan's guilty feelings about pushing his sister out of the only home I had ever known would allow for nothing less. I imagine Lilith thought it was a small price to pay to get me out of their lives.

Too soon, the day of departure arrived. Ethan had tears in his eyes as he hugged me good bye.

"I'll miss you!" he exclaimed. We both knew that it would be a long time before we saw each other again, maybe never. "I've sent a letter to Robert. He will be expecting you, and can make the proper introductions. Be well Grace."

I boarded the coach and waved good bye to the only life I had ever known. In reality, that life had ended when my father died and Ethan inherited everything. Still, it was familiar, and leaving was difficult. I wanted to be excited about the next chapter in my life; instead, I was ambivalent. It felt too much like I was being pushed, not too gently, out of the nest. I settled into the otherwise empty coach and let grief overwhelm me.

Chapter 7

Lilith left Ethan alone to deal with his feelings about Grace's departure. She knew that he felt guilty, but he would get over it. She couldn't be happier. He would be so much easier to handle without his sister around to complicate her plans. Lilith excused herself and went to meet with the man she had contacted several weeks before. As she handed the man the bag with his payment, she instructed him again.

"You know what to do, don't you? I don't want her showing up anywhere near here. I know my husband will look for her when he finds out she has gone missing. Make sure he cannot find her."

"Wouldn't it be easier for you to just kill her?" the man asked. "It seems like a lot could go wrong with this plan, too many loose ends. I don't want anyone coming after me. You're not paying me enough for that."

"No, dying is too good for her!" Lilith exclaimed. "I want her to regret every suitor she rejected while she works on her back, servicing low-life strangers. Make sure you sell her to the foulest brothel you can find." She sneered. "She'll regret being so picky. Marry for love! What a naïve little girl. Position and wealth are the only qualities that matter in a husband. Too bad she didn't realize that sooner. She could have had a comfortable life. Now... Well, we won't think about that, will we?" Lilith chuckled.

"She won't sell for much at a place like that. I was supposed to make good money on this deal," the man whined.

"I have increased your payment to compensate. Besides, anything you make until you sell her is yours to keep. I'm pretty sure she is a virgin. That should count for something; unless, of course, you decide to consider that part of your fee. Now go and finish the job, and don't forget the last thing," Lilith said as she turned away.

"You must really hate her," the man muttered as he walked in the opposite direction.

"I don't hate her" Lilith responded. "She is an inconvenience, and I hate being inconvenienced."

Chapter 8
Grace

I collapsed onto the seat as soon as the door to the coach closed. The effort required to look excited for this "adventure" had been exhausting not to mention that the anxiety had kept me awake the night before. I put on a good face for Ethan. I knew he still felt guilty. I didn't want to add to his discomfort. However, I was angry that Lilith's was the letter which produced results. It was his responsibility to take care of me – definitely not hers. He gratefully accepted the serendipity of the solution and never questioned the motive. I, on the other hand, obsessed over it, and a little voice in my head refused to stop reminding me that it was too good to be true. Since I would never convince Ethan that his wife had anything but good intentions, I didn't even try.

An hour into the trip, I finally stopped sobbing. I knew it was time to pull myself together and accept my fate. As the only passenger, the privacy of the coach provided the ideal place to let go of the feelings I had held in check for the last few weeks, but self-pity wasn't going to change anything. Now besides the dark circles indicating my exhaustion, my eyes and nose were red from crying. It was definitely not the most attractive look. At least now I felt like I could face the world again, even if I did look a little worse for wear. With any luck, I would be presentable by the time the coach took on more passengers at the next stop.

The gentle swaying of the coach should have been comforting, but it took some time for me to acclimate to the movement. The book I brought to occupy my time lay unopened on my lap. The unfamiliar movement and stuffiness inside the confined space made me slightly nauseous, and I could smell the previous occupants, which didn't help. Body odor and cheap perfume permeated the interior. Anyone that considered this mode of transportation "first class" had to have very low expectations. I wondered what second class was like. Maybe it meant sitting on top of the vehicle with the taciturn driver on a hard wooden bench listening to the horses fart. At least in here I was protected from the elements and had a padded seat. But fresh air seemed like a good idea, so I opened the small window and inhaled deeply and then opened the textbook which sat neglected on my lap. It was not engrossing reading, but if I was going to be a competent governess, I needed to brush up on a few things. I might not have the opportunity to study when we took on more passengers. However, it was difficult to concentrate on studying, and the swaying of the coach eventually did its work and lulled me to sleep. The oblivion was a welcome respite from grief and anxiety, not to mention the discomfort and boredom of the journey. As I drifted off, I looked forward to sharing the coach. Any distraction would be welcome.

I woke when the coach came to an abrupt stop. The view out the window didn't look like a promising location for us to pick up passengers. Where was the station? We appeared to be in the middle of nowhere.

"What is the matter?" I called out the window to the driver. "Is there a problem?"

A stranger appeared at the door of the coach and opened it extending his hand to me.

"Nothing to worry about, miss. Your sister-in-law arranged other transportation for you. Come on out."

I couldn't imagine that Lilith would have done something nice for me, even if she had been rather friendly the last few weeks, so I resisted the invitation to leave the coach

"I'm fine here. My brother has already paid for this trip," I replied and moved as far from the door as possible.

"I was hired to make sure you get where you are supposed to go," he said as he reached in and pulled me roughly from the coach. Before I could protest further, he placed a foul-smelling rag over my mouth and nose. Just before I lost consciousness, I caught a glimpse of a blurry figure off to one side – then nothing.

I regained consciousness some time later to find that my mode of transportation had taken a turn for the worse. The wagon in which I found myself was filled with straw and did not provide much of a cushion. In addition, there was a gag in my mouth, and my hands and feet were bound. I was covered with a rough blanket but could still tell it was getting dark. That meant I had been asleep for most of the day.

The gag in my mouth did not allow me to make much noise, so I kicked at the covering until the driver noticed the movement. He stopped the wagon and pulled me out. It took a few moments to regain enough equilibrium to stand on my own without leaning against my captor. I pulled away as quickly as I could and almost lost my balance.

He laughed as he grabbed me and said, "Don't worry. You'll get used to me. We're going to be spending a lot of time together."

I looked around at the desolate surroundings as the man removed the gag.

"You can yell all you like. You can even try to run away, but there is nowhere to go and no one to hear you out here. You might as well do this the easy way. I'm not so bad once you get to know me." He laughed again. I stood unmoving as he untied my hands and feet. "I imagine you need to relieve yourself by now. You can go on the other side of wagon."

I was still unsteady on my feet, but he was correct. I thought I would burst if I didn't do something soon, so I slowly made my way as far around the wagon as possible. The sweet taste and smell of the drug made me nauseous again, and the residual dizziness made it difficult to think. I felt a little better once I vomited. It was humiliating having to relieve myself with the strange man on the other side of the wagon, but I knew I couldn't wait forever. My captor didn't make any move toward me, so I just got on with it. He was right. If I wanted any illusion of privacy in this open wasteland, the far side of the wagon was my only option.

As my head cleared a little more, I became aware of the sharp pain on my cheek. I put up my hand to determine the cause and pulled it away quickly as I experienced a more acute pain. My hand was bloody. *WHAT HAPPENED?* I wondered. I was now confused and angry.

"What is going on?" I demanded. "And who are you?"

Unconcerned by my anger, the man asked, "Are you hungry? It would appear you now have an empty stomach," as he held out some dried meat. "I'm Arthur, by the way, and I will be escorting you to Hightower at my employer's request."

I slapped his hand away.

"I don't want food! I want you to tell me what's going on!"

"You might as well make yourself comfortable. This could take a while. Besides, we're not going any farther tonight."

I settled on the ground while he unhooked and hobbled the horses and let them loose to graze on the dry grass. It was not the most comfortable seat but better than the wagon which smelled like vomit and other substances I would rather not consider. It was unfortunate we had to use that area as a make-shift latrine, but the wagon provided the only privacy for miles. This situation was horrible enough without that added embarrassment.

"There is no governess position waiting for you and no one is expecting you," the man began as he worked. "Your sister-in-law wanted me to make sure you knew what was going to happen and why." Arthur took a crumpled piece of paper out of his pocket and continued, "She wanted to make sure I got it right. She never wrote to Robert, and she forged his response. She never sent a second letter to him either. Then she hired me to get you out of her way. She thinks your brother will be more easily handled without you around."

My heart sank.

"Are you going to kill me?" I inquired weakly.

"No," he laughed. "But if you ask me, you would be better off. Her plans for you are much worse."

"What could be worse?" I wondered out loud. As I touched my cheek, I was reminded of the injury there. "What happened here?"

"Oh, that's all part of the package – complements of my employer. It seems like you pissed her off when you refused to marry." He pulled out a fragment of mirror and offered it to me so that I could examine the damage. "Here take a look," he said.

I looked, horrified, at the long gash across my cheek. It was much worse than I expected. It was difficult to hold back tears as I realized what Lilith had done. I had been told I was a very attractive woman. The scar which would be left from the cruel and unattended cut changed that forever.

"I'm to sell you to a brothel. Your sister-in-law figured, with a scar like that, no madam who catered to high-class customers would give you a second look. That leaves the ones who only care if you can spread your legs or bend over," he continued crudely. "I gotta ask. What did you do to deserve this?"

I had been wondering that myself. Why me? Lilith exhibited disdain for everyone she encountered, so what had I done to provoke her to such drastic lengths? Did Lilith resent that I had someone in my life who indulged my dreams no matter how unrealistic? Maybe I presented Lilith with a convenient opportunity to express her contempt for all people.

"I can't think of anything I might have done to her. My instincts tell me that she is just evil, and this is an unprovoked act of cruelty by someone who enjoys inflicting torment." That explanation gave me little comfort, even if it did accurately express my feelings about her.

I was relieved I had declined the previous offer of food, as I was very close to vomiting again. Given my very sheltered life I knew little about what went on in the kinds of places the man was hired to take me, but everyone had heard stories. None of them were good.

"By the time we get where we are going, you won't look much different from the other women who are for sale. Even that fine dress you have on won't look so good by then. No one will ever suspect you're a well-bred lady."

Arthur offered the jerky once again.

"You gonna eat or should I tie you up? I need to get some sleep, and I don't get the rest of my money until you're sold. It would be foolish of you to attempt an escape, but you look like you just might try. Take a good look around. There's no place to go. I'd be able to spot you wherever you went. But should you manage to get far enough away, you'd die before you got out of this wasteland without a guide."

I grabbed the meat and began to chew slowly. I was definitely not hungry, but eating would prolong my freedom and give me more time to think. Besides, my wrists and ankles were already raw, so I didn't look forward to being tied up again. I had to admit that my chances of escaping were next to none. Even in the fading light, I could see that the man was right. There was nothing around but flat land and dry grass. The only landmark was a narrow ribbon of a darker shade of gray ahead that must have been a river or stream. Other than that, there was nothing that would indicate a path forward. Survival, for the time being, would depend upon my captor, so I would play the cooperative prisoner for as long as necessary. After admitting there was nowhere I could go and promising not to try and run, Arthur agreed to leave me unbound.

I woke the following morning, stiff from sleeping on the hard ground. I was also incredibly thirsty and hot. Not just hot, burning hot.

"Hey you," I managed to croak out through my parched lips." I need water!" I felt my cheek and realized the source of my discomfort. My finger came away covered with a sticky yellowish substance. I had seen enough inflamed wounds to know that this was a serious threat. I swallowed and got enough moisture in my mouth to yell louder. "Hey Arthur, I'm sick."

Arthur rolled over reluctantly. He took one look at me and immediately got up.

"Oh shite!" he exclaimed as he saw my face. He grabbed a flask from his coat pocket. "I hate to waste even cheap whisky, but it's all I can think to do. You're not dying until I get paid." He uncorked the flask and poured a little of the harsh alcohol over the festering cut. "It is at least two days until we get anywhere with a healer. When we get to the stream, you can clean it up some. That should buy us some time."

I refused to drink the whisky he offered.

"Water" I asked hopefully? Arthur helped me get up. We walked over to the wagon and he put the waterskin to my parched lips, so I could drink. He looked alarmed. If I looked as bad as I felt, he must really be concerned.

"We need to go, now!" He helped me into the bed of the wagon then collected and harnessed the horses. Before I knew it, we were bumping over the hard ground, heading in the direction of what was now a green ribbon.

By the time we arrived at the stream, things were noticeably worse. Arthur pulled me from the wagon, and I could see the apprehension in his expression. He helped me walk to the bank, where I sank to my knees in the cold water and splashed it over my face. It didn't matter that the only dress I had was soaked by the time I finished. It was such a relief to feel cool. Arthur's prediction that I would look like any other peasant by the end of the trip was undoubtedly true. The wet dress would collect all kinds of grime.

The next two days were agony. The dress dried quickly, and I was soon burning up again. Arthur offered me food, but I could not eat. Fortunately, there was ample water available along the way, and he doused me liberally whenever we stopped. While I still could, I attempted to rinse the wound and then apply some more of the precious whisky. By the second day, however, I could barely lift my head to drink.

Looks like Arthur won't get paid, I thought. *And Lilith can't make my life a living hell.* These thoughts struck me as incredibly funny, and soon I was laughing hysterically.

Chapter 9

Grace's crazy laughing, more than her appearance, scared Arthur. He was truly alarmed by the delirium she was exhibiting. Unexpectedly, he had actually come to like her. She was not like other women he had encountered. She seemed kind, unlike her sister-in-law, and he regretted taking this job. Arthur was a pickpocket and thief, not at kidnapper and slave trader. If only he hadn't desperately needed the money. Guilt was not an emotion with which he was acquainted. Although Lilith had taken things into her own hands by actually cutting Grace, Arthur felt some responsibility for the injury which might end her life, so it was with a profound sense of relief that they reached the village, and Grace still lived.

"I need a healer!" Arthur shouted in the center of the market. "I can pay." He knew those were words which would get almost anyone's attention.

A crone of indeterminate age approached the wagon.

"I'm the healer. What do you need?"

He pointed to Grace.

"Can you help her?"

The woman peered in the wagon and shook her head.

"She's pretty far gone, but I may be able to help her pass comfortably. She your woman?"

"She may not look like it now, but she's a woman of position! I'm her servant, and I was hired to see her safely to Hightower. She had an unfortunate accident, and her coach was lost. This was the best I could find to get her this far. She can't die. Please help her. I'll make it worth your while." Arthur pleaded. *It's mostly true*, he thought.

The crone looked at the cut as she nodded toward a cottage down the way. Arthur could see she doubted the story, but it didn't matter to him what she thought as long as she agreed to help.

"Take her there. I'll be along after I gather the herbs I need. Try to keep her cool. Do I get paid even if she dies?"

She knew it was an odd injury for a woman of means, and it didn't look like anything she would have sustained in a coach accident. Arthur could tell the healer thought it looked like the deliberate injury it was. She probably wondered if he was responsible, but regardless of any reservations she might have, money won out.

"You'll do better if she lives," Arthur responded.

Grace

I was barely aware of what was happening around me as Arthur lifted me from the wagon bed and carried me into a dark cottage. By now the pain in my head was excruciating. The darkness in the interior was a welcome relief. Some part of me was aware that I was hallucinating when I heard the sweet voice of death calling to me. It would be so easy to just let go and follow. The life which was waiting for me if I recovered was not particularly appealing. Oblivion seemed the better option. However, there was something that would not let me die.

Arthur beat a hasty retreat when the crone ordered him out. She looked me over carefully.

"I have been waiting for you. It is for you that I was called here. She does not mean for you to die. You have a greater purpose. Be brave. The next few hours will be painful, but you will recover. She does not abandon her children."

Then the crone uttered a name which carried the full power of creation, and the war for dominance began as death and life battled within me. Gradually, the voice luring me away from this existence faded. Life prevailed.

Chapter 10

Between the copious amount of whisky Arthur consumed and the expense of Grace's care, most of Lilith's money was gone. Arthur had to consider what he would do once Grace recovered as it seemed she would. The healer turned out to be more than competent. He suspected she might have other resources at her disposal that he didn't want to consider. He was not one to believe in magic, but Grace's recovery did seem miraculous, and he expected the resulting fee to take his remaining resources. *How much was the woman's life worth to me?* he wondered. He was pleasantly surprised when the healer refused further compensation and returned some of the money he had already paid.

"I had a dream about her," the crone said as she pushed the money into Arthur's hand. She seemed reluctant to keep it, as if by accepting the money, she was taking some responsibility for the woman's life. "This one is special. Bad things will happen if you don't get her to Hightower, so she can fulfil her destiny. Someone there is waiting for her."

"Who could be waiting for her?" Arthur asked. "I didn't tell anyone where I was taking her, and what could her destiny be, old woman?"

"The one who waits will know her when she gets there – the rest will be her story to write," the crone said. "Her role in the future is not yet clear, but it depends on you."

Grace

The following day, Arthur and I left the village and journeyed on to a place called Hightower. I had no idea what had transpired between Arthur and my healer, but he was different. He kept sneaking glances at me as if he was expecting me to do something unusual. I felt better, but I was not up to much beyond putting one foot in front of the other to get me where I needed to go. If he was expecting anything else, he would be disappointed.

Chapter 11

The land mass referred to as the Known World was divided into four segments by two intersecting mountain ranges. One range extended from northwest to southeast and the other from northeast to southwest. For centuries, this seemingly impenetrable barrier kept the knowledge of one area from the other. But the Creator foresaw many things, not the least of which was the curiosity of the creatures She had made. In anticipation of the time when they would want to know what lay on the other side of the mountains, She created four passes which led to a high plateau where the ranges dividing the Known World crossed. As She anticipated, adventurous explorers began expeditions into the mountains to determine if they were alone. Few of them came back. They were prepared for neither the harsh weather conditions nor the fierce inhabitants who managed to exist there. Eventually, a small group found the first pass, the one which led from the north to a plateau in the middle of the mountain range. From the vantage point of the plateau, they then discovered the others. This marked the beginning of one of the greatest advances in their civilization.

The discovery of the passes now allowed people from the four kingdoms to travel into the others without having to brave the perpetual winter of the mountains. Eventually a city grew on the plateau. The city which was to become Hightower attracted merchants and traders of all sorts with many remaining to set up shops or permanent booths rather than face a return trip home. Businesses catering to travelers and tradesmen were established next and flourished. Thus the city became a thriving metropolis – at least by their standards.

But even with the passes, getting to Hightower was no easy journey. The mountains were surrounded by barren foothills that could sustain nothing more than tall grass and provided little in the way of food or shelter. There was ample water due to runoff from the snow higher up in the mountains so travelers were not likely to die of thirst, but there was little in the way of landmarks to follow. It was easy to lose one's way unless there was a knowledgeable guide in the group. A caravan could wander for days looking for a passage through the mountains. In the beginning, only the hardiest would attempt the journey, and that group rarely included women.

The burgeoning city's population was both a blessing and a curse. The success of the city at the center of the Known World also attracted less desirable elements. The wealth there drew unscrupulous men whose only goal in life was to relieve the merchants of their profits. There were others who were greedy for power and realized if they could control the city and the passes, they could dominate the other kingdoms. Those who possessed the real power in the Known World quickly determined that it needed to be protected and kept neutral. The tower for which the city was eventually named was built and a wall circling the city came next. No one really knew how all this happened nor did they care. They were happy for the protection, so they didn't question the source. The result of this progress was the establishment by the immortal population of the Middle Kingdom.

As the market grew, it became necessary to set standards for doing business. Eventually merchants formed guilds to ensure fair business practices. From those guilds, a small group emerged whose purpose was to ensure that prices were appropriate and merchants and buyers alike were treated fairly. Some of the greedier merchants refused to join the guilds or adopt the standards set by this group. It did not take long for word to circulate that they operated a disreputable business, and they soon capitulated or left Hightower for less regulated markets. Finally the group established standards for the treatment of livestock of all kinds while awaiting sale. It was a good system and almost everyone benefited.

Much to the dismay of many, the category labeled "livestock" included not only animals. To satisfy the need for affordable labor, domestic help, and other types of employment, Hightower also became a center for the buying and selling of humans. Most people, regardless of their personal preference, conceded that slavery and indentured servitude were necessary evils. Even if they refused to own another human being, they turned a blind eye to the practice and many had friends and business associates who owned slaves. The economy could not exist without a cheap source of labor – deplorable as that practice might be. Healthy males with skills brought the best prices, and since it seemed there was always conflict somewhere, captured enemies provided a steady stream of men who would rather work than waste away in a prison cell. Household servants, especially skilled women and field workers were also in demand but not as plentiful.

But tolerance had its limits. What the people of Hightower could not tolerate was the trade in unfortunate women who were destined for the lower class brothels throughout the country. So that the residents could ignore its existence, this trade was conducted outside the city walls. The officials who monitored the conditions in the city market did not bother with the black market outside. As a result, the accommodation for the women awaiting sale there was less than desirable. The lucky ones were housed in a poorly constructed, drafty lean-to with straw on the floor which was rarely refreshed. Those who could not find room there had to make do in the pens outside the structure and hope to be sold soon.

It was to this market that Arthur brought Grace.

Chapter 12

Higgins read the note a second time. He was surprised that Arthur would even dare approach him after their last encounter. He was sure that the request must involve money. It usually did. He sighed and read the message one more time. *NEED YOUR HELP. LIFE OR DEATH – NOT MINE! MEET US AT THE MARKET OUTSIDE THE GATES.* This was melodramatic, even for Arthur. Higgins was curious about the other party, the "us" implied, and Arthur was, after all, his brother, so he set out to the requested meeting. He did not have to grant his brother's request, whatever it was, but he could listen and find out what he was up to this time.

Higgins stood in the shadows across the square from Arthur and Grace. He had not seen his twin for several years, and he still had mixed feelings about this meeting. He and Arthur had gone very different directions, and Higgins didn't approve of what his brother had done with his life. While Higgins had a very respectable job, even if his employer was somewhat unorthodox, Arthur had chosen to make his way using questionable, if not downright illegal, means. From the looks of him, his choice didn't seem to be working out too well for him. Higgins wondered about the woman with him. He couldn't imagine Arthur tying himself down, so he must be looking to get rid of a bad investment. Or maybe she was with child. That would certainly complicate Arthur's life. Higgins could not imagine his brother as a father. That would make Higgins an uncle – perish the thought!

Arthur was anxious. What if his brother refused to meet him? They had not parted on good terms. In reality, they had not been on good terms their entire adult lives. Higgins did not approve of Arthur's choices, and Arthur thought his brother was a pompous prig. While he and Grace waited, Arthur paced and fretted. What would he do with Grace if his brother didn't show up? Despite the scar and her disreputable looking condition, anyone who spoke with her would know that she didn't belong here, and she certainly didn't belong with him. If Higgins didn't respond, Arthur guessed he would just have to go through with selling her. Even if he let her go, she would be in danger and probably end up no better off.

Higgins continued to observe the two from across the street. His eyes kept coming back to the woman. Despite the condition of her hair and clothing, she didn't fit the part. It looked as if she had attempted to make herself presentable. Her hair was braided, but without the assistance of a comb or mirror, it was still in disarray and stray pieces of straw stuck out in various places. In addition, she looked ill or as if she were recovering from an illness. She was very pale and thin. The dark circles under her eyes could just be the result of sleeping poorly during the journey, but he doubted it. Maybe that was the "life or death" to which Arthur referred in his note. Higgins could certainly show some compassion in that instance. But there was something else about her. The dress she was wearing fit so it had been made for her. And she held herself in a manner which did not indicate a life of poverty and servitude. Higgins could see that she was attractive despite the scar on her cheek. He held his hand up to cover the disfigured side of her face and gasped. She was beautiful, or had been!

Arthur sensed eyes on him and looked up to see Higgins across the way. He saw the raised hand and interpreted it as a greeting. He was surprised but relieved his brother had responded to his message. Curiosity must have gotten the better of him because it certainly wasn't brotherly affection that motivated him. The two men eyed one another warily as they walked toward each other.

"To what do I owe this rare pleasure?" Higgins said sarcastically. "Life of crime not working out so well for you?"

Arthur bit back a caustic retort. This was, after all, about Grace. He realized the depths of his feelings for her as he addressed his brother with a rare hint of humility.

"I need to request a favor, and you know how hard it is for me to ask. But it's not for me," he added hurriedly as he nodded toward Grace. "It's for her."

Higgins looked down his nose at the bedraggled woman Arthur indicated. He wanted to make sure that he wasn't getting sucked into another of Arthur's scams. She could be in on it.

"So, what's the story here? Why do you need my help?"

"I accepted a job which I now regret," Arthur began, "and before you say anything, regret is a rare thing for me. This woman's sister-in-law hired me to get rid of her. I thought it would be easy to just kidnap her and take her somewhere far away, but there were other conditions. The sister-in-law wanted her sold to some low-class brothel, and she wanted me to scar her, so she would not be able to work in a more respectable establishment."

Higgins was shocked.

"I never approved of how you made your living, but I didn't think you would stoop this low you bastard!"

Arthur raised his hand to silence any further comments.

"Will you just listen to me for once before you judge? My employer didn't trust me to carry out her instructions, so she insisted that she come with me when I abducted Grace. I drugged Grace, but I couldn't injure her. Although she wouldn't feel it, I couldn't bring myself to do that to a defenseless woman. Her sister-in-law grabbed the knife from me and did it herself. I think she actually enjoyed it. She had this kinda crazy look on her face. I think she would have done more if I hadn't lied and told her I thought someone was coming. I was afraid for Grace. I know you don't think much of me, but I could never do that. Grace is a decent sort, and I couldn't go through with the rest of the job. I know your employer hires women for his establishment. Couldn't you take her? I know she would be treated well there. She doesn't deserve what her sister-in-law planned for her."

Higgins still couldn't believe what he was hearing.

"Her family did this to her? Won't her brother be looking for her, or was he in on it, too?"

Grace had been quiet during the conversation. Some of the details of Lilith's plan still shocked her. Arthur had previously omitted the more gruesome details, so this was the first she heard of them. She knew Lilith resented her, but Grace didn't think her capable of such cruelty. When Higgins suggested her brother Ethan might be involved however, she could not remain silent.

"No!" Grace exclaimed. "Ethan would never have a hand in this. He thinks I've accepted a position with a friend of his. It will be months before he even suspects anything. Of course, Lilith undoubtedly concocted some story about my abduction and probable murder to keep him from even looking for me. Now that I know she was there, she would even have bloody clothes to provide as evidence of my demise."

Arthur pleaded, "If your employer will just buy her from me, I will be on my way. She has many fine qualities. She is well educated and managed a large household for her father before he died and left her without prospects. I believe she is just the kind of woman Hightower House could use."

"That's quite a sales pitch. Maybe you could have an honest career as a horse trader. Should I look at her teeth, too?" Higgins asked sarcastically, as if he were buying livestock. But he was considering the possibilities. Mr. Ross was looking for someone to run the house. The previous chatelaine found a husband and left a week ago, and the house was in turmoil. Higgins didn't think Grace's appearance would be a problem since she would not be expected to mingle with the patrons. It might even work in her favor – a little sympathy could go a long way. It was working on him. He suspected the scar would be less noticeable once the swelling went down and it finished healing. None of the other women employed there had the skills to manage such a large operation with its unique requirements. Grace just might be what they needed. It was at least a short-term solution until Mr. Ross returned.

Still Higgins hesitated.

"Mr. Ross doesn't buy slaves. I don't know that I can talk him into taking her under these circumstances no matter how unfortunate."

"I'm not really selling her," Arthur reasoned. "I just need enough to keep me until I get another job."

"In his defense," Grace interjected, "he did spend a great deal of the money for a healer when I became ill. He didn't have to do that."

Higgins looked surprised.

"You did that, Arthur? That's unlike you. Well, I suppose I could check with Mr. Ross when he returns, but I can't make any promises."

"What am I supposed to do with her until then?" Arthur said, beginning to panic. "If we stay here, someone will assume she's for sale. You have to take her now. I don't have enough money to keep us both for a couple weeks until your employer returns." Arthur knew that Higgins must have some household funds at his disposal. He hoped his appeal and Grace's unfair situation would convince him to risk the wrath of this employer and take her on. He could see that his brother was considering it but was not sure if he should press harder.

Finally, Higgins shook his head.

"How do you feel about this, Grace? If I'm going to have to explain my impulsive behavior to Mr. Ross, I have to be sure you're here voluntarily. We are not likely to have another qualified applicant drop on our doorstop, but I have to be sure you won't run off as soon you are free of my brother."

Grace looked at both men and responded, "I don't want to sound impertinent, but it's about time someone asked me what I wanted. As I see it, my options are limited. I can't go back to my brother's house where I am definitely not wanted. I am without a male protector or money, so I can't travel safely in order to seek a position. I have no one to arrange a marriage for me, so it would appear that my only real prospect is to work for you. Give me a trial. If I prove unacceptable, you can sell me where you will and recoup your expense. I assure you, I am not likely to run off."

So it was settled. The brothers concluded their business, and Arthur left Grace without a word. He realized he would miss her, and he didn't want to risk an emotional goodbye.

"Come with me, Grace, and we'll get you settled," Higgins said as he took her elbow and ushered her through the gates of Hightower.

Hightower House

Chapter 13

Grace

The sprawling structure to which Higgins took me could hardly be called a house, even if it did bear that name. The formidable-looking "Hightower House" resembled a fortress and surrounded a large courtyard and the tower. There was little continuity to the architecture since there had been numerous additions to the original structure. Each addition reflected the purpose for which it was built, but most seemed to favor function over form. I could see that some of the sections had several floors and appeared to provide housing, but the majority had a single level, and I would only be able to determine their purpose from the inside. At my apprehensive look, Higgins cautioned me not to judge its comfort level by the austere exterior. However, it was not the house's appearance which concerned me, but it's massive scale. Hightower House was much larger than my family home, and I was beginning to doubt my claim that I could handle its management efficiently.

When I voiced my concern, Higgins was quick to reply, "Don't worry. We do not use everything, you see. In times of war, the army is housed here, so forces can be deployed in any direction needed. Only then do we require the use of all the additions. Even then the troops take care of themselves. Your responsibilities will only include the public rooms, the living quarters, and kitchen gardens. The remainder of the building is unoccupied or off limits."

We approached the entrance to the main house, and Higgins stopped to unlock the door, which appeared solid enough to withstand a battering ram. He pulled it open and ushered me into the foyer. Rather than the Spartan, militaristic décor I anticipated, it was lavish. Thick carpets covered the stone floor and faded tapestries covered the stone walls. My first impression was of welcome, warmth, and sophistication. This was nothing like my provincial home in the north.

Belatedly, I realized that my mouth was gaping open in amazement.

Higgins just laughed and quipped, "Not what you expected, eh? This part of the complex was the tower-keeper's house when there was one. Everything else was added as needed. As for the current furnishings, your new employer is a very wealthy man with exquisite taste. Come along. Let's get you cleaned up and settled in. Then I can explain your responsibilities."

I followed Higgins through corridors, which appeared as random as the outside implied. As we walked, he provided a running commentary on my new home.

"Since the house grew as needed over time," he explained, "there is little continuity or rationale to the room placement. It is sometimes inconvenient, but makes it much harder for invaders to easily find what they are after. You will get used to it."

"I have a rather good memory," I responded. "So would you explain what I am seeing as we pass? I will do my best to remember it."

Higgins nodded to a large set of closed double doors to our left.

"That is the salon. That room is the real reason Hightower House exists and where Mr. Ross entertains his important guests. Your responsibilities in the salon are limited to the daytime hours, when it is being prepared for the night's activity. You will be responsible for scheduling the staff and coordinating with the cook for the food that will be served, but you will not enter while he is entertaining unless instructed to do so."

I made a mental note. *Stay out of the salon at night.* I wondered why.

As we continued, he pointed out the kitchens and cook's quarters, which were to the right. A refectory for the staff was positioned next to the kitchens. To the left, adjacent to the salon, was a large library. I made another entry in my mental notebook to check it out as soon as possible. Access to books might make my employment here enjoyable, and the selection of books and manuscripts was extensive. The hall took an abrupt jog to the right then to the left and dead-ended at a wing with two floors of guest rooms. This had to be the first addition to the original house. Most of the doors were open, and the rooms looked as if they hadn't been used in a very long time. Higgins explained that this wing was built to house military officers during some previous conflict long ago. It was one of the two additions that had more than one floor.

"Don't Mr. Ross's guests stay overnight?" I inquired.

"Rarely," he replied. "When they do they are accommodated in a different part of the house. You needn't worry about them."

At the end of the hall were the stairs leading up to the second floor. There, we turned left and continued along the guest wing and dead-ended at another flight of stairs. We turned left again and the corridor continued along the other multi-level addition. The rooms in this wing were smaller and rather sparse in comparison to the ones we had just passed. They also appeared to be in use, as most of the doors were closed. I guessed, correctly, that these were the quarters for the staff. Higgins ushered me to a room that was larger than the others I had seen, but just as sparsely decorated.

"These are the chatelaine's quarters," he announced. At my lack of response he said, "This room is yours. It looks a little bare right now, but you are free to decorate it as you wish. There is a storage room full of furnishings at your disposal. We want you to feel at home here."

The most surprising and welcome revelation, as far as I was concerned, was that the Hightower House compound was built over two springs, which provided an inexhaustible supply of water. The fresh water spring provided drinking and cooking water for the kitchens, which meant the staff did not need to carry water from the well in the middle of the courtyard. In fact, a pipe ran directly to the kitchen. The other spring, Higgins explained, was a hot spring over which was built a bath house. This building, much to my delight, was our next destination.

At his knock, the door was opened by a lovely young woman. Higgins ushered me in. No one seemed to object to his presence even though most of the women were in some state of undress. It seemed he was a frequent visitor.

He adopted a commanding tone and announced, "Ladies, this is the new chatelaine, Grace. She will be supervising you. As you can see, she has had a difficult journey and is in need of a good soaking and some clean clothes. Please make her welcome." He then addressed a woman by the name of Aubry, who was the resident seamstress. "Please find a uniform that will do until we can have Grace fitted for her own."

Higgins then left me in the care of my new staff.

Chapter 14
Grace

There were several groups of women in the bathing house. Their reactions to Higgins' announcement varied from curious and friendly to openly hostile. There was one group in the far corner that was clustered around a stunning and voluptuous woman who appeared to be their leader. She tossed her head and mouthed, "We'll see about that." I imagine my present appearance had something to do with the disdain emanating from that corner of the pool, but I didn't understand the hostility toward someone they had just met and didn't know. The management skills I had developed running my father's house would certainly be put to the test with this group of women. I had the feeling that handling the staff on my own was the first test of my suitability for the position. My job here was not assured yet, and I would need to prove I could manage a diverse group of employees without Higgins' help. But that was a problem which would not be solved immediately. I had other priorities at the moment.

I felt a sense of relief as I removed the stained clothing and lowered myself into the pool. It felt like heaven. The warm water eased my muscles, which were still aching from the arduous journey. I dunked my head under the water to wash my filthy hair and looked for soap. One of the other women in the pool looked me over and then reluctantly handed me a bar. I thanked her politely, but since she made no other overtures, I returned to my bathing. I couldn't remember when I had last felt clean, and I was in no hurry to leave the water. Eventually, the prune-like appearance of my fingers convinced me that I needed to get out.

The woman named Aubry approached me with several dry towels and some clothing. I dried myself off and donned my "uniform." The gray watered silk dress apparently marked my position in the household. The dress was not unattractive, even if the color was drab. The high neck and cream cuffs were lined in exquisite and expensive lace. The seams, which gave the garment some shape, were accentuated by maroon braid. I thought the dress resembled a military uniform. Minus the lace, it looked very... authoritative. I wondered drolly if that made me the general of the staff. The dress was not unfeminine, however it did convey the message that I was aloof and untouchable. I wondered what that was supposed to mean.

Aubry waited quietly while I dressed.

"We will need to do something with your hair" she said. "Sit."

I sat on one of the benches arranged around the pool.

"Are you my servant? I wasn't aware that benefit came with the job."

Aubry paused from running the comb through my wet tangled hair.

"I'm just trying to be nice. I think you could use a friend. There are some here who resent you already. They wanted the job Higgins gave you, even if they lack the qualifications. They thought they could convince Mr. Ross to choose one of them, but Higgins, announcement made it sound like it was already settled."

I sighed.

"I didn't ask for this. It was not my intention to apply for this job. I was brought here as a favor to a friend. To be honest, I thought I was destined for another kind of ... service. I'm only here until your Mr. Ross returns and makes the final decision. He has ultimate approval, so your friends need not be concerned."

"They're not my friends," Aubry replied bitterly. "They're friends to no one, so watch your back, Grace. You seem like a nice person. They eat nice people for dinner."

"If we are to be friends, may I ask what you do at Hightower House?"

"Besides my job as seamstress, I am one of the many companions for Mr. Ross's guests. You have only seen a few. You can tell us by our blue dresses – that is when we are clothed, of course. They can vary in style according to body type and taste, but everyone here dresses according to their position. You are the only one entitled," Aubry laughed, "or maybe condemned to wear gray. I guess the unattractive color is supposed to enhance your air of authority." Aubry paused, assessing my appearance and then asked tentatively, "What happened to you?"

The question was not unexpected still I had been dreading it. Although Aubry seemed sincere in her attempt at friendship, I was not sure how much I was prepared to reveal until I knew how things would go. Fortunately, I didn't have to make that decision just yet. The tinkling of the bell and knock at the door interrupted our conversation.

"I imagine Higgins is waiting for me. My story will have to wait for another time."

I was relieved to have an excuse to leave the bath house with the question unanswered; however, I would have to decide on my version of the story soon.

Chapter 15

Grace

Now that I was clean and properly dressed Higgins escorted me back the direction we had come. I was pleased to realize that I remembered the way. It would not be that difficult to find my way around on my own. The layout was not as confusing as Higgins implied.

It was mid-afternoon, and the only people I saw were working in the kitchen preparing for the evening meal. Higgins noticed my surprise.

"It's very quiet around here in the afternoon," he stated. "Most of the women are resting in their rooms or in the bathhouse. As I may have explained, Mr. Ross entertains in the evenings since his guests are – ah – otherwise occupied during the daylight hours, so the women are not needed until then, and they often work late. I hope you are an early riser since your responsibilities begin first thing in the morning. The cleaning staff arrives in the morning after the guests leave. You will meet with them tomorrow, so they can show you what they do, and you can let them know your expectations. Keep in mind, Mr. Ross is rather fastidious, so the salon must be pristine. Then you will need to consult with the cook and make sure she has everything she needs for the meals that will be served. Finally, you must determine which of the staff will be available for the evening. You may need to make adjustments depending on the women's activities the previous night. As with all positions of this kind, there may be other duties as unexpected situations demand. Thinking on your feet is a necessity. Arthur said you ran your father's house, so you should have an idea of what is required. I hope the size of the house and staff is not too intimidating."

Before I could become too overwhelmed by the magnitude of the job, Higgins took me into our second destination, the kitchen.

"It's time for you to meet the chef. You will be spending a great deal of time with her, so it would be good to have her on your side. She can be a little grumpy at first, but she has a good heart. I think you'll like her – eventually."

The person to whom he referred was a portly red-faced woman in her middle years.

"Mrs. Miller, I would like for you to meet our new chatelaine, Grace."

Mrs. Miller looked up from the pot she was stirring.

"Well, that's a relief. Those girls have been at each other's throats. Now they know the position is settled, maybe they'll calm down." As an afterthought she looked up from stirring the pot on the stove and added, "It's good to meet you, Grace."

Standing in the kitchen amid the aromas of cooking, I realized I had no idea when I had eaten last. I was very hungry, and my stomach growled loudly to confirm it. Mrs. Miller looked up in concern. She was firmly convinced that the solution to any problem was food.

"What's wrong with you, Higgins? This girl is half starved! Sit here and eat something, Grace. Can't you see how thin and pale she is?"

As the two bickered back and forth like an old married couple, I looked longingly at the bread on the table, then looked hopefully at Higgins, and he nodded his consent.

"You don't need to hover while she eats. Leave us to get to know each other." She turned to address me. "He's afraid I'll bite your head off."

She laughed as she hustled Higgins out of the kitchen. Then Mrs. Miller ladled out a generous bowl full of stew and set it in front of me along with the large piece of bread I had been eyeing.

"I'd ask you how you got here, but I think you'd best eat instead of talk. You do look a little pale."

I tried to restrain myself from shoveling Mrs. Miller's delicious stew into my mouth. The longer it took me to eat, the longer I could avoid the uncomfortable questions that would undoubtedly come. I really would have to come up with a believable story to satisfy my new acquaintances. My silence would just lead to speculation, and I didn't need that. Although I avoided them when possible, I was well acquainted with gossipy women. I didn't want to provide fodder for the stories they could invent when facts were unavailable. I knew I would have to be honest with my new employer. That interview would be uncomfortable enough without worrying about how much to trust the rest of the staff. Aubry's warning still rang in my ears.

All too soon, the stew was consumed, so I turned to Mrs. Miller hoping to ward off questions with one of my own.

"I imagine this is what you will be serving for dinner. It is delicious. Will the guests be having it also?"

Mrs. Miller hesitated before responding.

"The stew is for the staff. The guests arrive well after the dinner hour and have somewhat different tastes, so no. I have been providing for Gabriel's guests for many years and am well acquainted with their requirements. You will not need to concern yourself with them."

I chose to ignore the blush on Mrs. Miller's cheeks as she realized her verbal slip. I wondered just how well the chef knew the master of the house. Obviously well enough to call him by his first name. There was a story I would love to pursue sometime in the future. Perhaps I wasn't the only one with secrets. I pretended to ignore the *faux pas* and we went to work discussing how our individual duties would be carried out.

So, the master of the house and my potential employer was named Gabriel Ross.

Chapter 16

Higgins was waiting at the door when his employer arrived later in the week. He greeted Mr. Ross and took his cloak and gloves then inquired, "How was your trip, sir? You're back early."

"The usual. Travel is always tedious, but my business was concluded successfully and ahead of schedule. The Council will be pleased. How are things in the salon tonight? Anything I need to deal with right now? I would love a drink and some peace and quiet."

Higgins hesitated.

"I'm sure Mrs. Miller has what you require in the kitchen. Why don't we go there, or I can have something brought to your rooms?"

Gabriel was not pleased with that suggestion. He noticed Higgins seemed a little out of sorts. He was hiding something.

"You know I never eat in the kitchen or my rooms. I would prefer some quiet time in the library."

Higgins was not sure how his employer would receive the news that he had acted on his behalf without permission. He could no longer avoid it since Grace was spending some of her free time this evening in the library, so he decided to get right to the point.

"I've taken on a new chatelaine. Before you object, she knows her employment depends upon your approval. She has been here two weeks and is quite competent. I think you will be pleased. She has even been able to handle the, ah, politics, if you know what I mean."

"Ah, the joys of a house full of women. I know what you mean. I can ignore them most of the time. You have to deal with them all day. I suppose you're glad to have someone else to help herd the cats," Gabriel replied without humor.

"Assuredly, but I'm afraid you are insulting the feline species." Higgins hesitated again. "Her name is Grace Pryce, but there is something you should know. I don't want you to meet her unprepared. She is disfigured. Not alarmingly so, but some might find it distasteful."

"I can determine that for myself." Gabriel sighed. He was hopeful that she would be adequate. It had been difficult around Hightower House without a chatelaine, and candidates for the position were not lining up at the door. They both knew that some of the staff desired the position for the status they thought it would bring them, but none had any of the skills that were necessary. Higgins was doing a splendid job of covering, but things were starting to slip through the cracks, and soon the patrons would begin to notice. "When will I speak with her?"

"She is in the library. You can speak with her now if you wish."

"Well, that explains a lot."

Chapter 17
Grace

I was anxious and tired of waiting. Higgins warned me that my interview would depend on the mood of Mr. Ross when he arrived, which was earlier than anticipated. I was hoping that meant we would talk tonight. So far I was enjoying my position at Hightower House and was in no hurry to lose it. Any anxiety I had over the hostile reception by some of the staff was gone. It would be a relief to have the matter of my employment settled so that my authority could not be challenged.

I got up from the chair in which I was sitting and began to pace the beautiful library. From the size of the collection, it appeared that Mr. Ross loved books as much as I. Learning the requirements of running the house had consumed my time, so I had not had the luxury of spending much of it in this lovely room. It had certainly been on my list of places to explore when I could. There was no time like the present, and I decided to expend my nervous energy by examining his favorite books.

It was obvious which books had been well-read and which were mostly abandoned on the shelf. Some of the spines were cracked and the pages dog-eared, while others looked like they had been bound yesterday. By looking for the ones which appeared to be opened most often, I should be able to get a feel for the tastes and interests of the man I would soon meet. The books were organized by subject and then language. It seemed that Mr. Ross was extremely well educated and could read a number of different languages. His interest in such a wide variety of subjects both awed and intrigued me. I thought myself reasonably well educated, but this was intimidating. It was hard to imagine how anyone could have read all of these volumes enough times for them to show wear. I was growing more impressed by this man by the moment, but I wondered what he would make of me. I hoped that he could see past the scar. I wanted him to approve of me more than I was willing to admit.

My wait finally ended when the door to the library opened. I was reluctant to reveal my face, so I observed the man from behind the book I was holding. Even that limited view was surprising. The doorway framed the most beautiful man I had ever seen. I realize we don't usually describe men as beautiful, but I had no other word to describe him, even those I had in my extensive vocabulary were insufficient. He was more than handsome. He was tall and slender in an athletic kind of way – not bulky, but still muscular. He conveyed an aura of strength and authority, and his elegant, almost effeminate, attire did nothing to disguise the impression that he could be very dangerous if provoked. His dark brown hair was pulled back and tied at the nape of this neck. A few strands had escaped and gave him a rather boyish look. I noticed that he seemed unusually pale, which was probably the result of his travels, as was the shadow of a beard. His most striking feature was the odd golden color of his eyes. Although they reminded me of an animal of some sort – a wolf or cat – they conveyed his obvious intelligence. But there was more to it than that. As he appraised me, there was also an unexpected humor and kindness. I was surprised, and I hoped he didn't notice my reaction.

However, my surprise had nothing to do with any of those things. It was his apparent age. I was expecting a grandfatherly type based on the contents of his library. Even if a number of the well-used volumes were hand-me-downs, he had still read and studied a great deal. Someone who had read as extensively as he, must be at least in his sixties. Gabriel Ross appeared to be no older than his mid-thirties.

I was holding the last book I had taken and deliberately delayed lowering it. As a result, my injured cheek was obscured when Mr. Ross entered the room. As he addressed me, I lowered the book and turned toward him. The eyes which had appeared so benevolent before took on a momentary hardness. I could see the anger as he realized my "disfigurement" was the result of a deliberate act and not a defect of birth. Higgins must not have told him of my circumstances. The moment passed quickly, and Mr. Ross adopted an impassive expression as he motioned for me to sit. He took the chair opposite mine.

"Higgins has good things to say about your work. He is encouraging me to make you an offer of permanent employment. But before I make up my mind, it is clear you have a story to tell. I would like to hear it."

The moment which I was dreading was finally here. I was prepared, but how could I possibly sit across from this extraordinary man and tell the tale I had to tell?

Nothing that happened to me was my fault, but I refused to play the victim either. After taking a deep breath, the story poured out. For the next hour, I told him the story of my life. I did so with as little emotion as possible, almost as if it had happened to someone else. I watched him closely during my narrative to see his reaction. I thought I could see the same hardness in his expression at certain parts of the story, particularly those involving my sister-in-law. Most of the time, however, he maintained a neutral expression that was hard to interpret.

I had been sitting on the edge of my chair while relating my story. At the end, I was emotionally and physically exhausted, so I relaxed with a sigh and let the large leather chair swallow me.

Mr. Ross sat for a moment with his hands steepled in front of him and regarded me. It was one of the most uncomfortable moments of my life. Time stood still as I waited for him to determine my future. But his response was unexpected.

"I see you like books, Miss Pryce. What do you think of my library? I assume you read."

I was offended, and I fear my response expressed some of my anger.

"Of course I read!" Then I caught myself and returned a thinly veiled insult of my own. "I am most impressed by the library, sir. Have you collected all of these volumes, or did you inherit them? Many of the books look well-studied. However did you find the time?" I still couldn't reconcile his age with the size of the collection, and I couldn't resist implying that he could not possibly have studied all of the well-used books contained on the shelves. It occurred to me that my veiled insult might not have been a good idea if I wished to gain the approval of this man, but my nature got the better of me.

The corner of Mr. Ross's mouth turned up in a suppressed smile. He caught the slight but found it amusing.

"It's good to see you have a little backbone. I was not sure by the way you told your tale. You will need it around here if you haven't already found that out. I see you are still clutching one of my books. Which one, if I may inquire?"

I decided that verbal sparring with the man who held my future in his hands was not a good strategy, so I merely responded with the truth.

"It is just a little book of poetry. It was the last one I came to before you arrived."

"It sounds as if you were making a thorough search. What was the purpose?"

He had caught me out.

I blushed furiously and then responded, "I was trying to find out a little about you by looking for the most-used items in the library. I apologize if I overstepped my bounds. No one seems to want to talk about you here. Are they afraid of you?"

Mr. Ross ignored my question but responded to the first part of my statement.

"I congratulate you on your incentive. Your methodology is impressive – very well thought out. Of course, if you were correct about my inheriting the collection, your suppositions would be incorrect. Ignoring that, what were your conclusions about me?"

That question was unexpected and took me completely off guard. What had I learned about him? I took a moment to collect my thoughts and try to remember the relevant volumes.

"I observed that your interests are varied. You are interested in philosophy, mythology, history, religion, and medicine. Those books showed the most wear, as if they were not just perused but studied. You also give a nod to poetry. Since I don't recognize some of the languages represented, I can't tell the subject by the titles, but since they were among other books dealing with a specific subject, I have to assume they were the same. Your cataloguing is methodical. To sum it up; you are well educated and well-read. From the subjects you have studied, you have a serious nature, which seeks to find answers to existential questions. The small section for poetry would indicate you might have a romantic side. I could not tell from the sample if you have a sense of humor, but I didn't make it through the entire collection."

He looked thoughtful for a moment and then burst into laughter.

"Where on earth did Higgins find you? You are a breath of fresh air." He continued to chuckle and responded with a twinkle in his eye, "You have discovered quite a lot about me, and most of it surprisingly accurate. I will have to be careful who I let into my library in the future. I don't want any secrets getting out."

He got up from his chair and extended his hand to me as I got up from mine. I wondered if the carpet had anything to do with the mild shock I got as our hands touched. Mr. Ross seemed a little disconcerted by it. As we walked toward the door, he said.

"However, it is late, and I have been traveling. You will have to wait a little longer to find out if I have a sense of humor."

Then he added, "Just so you can sleep tonight, I approve of your hiring. Welcome to Hightower House, Miss Pryce."

I decided to push my luck a little more.

"May I use the library? In my spare time, of course?"

He chuckled again and responded, "I would be insulted if you didn't. Good night Miss Pryce."

Gabriel

I had been in no mood for an interview but better to terminate the woman's suffering. I still longed for a drink and some peace and quiet, so I intended to keep this interview short. Higgins had already given a positive account of the woman's performance, and that was good enough for me. I would meet her and give my blessing. Two or three minutes at the most. That should be all it would take.

I opened the door to the library and startled the woman perusing my books. I was surprised, and just a little pleased. Maybe I would finally have someone in the house with whom I could discuss something of substance, someone who admired my books rather than my wealth and position. She seemed a little embarrassed, as if she had been caught doing something wrong. I doubt she met many men who were impressed by a woman with an education.

There was something appealing about her which had nothing to do with books. I found myself very drawn to her. Her profile was not classically beautiful, but she was attractive, and even though the "uniform" of her station was not designed to accentuate her female attributes, I could tell she had a pleasing figure. Her light brown hair was pulled back in a thick braid that was attempting but not quite succeeding, to control the wisps of hair which surrounded her face. I had the strangest desire to smooth the stray strands into place behind her ear. Fortunately, I was not close enough to indulge that impulse. She seemed reluctant to lower the book that hid one side of her face. She finally lowered the book, and what I saw was appalling. Higgins had warned me that she was disfigured, but I expected a birth defect of some sort. I did not expect to be confronted with a deliberate act of cruelty. I could not be sure, but I thought she caught the flash of anger in my eyes before I regained my composure. Despite my intention to make this a short interview, I knew I had to hear her story.

I gestured her to one of the chairs and took the one across from her. It was important that I see her face when I demanded she tell me how she came to be here. If this was some sort of plot to gain access to Hightower House, I needed to know. I was good at detecting a lie. Fortunately for Grace she told the story with an honesty that could not be questioned. It was obvious to me it was rehearsed, but I could tell it was her way of keeping her emotions under control. There was a current of betrayal and hurt under her composure that resonated with me. For the time it took Grace to recount her experience, I attempted to remain impassive while she led me through every emotion I could imagine. I could tell Grace was carefully wording her story so as to avoid villainizing the people involved. It was surprising that she could even see humor in some of her "adventures." Her ability to recount the tale without the anger and rancor I was feeling toward everyone involved deserved my admiration. She was, I had to admit, an extraordinary woman, and there was no doubt in my mind she told the truth.

Grace was drained when she finished, and I could see no reason to question her. Since I was now no longer in a hurry to end the evening, I opted to change the subject completely and asked her about my books. The subject seemed to bring her to life again. She responded to my questions with an energy I thought was beyond her at that point. It was obvious she was intelligent when she gave her alarmingly accurate description of me just from perusing my reading material. She exhibited a sharp wit and wasn't afraid to use it. She even managed a few well-placed verbal barbs in response to my own. She had a keen organized mind, much like my own, and I imagined what it would be like to argue, good naturedly, of course, the finer points of philosophy or religion. My friend Yi and I had debated most subjects *ad nauseam*, so there was little left for us to say. It would be nice to have a fresh perspective. Suddenly evenings at Hightower House promised to be much more interesting.

A lull in the conversation indicated that it was time to end the evening. I extended my hand to Grace to help her from the chair, which was threatening to swallow her small frame. I felt a tingle of energy as our hands touched, and I almost released her before she was out of the chair. She had a rather startled look on her face. She must have felt it also. *Interesting.*

Chapter 18

Gabriel would be the first to admit that he appreciated women. That is to say he enjoyed the company of sophisticated and educated women. Where the company of his associates triggered the aggressive nature he tried so carefully to suppress, a charming woman provided a calming influence in his often troubled world. He did not view women with the same disdain as many men of the time. He loved to hear them laugh and couldn't bear to see them cry. He was particularly enraged when they were discarded and abused.

Many years ago, Gabriel Ross had begun to provide refuge for women who escaped, with a little assistance, from deplorable conditions. He provided food, decent clothing, and a safe place for them to live. Some came from homes in which they were abused by family members. They felt betrayed by the institutions, which promised safety, and nurture but failed at both. The majority of the women, however, came from disreputable brothels that preyed on women without means or those who had been sold into sexual slavery. In order to provide employment and income for them until they could find suitable positions, he provided a safe place for them to do the only thing they knew. Prostitution was a way of life for them, and he didn't object to the profession as long as it was voluntary. It provided the only possible means of support for many unfortunate women. It had been that way for centuries. It was logical, then, that his collection of rescued females would evolve into a very exclusive club for his unusual visitors and associates.

At first, as well as providing the necessities, he employed a tutor to teach the women to read and write. They were willing until they discovered how difficult it was to become educated. The tutor, who resigned his position after only a few weeks, described the project as being like trying to teach a pig to play the piano – it just frustrated you and irritated the pig. It was not a particularly flattering comparison (one Gabriel would never share with his charges), but it proved to be true. Finally, Gabriel had to abandon formal education and concentrate on elevating basic social skills. Just getting some of the women who came from the poorest conditions to bathe regularly was a challenge. The men that gathered in his salon were very discerning and expected their companions to exhibit some social graces. It took several years to develop a group who met their exacting requirements.

Gabriel required that all of his employees be in good health and free of drugs. The women were permitted limited alcohol consumption, but drunkenness was not tolerated. Since many of them arrived at Hightower House undernourished and diseased, Gabriel brought his long-time friend Dr. Yi Sheng to Hightower as house physician. Yi treated both conditions. He was kind, empathetic, and non-judgmental. Since Yi's preference was for other men, he was the ideal choice for a house full of women. Gabriel also benefited by having at least one person in the house who was not embroiled or interested in the political mechanizations of the Hightower Council. The Council members were the most frequent visitors to Hightower House and conducted a great deal of business in the congenial environment of the salon.

However, accommodating the libidos of his clients was not the primary purpose of Hightower House. Gabriel also required clean, willing blood donors. Unlike the kingdoms outside the Middle Kingdom, the presence of vampires in Hightower was a not very well kept secret, so recruiting participants was not nearly as difficult as trying to teach the women to read and write. Fortunately, some of the women had already had experience with an immortal before they came to Hightower House and found it quite enjoyable. Those women were able to alleviate fears and convince others of the benefits. Of course, there were some who found both options unacceptable. Gabriel was able to provide kitchen and housekeeping positions for a few. The rest he placed elsewhere. No one was turned out without some means of support.

With so many available women at his disposal, Gabriel had entertained thoughts of a long-term relationship. Occasionally, he had taken lovers but never from his own household. That is not to say he didn't receive many offers. He was, after all, an extremely attractive prospect in many respects. The more ambitious women were looking to gain an advantage over the others in the house and a position well above their poor birth circumstances, a few offered out of pure gratitude. Gabriel declined all offers on the pretext that it would be bad business to exploit his own employees. They would have been insulted to know the real reason. He found them unspeakably boring.

Chapter 19
Gabriel

Recently, I found myself becoming increasingly irritable and restless. When in one of these "moods," my patience for the constant political wrangling was extremely limited, so I avoided the salon. I even occasionally lashed out at my employees – something I regretted later but never admitted to them. I couldn't help but notice that my current display of displeasure seemed to coincide with the appearance of the new chatelaine.

The nature of my assignments for the Council required a certain ruthlessness that tapped into my less desirable instincts. It also threatened to suffocate what was left of my veneer of humanity. I found that female company helped me to hold on to the less aggressive, more rational side of my nature, so Higgins suggested that perhaps it was time for me to take another lover, even for a short time, to lighten my disagreeable mood a bit. Little did Higgins realize that the cause of my discontent was a woman, and taking a lover was the last thing I wanted to consider. The woman I wanted to take would require breaking my own rules. I was pondering this dilemma when I encountered Grace in the library the following evening.

Grace

The solitude of the library was a welcome respite. My duties had kept me busy, and I had not been able to spend much time there lately. I had already examined most of the books on the shelves and made a mental note of the ones I would like to study further. One of the lower shelves remained untouched and was the current focus of my attention. This shelf contained an odd collection of books and manuscripts that defied the other methods of categorization. One item in particular drew my attention. It was a small book with no title on the dark blue leather cover. It looked more like a diary or journal. I opened to the first page and was surprised to see that the title was hand-written. What was even more surprising was its title, *The Truth about Vampires*. There was no author. What an odd thing for Mr. Ross to have in his library. Someone must have written this as a joke. Everyone knew vampires were the subject of myth and fantasy, nothing to be taken seriously. I wondered why this volume – if you could call the slim book a volume – was not in with the other extensive collection of books on mythology. Mr. Ross did seem to be fascinated with myth. Maybe he was the author and trying his hand at a fictional work based on his knowledge of the fantastic. It appeared to be a work in progress, so maybe that explained its odd position in the library. This required further investigation.

I took the small book and sat in a chair to try to decipher the writing. I was so engrossed that I didn't hear the door between the salon and library open or the approaching footsteps muffled by the thick carpet, so I was startled by the voice of my employer.

"Higgins thought I might find you here. What has you so absorbed?"

"Oh, nothing, sir," I replied a little embarrassed. "It's just a little work of fantasy I found on the shelf. Did you need something?"

Gabriel threw himself into the chair opposite me, closed his eyes, and sighed.

"I've just come from a frustrating meeting and need a little distraction. Would you be good enough to read to me? Maybe that will put me in a better frame of mind. As it is, I'm liable to kill someone. An escape from reality sounds like just the thing."

I was doubtful that this particular book was what he had in mind.

"I'm not so sure. This doesn't seem like something you would enjoy. Wouldn't you rather hear some poetry?"

Gabriel opened one eye.

"Do you presume to know me well enough to decide what I would and wouldn't enjoy?" he replied with irritation.

"In my defense, sir, I have been spending a lot of time looking at your collection of books. This one seems rather out of character, but I apologize if I am being presumptuous," I replied sweetly.

Now I had his complete attention. It was not what I intended.

"Oh? And how would you describe my character?" he asked with a cocked eyebrow.

I thought it best to avoid answering his question, so I continued, "Besides, this one is hand written, and I'm still trying to decipher it. The writing is not always clear. It might be difficult for me to read it out loud."

He opened both eyes this time and looked at the book in my hand. He had an amused look on his face as he replied, "That will do just fine."

Reluctantly, I reopened the book and began.

Chapter 20
The Truth About Vampires

I

The truth about vampires is shrouded in mystery, myth and superstition. This treatise is an attempt to set the record straight for those who are open-minded and adventurous enough to read it. I will admit that our kind have played on the fears of mortals as a means of self-preservation. It is easier for humans to ignore us if the legends are too horrifying or ludicrous to believe, but for those humans who live in close contact with us, it is important to know where myth ends and reality begins.

Most of what is known (or believed) about vampires is based on stories that originated a long time ago and were passed on by oral tradition – a notoriously inaccurate method of relaying facts. It seems that early cultures needed someone to blame for misfortune, so they created fantastic creatures to explain the vagaries of nature, disease, and death. Why are so many children stillborn? Blame it on some blood-sucking demon. Why do so many women die in childbirth? Same answer. The list goes on and on. Since no one has ever bothered to ask us, there is no one to refute these absurd accusations.

The organized religions in our time presume to teach that the original vampires were spawned by the devil or, at the very least, demons. That would make us inherently evil. I guess that makes sense to the theologians since we are blamed for every bad thing imaginable. The oldest of our kind are unable to remember back that far and therefore cannot verify or refute the claim. However, I do not think myself any more inherently evil than many mortals I have met. Maybe the clerics' doctrine of original sin applies for both of us.

Others believe that we were created before mankind and given dominion. We were the first gods. So that we would not be tempted to believe that we were equal with our creator, we were given certain vulnerabilities. We need the blood of other warm-blooded species, preferably humans, and we cannot tolerate the sun.

It is true that vampires are parasites. We don't like the term, but let's call a spade a spade. We must consume the blood of another living entity to thrive. It is the curse of our existence. However, we do not need to kill to survive. An older, civilized vampire can even ensure that their donor is not aware that they have been bitten. They may feel a little "under the weather" for a few days but no worse off than before. Since our blood can heal a mortal's external injuries, we can remove all physical evidence and even alter their memory of the encounter.

Younger vampires (those who have been recently sired) are insatiable in their bloodlust. If left unsupervised during the first few years after rebirth, they can terrorize a whole region. It is the responsibility of their sire to lead them through the early years, during which they lack self-control. Most sires accept this responsibility gladly. We do not create others like us lightly and strive to ensure that their transition is as painless as possible for all concerned.

Although many changes take place during rebirth, the process does not change the person's essential nature. Occasionally, a vampire has attempted to create a formidable tool by siring an unconscionable madman. It has not gone well and eventually the child has to be destroyed. It is not to our advantage to draw attention to ourselves. It does occasionally happen that even a carefully chosen subject has unsuspected flaws and resists the guidance of the sire. Then chaos ensues. It is those exceptions that have caused us to be viewed with fear and suspicion. I could cite examples of mortal governments or outlaw groups who have done much worse but I will leave that to your knowledge of history.

At this point, I stopped reading and said, "You've got to be jesting! No one could possibly believe any of this. I'll admit it makes for interesting conjecture but, really!"

Gabriel opened one eye and responded, "You need to have an open mind Grace. It sounds plausible to me. Do you mind continuing?"

I sighed and went on to chapter two.

II

It should be noted that although vampires prefer to refer to themselves as "immortals" we can be killed. It is just very difficult to do so. Most of us fall at the hand of another vampire. Mortals have neither the strength nor knowledge of our nature to dispatch us. They do feel compelled to try, and their inability to do so has led to much of the fear concerning us. The legends of successful vampire hunters are grossly overstated. Best leave us alone if you are able.

There are two things that can kill a vampire – beheading and fire. Both methods are gruesome to behold.

As previously stated, most mortals do not have the strength to cut off a vampire's head on the first try. Make no mistake, it had better be the first try. We heal quickly. We also find it rather irritating to have someone hacking at our necks, so the assailant is not likely to survive the attempt. It is also unlikely that a mortal would be skilled or fast enough to get a blade close enough for a lethal blow. We are very fast, and we can sense an enemy before they can get close. There will be no element of surprise.

Fire is the most practical way to destroy a vampire. (I hesitate to instruct the reader about this since it could be used against me.) It is true that we have an aversion to the sun. If exposed, the heat of it can burn us to extinction. Even if we are not exposed, the daylight hours sap our energy. We don't know why. For this reason, we must retire during daylight hours. Younger vampires must truly sleep. Older vampires are able to stay awake but need to rest some of that time. The truly ancient among us can go out in the sun if protected. They are the "daywalkers." However, the majority of us are vulnerable during the day. If you can find the location of a sleeping vampire, you may be able to destroy them. As a precaution, we usually choose resting places that are impervious to fire and very difficult to locate. Don't look for us in our family crypt.

You can also forget about the stake through the heart. That wound can also heal. You might be able to pin the vampire to the ground for a moment or two, but you'd better get as far away as possible before they recover, or you're dead. That method really makes us angry. That particular myth involved the use of iron stakes to pin suspected vampires in their coffins, so that they could not escape. Sad but true.

You may be wondering what happens if a vampire is denied blood. There have been stories of vampires being trapped for centuries without sustenance. Eventually, the body shuts down to allow the brain to remain functional, but the vampire does not die. If found and revived with fresh blood, they will return to their previous condition. The speed of recovery is enhanced if the blood comes from another vampire. They do tend to wake up rather grumpy.

I stopped reading and looked for something to drink. I was hoping to find a decanter of wine, but anything wet would do. I was parched, and my voice was tired and a little raspy. I had probably continued much longer than I should have, but Gabriel seemed to enjoy listening to me, and I could tell he was much more relaxed than when he entered the room. Noticing my distress, Gabriel came to my rescue.

"Here, let me have the book. You have read long enough. There is wine on the table in the corner. Please help yourself. I will give you a break."

I located the decanter of wine and two glasses.

"Can I bring you a glass also or do you prefer something else? I usually see you with whisky."

"Wine will do. This vintage is one of my favorites. So what do you think of this, what did you call it, 'little piece of fantasy'?"

"To be honest, I don't know what to make of it. Who would write such a thing? I will admit that the writer has a sense of humor about the whole subject. You'd think he truly was a vampire. I can't imagine a mortal making some of the same observations, no matter how vivid their imaginations. But still, I was raised to believe vampires were just myths designed to scare us. It is unsettling to believe they might be real."

"As I said before, keep an open mind. It will allow you to accept truths you had not considered before. Now sit. I will read to you."

Gabriel opened the book were I had left off and began. He had the most wonderfully mellow, baritone voice. His tone was well modulated, his articulation clear. If I didn't know better, I would swear that he was a trained orator. I was shocked when the word "sexy" came to mind, and I nearly choked on my wine. I was sure Gabriel noticed and probably wondered what I was thinking. On second thought, from his sly smile, I suspect he had received that reaction before and guessed exactly what I was thinking. His voice was seductive though, and I sat back in the chair to enjoy it.

Gabriel continued to smile at me as he began. "Chapter Three…"

III

When a vampire is sired the senses are enhanced. For the first few months, sound, smell, taste, feel, and sight are acute to the point of physical pain. Everything is overwhelming. Many newborns spend the first week or so after their rebirth whimpering in a dark corner, trying to avoid any stimulus. The sire must teach the new vampire how to harness the current that runs through his or her new body to create a protective shield. Once that is accomplished, the environment is less threatening, and they can begin to function normally.

The heightened senses help with the other major change. Vampires become more creatures of instinct than thought. In order to coexist in a world with mortals, we must learn to suppress our heightened animal instincts. Even the oldest vampire's strongest motivation is to hunt and feed. Equally strong are the instincts to protect and possess.

Vampires are social animals. Our community structure is much like that of a wolf pack. That wolf-like behavior, particularly while hunting, probably led to the wolfman myths. (Werewolves do not exist, by the way.) Our close identification with the wolf influences our mating ritual as well. We do not embrace marriage in the way it is understood by mortals. Since we cannot procreate, there is no need for a social structure to provide a stable environment for children. Also, the strength of a vampire is determined by the strength of their sire's blood and the vampire's age. Female immortals may be stronger than their male partner. There is no need to protect them by imposing an artificial social institution.

Like wolves, vampires mate for life. With an indeterminate lifespan, it is very important that the decision not be based on mere attraction. The compulsion goes much deeper. I know of no mated vampires who did not know immediately that they belonged together, even if they tried to deny it. It is not uncommon for a vampire to wait hundreds of years for a mate. Our version of marriage (if you dislike the more primitive term mating) only requires that both parties commit to each other. This need not be a public announcement. Once the pair begins sharing blood (yes, we drink from one another during our more intimate moments), other vampires can detect the mingling of scents and acknowledge that they are mated.

Although not ideal, a mortal and vampire may be so drawn to one another that they become a couple. We refer to this as "binding" instead of mating, and the human terms of husband and wife are used. Since one party will outlive the other, the term mate is generally reserved for vampire relationships. This is not to say that the binding is not as strong as mating. It is probably much more difficult to make the decision to enter into this kind of relationship since the death of a partner can create a suicidal despair in the survivor. Immortals have been known to walk into the sun after the death of their mate rather than face the rest of their extended life without them. As a result, the mortal partner almost always eventually chooses to be reborn.

Even though a vampire may wait a long time to mate, that doesn't preclude relationships. Many vampires have a succession of both mortal and immortal lovers. As I said, we are social creatures.

Gabriel stopped reading and looked over at me. My eyes were partially closed, and I was so relaxed that he must have thought I had fallen asleep. But I saw a look of longing on his face. This section on taking a mate seemed to unsettle him. I wondered about his apparent distress. Perhaps he was remembering a lost love or someone he desired but could not have. I could hardly imagine that. He was perfect. But some people could not see beyond his physical beauty and as a result could not have a relationship except on the most superficial level. He would never accept that. But the desire was there and something else I couldn't quite put my finger on. Could it be that he was lonely?

Gabriel must have noticed that my attention wandered.

"Should I continue, or do you wish to retire? You appear distracted."

"Oh no, please go on. Your voice makes even the most absurd subject appealing. I could listen to you all night."

At that, Gabriel's expression lightened. No doubt, like most men, he could always use a little affirmation. His expression, however, was still a little odd as he continued.

"Chapter Four."

IV

Since we are creatures of instinct, we are attuned to the elements around us. We gravitate toward cultures that worship the forces of nature. Like them, we are most effective when there is a balance in our lives. While we are made up of all four elements, earth, wind, water, and fire, each immortal has a preference for one above the others. A vampire sired to earth can, literally, move mountains. You can imagine the rest. Most of the "lesser gods" of myth are the result of mortals observing a vampire manipulating their element. Who are we to argue?

The scholars of the East Kingdom identify a fifth element — the energy that animates us. It is this current which allows us to moderate our senses and control our element. That energy originates in the brain, which is why beheading is one way to kill us. If you separate our bodies from the source of our animating energy, we die. Likewise, if the brain is separated from its source of sustenance, the blood, it cannot create the energy to maintain itself. The scholars theorize that it is not the blood itself but the energy it contains that sustains us. They also believe that there are vampires who are able to drain the life-force from a human without even consuming their blood. I have never encountered this variety, but I suppose it is possible they exist. After all, many humans deny the existence of any of our kind. As belief in magic is replaced by a demand for empirical proof, belief in magical creatures is regarded as nothing more than fantasy. We prefer it that way. It is our protection in a world which we no longer dominate.

By this time, I was barely able to concentrate. Gabriel's mellow voice had lulled me into a state of relaxation nearing sleep. *Magical creatures,* I thought. *That voice is enough to enchant anyone.*

I yawned, "I'm sorry Mr. Ross, but I think it is time for me to retire. I can barely keep my eyes open let alone drag myself to my room. Can we continue another time?"

"I would be delighted," Gabriel responded. "But it will have to be some other text. It seems the author has left off at this point. It is unfinished. Do you like poetry?"

"I will leave the choice to you. Good night, sir."

He surprised me when he responded, "Tomorrow then."

Chapter 21
Gabriel

It was such a pleasure to share time with Grace in the library, and since there were no immediate demands on my time, I was delighted to spend it with her. Over the past weeks, our evenings together had become a daily ritual. Having someone with whom I could share my favorite books was a rare treat. I enjoyed discovering what her choices would be. I did notice, after reading *The Truth About Vampires*, she avoided anything from the mythology section. The library was the one place I could be completely myself – well almost. I could not avoid the feelings I was developing toward her. My intention when she came here was to find a suitable husband or position for her. Reading *The Truth* made it clear to me that she was not prepared for a full disclosure of life at Hightower House. It was also obvious I didn't want to let her go. I tried teasing her now and then to establish a more brotherly relationship. It might have worked for her, but it did nothing to lessen the growing attraction for me. I did not feel brotherly in the least.

Chapter 22

It was late afternoon, and Jayne was holding court in her room. To say that Jayne was beautiful was an understatement. She was stunning. Her pale skin was flawless and provided a contrast to lush red lips and her large dark eyes, eyes that could mesmerize and ensnare even the most hard-hearted men. She had long auburn hair that curled enticingly down her back to her full hips. She was the perfect courtesan.

She had learned early on how to use her physical attributes to her advantage. As such, she attracted a following, especially among the younger women there. She was always surrounded by admirers who hoped to advance their positions in the house just by association with her. They worshipped her as their queen.

Jayne was not well-educated. She could neither read nor write. She grew up on the streets without benefit of even the most basic education. Nevertheless, her followers hung on her every word as if she possessed the answer to the secret of life itself. What Jayne lacked in knowledge, she made up for in cunning and creativity. She was a master at spreading malicious gossip. The current subject of her derision was Grace. Since the new chatelaine had not been forthcoming about the details of her past, Jayne and her little group created them. Had she known, Grace would have been amused at what an interesting life she had lived before coming to Hightower. Her exploits were legendary. The group's make-believe could not have been farther from the truth and centered mostly around Grace's scar. The most popular story involved a liaison with a married man and injury at the hands of a jealous wife. That narrative was the most believable for most of the women since they knew of similar cases in their own experiences. No one expected that the real story would involve a jealous and greedy sister-in-law who felt the need to control her husband and his wealth. Perhaps if they had known, they would have been a little more charitable. They had all been an inconvenience to someone.

But Jayne was the self-proclaimed queen at Hightower House, and she was not feeling charitable. She had been hoping for some time to catch the attention of her employer. She was sure that she could entice the confirmed bachelor into a relationship, which would be of benefit to her. She didn't expect marriage. She didn't even want it. She did want influence. Her current station in the house did not allow the access she needed to make that a reality. Now another obstacle stood in her way: Grace. Jayne noticed that Mr. Ross observed her with something approaching admiration. Jayne resented the time he was spending with Grace in the library. That just would not do. He never looked at Jayne the way he looked at Grace and probably never would. Jayne had to find a way to wipe that admiration from his face or get rid of Grace altogether. Maybe…

Chapter 23
Grace

Next to the library, the kitchen garden was my second favorite place to spend free time. Because of her bulk, the chef had never enjoyed gardening, and as she aged her knees were no longer up to the task. Mrs. Miller was more than happy to turn the gardening duties over to me, and tending the garden became part of my job. I enjoyed the exercise and the time outside, so I was happy to oblige.

I was weeding one afternoon. It had rained for several days, and this was the first chance I had to rescue my new seedlings from the encroaching weeds. It looked as if it would rain again this evening, so I was determined to finish even though it was getting dark. I managed to pull the last weed just as the remaining light faded and then went into the kitchen.

Mrs. Miller looked up.

"My, but you are a mess!" she exclaimed. "You'd best clean up before Mr. Ross sees you. You look like a farm hand."

"Mr. Ross!" I exclaimed. "I was supposed to be in the library by now. I'd best make my excuses before I do anything else. I hope he won't be angry thinking I stood him up for no good reason."

Gabriel looked up expectantly as I rushed into the library wiping my hands on a towel.

"I'm so sorry, sir. I needed to finish in the garden before it rains again. I didn't forget about you. My hands are a fright. I don't think I should be handling any of your books. Perhaps we should wait until tomorrow."

"I wasn't aware you were so passionate about gardening," he said as he looked up from the book he was reading. "I happen to like gardens myself. I don't get a chance to enjoy them much anymore, but I have fond memories."

I guess I got a little dreamy-eyed as I replied, "I love the feel of my hands in the dirt – as you can see." I held up my hands. "I feel connected somehow. There is something very satisfying about helping little tiny seeds come to life and become something new and different. Besides, I love to feel the warmth of the sun as I work. It just feels… right somehow. I don't believe we were meant to stay cooped up in a house all day."

Gabriel was not to be deterred from our evening together.

"Well, I don't believe a little dirt should get in the way of a good book. I have chosen one I think you will enjoy, so sit down, and I will read. You don't need to touch a thing. You can clean the dirt from under your fingernails later."

And that was that.

Gabriel

Grace never failed to surprise me. Rushing into the library with dirty hands was unexpected – I thought it best not to point out the mud on her dress where she had been kneeling. Mrs. Miller forgot to mention she had turned the care of the garden over to Grace. Grace's face, flushed with excitement as she talked about her new duties, made her very appealing. It was her scent, however, which nearly overwhelmed me. She smelled like growing things and sunshine. I wondered.

I knew she was embarrassed to be seen in her current state. She always looked so neat and proper, especially around me. I was flattered that she wanted to look her best for me, although I had to admit it was probably because I was her employer. I could still wish it were otherwise. She had no idea how it delighted me to see her glowing with excitement, and I had no intention of letting her leave the library even to clean up.

And that was that.

Chapter 24
Grace

The following afternoon, Gabriel sent a note asking that I meet him in the kitchen garden instead of the library. He had a surprise for me. I was excited about this deviation from what had become a pleasant but predictable routine.

We met outside the kitchen as the sun was setting. There was still enough light as we walked through the garden for me to indicate the new sections I was cultivating. I pointed with pride at the section containing the new herbs I had just planted, the ones which had made me late to our appointment the previous evening. Mrs. Miller was anxious for the new additions to get large enough for her to incorporate into her latest recipes. I suppose I was bragging a little, but I was proud of the improvements I had made and hoped for my employer's approval.

At the far end of the garden was a wall with a formidable looking door. Gabriel took a key out of his pocket and unlocked it. It didn't look like any of the keys I carried, so I was intrigued.

"Close your eyes, Grace," Gabriel instructed as he led me through the opening and relocked the door. "I want to see your expression when you see the surprise." I did as instructed. However, I could not help but notice the lovely fragrance that greeted us.

"It has to be some kind of fragrant garden," I exclaimed. "You might cover my eyes, but you can't cover my nose! What a glorious smell. It's almost intoxicating."

Gabriel chuckled, "You can open them now. You're a hard woman to surprise."

I was stunned by the sight that greeted me. I never would have guessed that this paradise existed behind the sturdy door. The large, carefully planned garden was magnificently planted with a large variety of night blooming plants. I was able to identify moonflowers and jasmine as well as queen of the night and lady of the night cactus, but there were many others I had never seen before. Surrounding the formal garden was a wild perimeter, which allowed plants to grow in a more natural environment.

There was a large pond in the center of the formal portion of the landscaping and walkways radiated from it. The paths created sections which contained plants with similar growing requirements. There was a section which must have been shaded most of the day, and one containing plants that needed full sun. There was a section for succulents and cacti, and another for water-loving varieties. These separations made life easier for the gardener since everything in each section required the same care. The pond created the final growing environment and contained several types of night blooming water lilies. Its fountain added an additional element, the sound of splashing water. The overall effect was ordered and tranquil.

"I chose tonight to bring you here because the moon is full," Gabriel explained. "You don't get the full effect without it. The moonlight creates a lovely effect with the white flowers. They almost seem to glow. I am in awe whenever I come in here. Believe it or not, one of my gardeners created it on a bet. No one thought he could design a garden that could only be truly appreciated by moonlight. As you can imagine, he won the bet. It has been one of my favorite places ever since it was created. It is my refuge from the insanity, which can be part of this place"

In addition to the plants, each section of the garden contained statuary. The figures represented various gods who were associated with different aspects of nature. All, that is, except one. Off to one side was the statue of a barely clad male without a head. It was a beautiful piece, even if it seemed out of place. Perhaps it represented a long-forgotten deity no one remembered. The sculptor knew what he was doing and had used a very appealing model. Something about it was strangely familiar, and I found myself drawn to the figure. The way the moon shone on the pale marble made it look alive. Like the flowers it almost glowed. I reached out and ran my fingers absentmindedly over the bare chest. I found it hard to believe chiseled stone could be so smooth and life-like.

Gabriel

I had trouble suppressing a smile as I watched Grace's intimate encounter with the statue. She was so focused I think she forgot she had an audience. Grace wore her feelings on her sleeve, and I observed when her dreamy caress ended with a look of disappointment and sadness. She had discovered that no matter how life-like, the flesh she hoped would be warm and yielding was anything but. Her reaction spoke of some unmet desire.

I was curious about her reaction, so I inquired, "What is it Grace? Is something wrong?"

The interruption shook her out of her reverie. Grace was blushing furiously. "Oh, nothing," she replied. "Certainly nothing I would share."

It was fortunate for her that moonlight did not enhance the color red, but I could still see her blush. I paused for a moment and then attempted to joke her out of her apparent embarrassment. "I suppose you are imagining a more intimate encounter with ..."

Grace

At that moment, I realized what about the statue seemed familiar. Even fully clothed in Gabriel's custom tailored attire, I could imagine what was concealed underneath. Lately, I had been considering it much more than I should. The probability that I would never find out for sure filled me with regret, unless this statue was the accurate representation I suspected it might be.

Gabriel stopped his inopportune jesting when he saw the tears in my eyes.

"Oh, Grace! I'm so sorry. Does it remind you of someone, a lost love perhaps?"

I sighed and admitted, "No, of love never to be. The problem with getting your ideas of romance from books and gossip is that no one will ever be able to live up to the ideal you have created. The subject of this statue is so perfect, but so unattainable. I was disappointed to find it so cold and lifeless."

Gabriel smiled, still trying to lighten the mood and salvage the evening.

"Don't sell yourself short, Grace. You wouldn't want this one," he said as he indicated the statue's missing head. "He has nothing up there, and I can't imagine you settling for brainless brawn no matter how perfectly formed."

I swiped at a tear that threatened to run down my cheek. He was right, of course, but the smile his comment elicited was still sad.

"Of course you're right, but there is no chance of a normal life for me, not now."

Now it was Gabriel's turn to look sad as he asked, "What do you consider a normal life? What is it you desire, Grace?"

"I suppose it is a husband, home, and children," I replied quietly. "At lease that is what I was raised to expect. What other option would I have outside of my current situation, that is?"

Gabriel was very good at hiding his emotions, but I was able to detect the disappointment he briefly exhibited before returning to his customary impassive expression.

I hurried on to add, "It's not that I am unhappy here. I appreciate everything you have done for me." I paused and then continued. "It's just not how I expected to spend the rest of my life. Still, I'm in no hurry to leave. I think my situation here is the best I can expect."

Gabriel looked down at the ground trying to hide his regret as he spoke.

"I'm glad that you are not in a hurry to leave. You have become indispensable here, but I can arrange a marriage for you if that is what you want. After all, I am the closest thing you have to a male protector now. It would be my duty to find you a suitable husband."

His response disturbed me, and I responded more harshly than I intended.

"That's just it! I don't want an arranged marriage. That is precisely what I had been avoiding all those years. What right do you or any other male have to choose a husband for me? I want to choose the man I marry. I know that is not the way things are done in our culture, but can you guarantee the kind of match I expect? I don't want to end up some exhausted drudge with children hanging on my skirts while my carefree husband takes a mistress to avoid the demands of his family. Is that asking too much?"

"You appear to have a rather low opinion of marriage," Gabriel observed.

"Don't take me wrong. I have seen good marriages, so I know they can exist. But I have seen so many more that only seem to benefit the men. Marriage as an institution was created to protect women and give children a safe environment in which to thrive and grow. Judging from the stories of the women you employ, it hasn't worked out that way for many."

Gabriel nodded.

"I have to admit you have a point. I also have very high expectations where relationships are concerned. I suppose that is why I never considered marriage, and I have waited much longer than you. That still begs the question, what kind of life do you envision for yourself? How can I help you obtain it?"

I walked over to the nearest bench and sat before I replied. He had a point. I knew what I didn't want, but did I have any idea what I did want? I took a deep breath to calm down and collect my thoughts then began.

"The marriage I want is a partnership. As far as what kind of man I would like, he would be kind and understanding. He has to be intelligent – at least my equal – or smarter. My husband must value me for my brain, not just my ability to run his house and have his children. Most of all, we have to respect one another. I have little experience with men. Tell me, does that kind of person even exist?" I stopped for a moment and continued, "I suppose I want a lot."

The admission brought tears.

Gabriel's response was gentle and not at all defensive.

"I'm afraid that you do expect a lot, but I don't believe it is impossible. I understand why you have never married. Have you considered that what you call a normal life as it exists in our culture may not be your ideal? You seem to be describing two very different types of relationships – the one you want and the one which is expected of you. Do you want the husband who expects you to run his house and have his children and little else? Or do you desire someone who will go through life with you as his partner and lover? I'm reluctant to suggest it. but the second option might not include marriage."

I looked at him rather amazed that he had grasped the situation so well. More importantly, he was actually taking me seriously.

"What do you mean? I never believed I would have a choice. My role in life seems to be written in stone with no exceptions unless I want to choose the life your courtesans have chosen."

"I can introduce you to some men who might be of interest. Not all men are looking for a wife. Some would be more than happy with a pleasant companion. I would not presume to arrange a marriage. But as long as you are here, you have a choice. It's a shame the other men in your life never really listened to what you desired."

Gabriel

It had taken a great deal of patience for me to listen to Grace's lament and respond with a degree of compassion. I guess I was successful, but a great deal of self-control was required. I had never been in this kind of situation before. I had never given a second thought about making the same offer to my other employees. But this was different. Everything in me cried out to satisfy my selfish desires and convince Grace to stay. There was no reason to disrupt the status quo. She could have the second kind of relationship here. With me. The nobler part of me argued that I would be just as bad as the other men in her life if I tried to limit her options.

It seemed Grace felt much better after expressing her disappointment with the direction her life had taken. It was cathartic for her. I, however, was a little hurt. I hoped she was not including me as one more man who disappointed her. Was she was judging me and perhaps finding me wanting? Before I became consumed with the question, I changed the course of our conversation. I was adept at changing the subject when things got too uncomfortable. It wasn't entirely clear which of us was the more uncomfortable at the moment, but Grace seemed to appreciate the abrupt change.

"This conversation is much too serious for such a beautiful setting," I stated.

"Take some time to think about what you want later. There is no rush. Let's just enjoy the rest of the evening. I have much I want to show you. We'll avoid discussing the statuary."

Grace got up from the bench and dried her eyes on her sleeve then walked over to where I stood.

"You're right. I can't believe I'm pouring my heart out when all you did was plan a wonderful surprise. I'm in danger of ruining a beautiful evening. I'm sorry."

I tactfully ignored the apology.

"We're going to take the path around the perimeter. It is where some of the rarer blooms are planted. It's rather uneven so I suggest you take my arm. There are many hazards that are difficult to see in the dark."

Chapter 25
Grace

Gabriel tucked my hand in the crook of his arm, and we began a leisurely stroll. I was grateful for his support. He must have excellent night-vision because I found it very difficult to navigate even with the full moon providing illumination, but then I suppose he had walked this path many times and knew the hazards. I also realized that until tonight, Gabriel and I had rarely touched, so the offer of his arm was surprising.

Gabriel steered me along the winding path and pointed out some of the flowers that I would not see anywhere else. There was no conversation other than his descriptions of the various species. He was cautious to say nothing that would disturb the fragile peace we were now enjoying, and I finally relaxed.

About halfway around the garden, I tripped and nearly fell. Gabriel instinctively pulled me against his chest to steady me. The next moments seemed to last for an eternity, and I realized two things as Gabriel held me. The first was that his embrace was lasting longer than necessary to return me to my feet – a fact I didn't mind in the least. The second was that even with several layers of clothing between us his chest felt very much like I imagined the statue would feel if it were indeed real. My hands on Gabriel's chest recognized the similarity. It was an absurd thought. Maybe it was due to my emotional state earlier, but I began to giggle.

Gabriel chuckled.

"I don't know what I did to lighten the mood, but it's nice to hear you laugh."

I could not contain myself. I had already confided my deepest regrets and desires to this man who I was only beginning to know, so what was one more embarrassing confession? The previous thought was just too funny not to share, so I blurted out:

"You feel just like how I imagined the model for the statue would feel. Did you pose for it?"

Gabriel

I snorted.

"Just how old do you think I am? That statue is several hundred years old. But thank you. I'm quite flattered. Frankly, I don't see the resemblance." However, I was well aware of the resemblance, and judging from the manner in which Grace was caressing the statue earlier, I was more than flattered. Finally, I leaned down and whispered in her ear. "You can let go of me now."

Grace put weight on her foot and winced.

"I would, but I twisted my ankle when I tripped. You may need to help me back." She looked at the distance to the garden gate and added, "You will definitely have to help me back."

Grace was struggling. and I could see her ankle hurt a great deal. Our progress back to the entrance was slow, and finally I picked her up in my arms and carried her. She snuggled against my chest, and I had the feeling she was still thinking about the statue.

"Mr. Ross," she began. "I'm terribly embarrassed about this evening. I'm sure your surprise didn't go exactly as you planned. I don't know what got into me. I shouldn't have gotten so melodramatic. I know you dislike hysterical women. And now, because of my clumsiness, the evening has ended too soon, and you are burdened with having to carry me back to my room like a child."

"Carrying you back to your room is the least of my concerns. It is my pleasure. I don't often have attractive women hanging onto me. However I'm concerned about your ankle. Shall I have Dr. Sheng take a look at it?"

"I think it will be fine once I can put it up. If it is not better in the morning, he can tend to it. Thank you for the offer though."

My surprises for Grace this evening didn't end when we left the garden. I had a request I was not sure she would be willing to grant. I wanted her to call me by my given name. I wanted to hear my name on her lips.

"I could never do that!" Grace exclaimed. "You are my employer! It would not be appropriate. What would the others think?"

I was disappointed by her reaction. I hoped this evening would mark a turning point in our friendship. She had been so open earlier. I did not want to return to our more formal relationship but I conceded that it was still necessary in public.

"I wouldn't expect you to do so in front of others, but at least when we are alone. I call you Grace all the time. Please?"

"But I am already unpopular with Jayne and her worshippers. I could just imagine what they would make of me calling you Gabriel. Even if the two of us are 'alone,' the house has ears. Everyone seems to know everything that goes on. I will consider it, but I'm still concerned someone might hear."

The walk back to Grace's room was quiet. She was lost in her own thoughts. Was she actually considering my request? However. I had come to an important decision and was preparing to act on it as I set her down in front of her door. Grace turned to me and thanked me again for the lovely evening. She raised herself up on her good leg and leaned forward to say goodnight. I knew she intended it to be only a chaste kiss on the cheek, something one would bestow on a relative or a child. At the last moment, I turned my head toward her slightly and instead our lips met, and it became more than chaste.

Grace

I wasn't sure who changed the intent. It had to be Gabriel because I certainly didn't know how to kiss like that. But how did it happen? Was it merely a reflex on his part, or did it mean something? Whatever the intent or reason it set my heart racing and took my breath away. As the kiss deepened, he pulled me tight against his body. I molded against him as if we had done this many times before. It seemed so natural. But my brain, which was nearly incapable of rational thought at this point, and the need to breathe, finally convinced me that I needed to break away. My gasp as I drew in much-needed air covered my disappointed sigh as I reluctantly ended the kiss. Gabriel's grip on my waist loosed, but he did not let me go.

"Don't," Gabriel whispered. "Not yet. I have wondered for some time what this moment would be like. Let me savor it little longer."

But I had finally come to my senses.

"I need to go. This is not proper. What would this look like to the others?"

Gabriel sighed as he released me and muttered, "I don't really care, do you?"

Reason dictated what I needed to say, even if my heart said otherwise. But I made one concession and responded, "Yes, I suppose I do – Gabriel."

I leaned against the doorframe for a moment and then reluctantly entered my room. I wanted to call him back. I wanted to invite him into my room. Most of all, I wanted him to kiss me like that again – and again.

Gabriel

I watched as Grace closed her door and then walked slowly down the hall to my own quarters. I knew she meant the kiss to be a peck on the cheek in thanks for the evening. It was an innocent gesture. I was the one who decided it should be something more. I had already decided that was how I wanted to end the evening. Grace just gave me the opportunity I needed without being too obvious. Was it wise? Of course not, but our evening in the garden had forced me to face the truth. The thought of finding a husband for her was intolerable. I couldn't imagine life here without her. In a few short months, she had become part of the fabric of Hightower House. When I saw the way she touched the statue… (Yes, I was the model. It was a decision I regretted every time I was in the garden and the reason I insisted the head be removed.) I wasn't surprised at my physical response. It was, after all, a very sensual gesture. It was the wave of possessiveness that overcame me that was unexpected. When she tripped, my need to protect her was almost overwhelming. The signs were undeniable. Possession, protection, my instinct to mate had been triggered. I hadn't even considered finding a mate since it had never happened in all these years. It would be extremely inconvenient at this point in my life. I now understood Yi's amusement when he teased me about my feelings for Grace. He saw it from the beginning. Was the kiss wise? The question no longer mattered. I could have done nothing else.

Chapter 26

Jayne stood in the dark doorway down the hall. She had been watching Gabriel's movements for some time, hoping to catch him alone. She was sure she could eventually seduce him into making her his mistress, which would elevate her above all the others. He had never given her any indication that he was interested, but she was determined to try. Failure was not an option.

If Gabriel had been paying attention, he would have detected her stalking. He could never imagine anyone in his house would stoop so low. He might have noticed if her scent was distinctive. He could pick out Grace's scent anywhere. But Jayne wore the expensive perfume he required all the courtesans to wear. It was difficult to find one that was light enough not to be offensive to his patrons' sensitive sense of smell but strong enough to cover the fact that some of the women still did not bathe regularly. As such, the scent he detected in the hall could belong to any one of the women. It permeated everything in their wing of the house.

But Jayne saw the kiss. She was devastated. *Grace is nowhere as pretty as I am*, she thought. *How could he possibly pick her over me? After all, I know who he really is, and it doesn't matter. She has no idea, but it's about time she did. The library was one thing, but this is intolerable.* Jayne was more determined than ever to get rid of Grace.

After trying her best to circulate rumors that put Grace in a bad light, Jayne realized she would have to devise another plan. Jayne had such a reputation for malicious gossip that no one outside her circle of friends took her seriously – least of all the two she wished most to influence. She discovered that Grace was not compelled to remain at Hightower House. Maybe if Grace found out what really went on here, she would leave on her own. It would not do to just tell her. Jayne needed to create a situation in which everything was revealed in a way that Grace could not ignore. Jayne was particularly upset after witnessing the kiss, so Grace also needed to know that Mr. Ross was a part of it.

After all her scheming, Jayne's plan was quite simple. She would lure Grace into the one place she was not supposed to go. Grace would then either face a severe reprimand from her employer and loss of his trust or confront a reality she might find unacceptable. Either scenario was a win for Jayne, but her first choice was that Grace would run screaming from the salon and never look back.

Chapter 27
Grace

As chatelaine, I carried a large ring of keys. Higgins and I were the only ones who could access all of the rooms and cupboards. Even Mr. Ross didn't have all the keys. I had been at Hightower House long enough that Higgins felt he could take some time off and was away from the house one evening. As a result, when I received the message that the salon was out of Mr. Ross's favorite whisky, I was the only one who could get it. I thought it odd that so much had been consumed that evening. I had restocked just this morning, but maybe there was a large party going on inside. Who was I to judge? Some of Mr. Ross's favorite guests rather enjoyed drinking up his expensive scotch, so I retrieved another bottle and decanted it. Then I looked for a steward to take the decanter in. Finding no one, I decided to take it in myself. I knew I shouldn't but surely a quick in and out would not violate my restrictions. There were extenuating circumstances after all.

I had been in the salon many times during daylight hours, but it seemed much different when populated. Like most of the public areas of the house the salon had very masculine décor with a great deal of dark wood and leather. There were a small number of curtained alcoves for private gatherings, but most of the large room was separated into small groups of tables and chairs where patrons met for conversation, a drink or cigar and, often, female companionship.

The most impressive feature in the room was the large sideboard, which dominated one wall. The structure was well stocked with every kind of libation imaginable. and the visitors were welcome to help themselves. From the items I had to replenish each morning, I discovered that Mr. Ross's guests were particularly fond of scotch and dry red wine. There were meticulously polished glasses at either end. and the decanted spirits were in the center along with bowls containing a selection of dried fruits and nuts. It seemed no other food was required.

I entered the salon and placed the decanter on the sideboard. I was relieved that Mr. Ross was deep in conversation with one of his friends and had his back to me. I could complete my task and be out before he was even aware I had been there. However, before I could turn to leave the room, Jayne looked up and gave me a malicious smile. At that moment, I knew that I had been lured into the forbidden room under false pretenses. Jayne had orchestrated this whole situation. I should have trusted my instincts about the unusual summons, but honestly, I was curious about what went on in here every night. This provided me with the excuse to find out.

Jayne chose my momentary hesitation to implement the second part of her plan. She held her wrist up to her companion's mouth. He bit and he began to drink. Jayne's triumphant expression said it all. She had gotten me. I felt the room begin to spin and then everything went black.

Chapter 28
Gabriel

Dr. Yi Sheng had been my friend for many years and was physician for the residents of Hightower House. Our topic for the evening was Grace and whether it was possible to remove her scar. I was not sure how to approach her about it. I didn't want her to think that I found her slight disfigurement objectionable. After the swelling went down, the injury was not all that noticeable. But I sensed that the scar both bothered and comforted her. She used it to shield herself from unwanted attention. But Grace had been raised in an environment where physical beauty was required to obtain a good husband or position and even a small flaw could remove a woman from consideration by some. As a result, she believed that a good marriage was no longer an option for her. She had already declared her belief that it was the whole person that should appeal to any man worth having. I had to admit I found her whole person very appealing. Leaving the scar might be a way to keep her here and discourage other interested parties.

Yi continued with his discussion of the medical options available to us.

"If the injury had been new, I could have healed it without a trace. But this is an old injury that has left a scar because of the clumsy way in which it was handled. I doubt she had the benefit of a competent doctor," Sheng explained. "The only real option is to reopen the original wound, remove the scar tissue and then seal the new injury with immortal blood. Do you think she would agree to that?"

"That discussion might be a little awkward since she is still skeptical about the existence of vampires. Some early lessons die hard. She certainly doesn't suspect we are immortals," I replied. "But I guess we don't have to tell her everything."

The next event rendered our discussion moot.

There was a commotion on the other side of the room toward the door. Yi and I both looked up and then I smelled it. Blood. Not just any blood – her blood! My first thought was, *Why is she in here?* But my instinct was to reach her before anyone else. An open bleeding wound in this room could be dangerous. When Grace fell, she hit her previously injured cheek on the corner of the sideboard, adding a new wound. The smell of blood drew the attention of every immortal in the room. Intrigued by the scent of new blood, they began to converge on Grace's still form. My shouted "NO" halted everyone's advance, allowing me to be the first to reach her. I snarled and bared my fangs at the curious guests. which left no doubt in their minds that I had just publicly declared she belonged to me as more than just an employee. They made room for me as I picked her up and quickly left the room. Yi followed immediately and closed the door firmly behind us.

I carried the unconscious Grace into the library and laid her on the couch there.

"Do you really want to do this here?" Yi asked.

"If she wakes, this would be the least threatening place for her to be. She doesn't know yet that I am an immortal. I'd like to keep it that way a little longer, but after tonight, she will probably suspect. She is irritatingly perceptive sometimes. Can you imagine how she would react with two vampires standing over her in her own room? Besides, it will be much easier to remove her blood from the leather. The scent of it is already driving me to distraction."

"So you've developed an attraction."

I nodded reluctantly.

"That is why I wanted to have the scar removed. I would like to find a position for her. A romance between the two of us would be extremely inconvenient. It would be better if I found a position for her somewhere else as soon as possible. Restoring her appearance would make that easier. The scar raises too many questions about her past."

"So, a position, not a husband," Yi said with a smirk.

"I don't think I can go that far. Every time I even consider the possibility of her marrying someone, the voice in my head screams 'MINE!'" I admitted.

"Are you sure you can let her go at all? Your protective instincts tonight indicate you have already claimed her. Besides, the others in the room have the scent of her blood. If she is that appealing to you, there are others who will pursue her wherever she goes. From this point on, she will need a strong immortal patron."

"I haven't had a significant relationship in a long time, Yi. I don't need one now. You know what I do for them. It makes me a target. Anyone I care for will be one also – even more so a mortal who could not possibly defend herself against my enemies."

"I understand that, but it seems that you already care for the woman and have demonstrated that publicly. She can be used as a tool to get to you if you do not keep her under your protection. Besides, you've been much more content since she arrived. She's good for you."

I had only one response to Yi's comments.

"Damn!"

"Well, we're not here to discuss your love life. We need to get started before she wakes."

"It's not my love life," I muttered *sotto voce*.

"Gabe, you to need to keep her unconscious while I work," Dr. Sheng instructed. "It shouldn't take long, and I suspect the head injury is enough to keep her under without your influence, but you should be prepared."

The procedure went quickly and without incident. Sheng bit his lip and prepared to seal the new incision on Grace's cheek with his blood. I gently pushed him back.

"I will do it."

"No, you're not smitten at all," Yi said with a smirk. "Congratulations."

"Oh, shut up and get out of my way!"

Chapter 29
Grace

I woke up the following morning in my own room. Aubry was sitting in the chair next to the bed looking concerned but relieved that I was finally awake.

"Mr. Ross asked me to look after you. You had quite an adventure last night."

"Am I the only one who didn't know about the, uh, unusual associates?"

"I'm sorry, Grace. I'm not allowed to talk about it. Mr. Ross said he'd talk to you tonight. I'm just here to make sure you're alright."

"Can you at least tell me if Jayne was behind it? Was Mr. Ross angry that I was in the salon?"

"Like I said, Mr. Ross will talk to you later. I can tell you that Jayne couldn't wait to leave this morning. She said she was going to live with her new patron."

"I guess that answers one question. I don't think she'd leave unless she thought she was going to be dismissed. What did she hope to accomplish?"

Just then Aubry started literally bouncing in her chair with excitement.

"But something good came out of all of it" she said as she held up a mirror. "Take a look."

I was astounded by what I saw. The woman looking back at me was completely unmarred. The ugly scar on my cheek was gone. All that remained was a barely noticeable thin line where it had been.

"How" I asked.

"When you fainted last night, you hit your head on the corner of the sideboard and hurt your cheek again. There was a lot of blood and that got everyone's attention. Mr. Ross had to rescue you from some of the more interested patrons. As it happened, Dr. Sheng was with him at the time, and he got rid of the scar while he healed the new cut."

"But, there is no evidence of an injury at all. How is that possible?" I was still staring at the mirror in disbelief.

"Vampire blood can heal mortals. Of course, you wouldn't know that since you didn't believe in vampires until last night." Suddenly Aubry realized that she had said too much. "Please don't let Mr. Ross know what I said," she pleaded.

"But why? I understand healing the new injury but why would he remove the scar? Was my appearance so distasteful? Wait. That means Dr. Sheng is an immortal, Mr. Ross too?" My head was still reeling from the idea that I had been healed, and by a vampire no less. It was hard to fathom. I grabbed on to Aubry's arm to make sure I was not dreaming. This was crazy!

"Who cares?" Aubry exclaimed. "You're beautiful again! Aren't you happy? As for the other question, you'll have to wait for Mr. Ross."

I put aside the question of my employer's immortality and focused on the removal of the scar. That was a question I had to consider carefully. Was I pleased? The scar had been a kind of defense. Most people, especially men, avoided me because of it. I felt safe hiding behind it. It was my mask and concealed who I really was. Maybe Lilith's parting gift to me was really a blessing in disguise. My former provincial life had not prepared me to face the wider world on my own. I knew nothing of courting or relationships outside of those in my family. My illusions of a love match rather than an arranged marriage were shattered by the abduction. If I was honest with myself, my knowledge of romantic relationships came from books. I doubted they were anything other than the fantasies of the author and probably unrealistic. I had never felt any real attraction to a man until Gabriel's kiss. So, was I pleased? That remained to be seen.

"I need to get up and get to work. I can't stay in bed all day," I announced to avoid thinking about my many unanswered questions and the implications of my changed appearance.

"Staying in bed is exactly what Mr. Ross wants you to do," Aubry said as she pushed me back down on the bed. "You have a nasty bump on your head. and you lost a lot of blood last night. You need time to recover. Mr. Ross said to tie you down if I had to."

Resigned, I settled back into the comfort of my bed and fell asleep.

Aubry awakened me a little before sundown.

"Get up. It's time to get you dressed. Mr. Ross wants you to meet him in the library as soon as you are ready. I hope you feel up to it. He was kind of insistent, but I could have him come here if you are still not feeling well."

I felt slightly dizzy as Aubry helped me out of bed, and I had a splitting headache. Aubry viewed me with concern.

"Should I tell Mr. Ross that you can't come? You are paler that usual. Maybe this could wait another day or two."

"No. I'd rather get it over with, and I don't want him to have to come here. I'll be fine in a few minutes."

With Aubry's help, I donned my uniform and tidied my hair. I had a sinking feeling that this was the last time I would wear the dove-gray watered silk dress. Despite the obvious disadvantage of working around a bunch of vampires, I liked it here. It was safe. *Odd that I should think of working around vampires as safe.* I didn't look forward to losing my position, but I had disobeyed an order from Mr. Ross. By rights, he should dismiss me. As I considered the situation, I realized that I had been there for three months and knew little about the creatures that came and went. They never threatened me before, so I had no reason to believe they would do so now that I knew what they were.

I walked down the hall with all the dignity and grace I could muster to face my uncertain future.

Chapter 30
Gabriel

I waited in the library considering how I should handle this interview with Grace. I considered talking to her in the library but decided, instead, that the salon would be the proper environment. She might as well face what remaining at Hightower House would mean for her. Despite my earlier intention to place her somewhere else, I realized she might make the decision to leave on her own. I hoped fervently that she would not.

Grace appeared nervous when she entered the room. I approached her and took her arm.

"Come with me. We have a lot to talk about." I opened the door to the salon and escorted her to my private siting area in a far corner of the room. Grace openly stared as we walked through the crowded room. She observed several of the guests feeding from the women in my employ and seemed surprised to hear moans of pleasure as the men took blood from either their wrist or neck.

"It's not polite to stare," I whispered in her ear. "Although, I understand why you would. I suspect you have a lot of questions."

Grace blushed and turned her attention to me.

"You are right we have a lot to discuss! You're exploiting these poor women! How do you get away with feeding them to vampires?" she whispered angrily. "Is that what you intend for me now that I know? This is nothing more than a brothel with different clientele. I haven't escaped that fate after all."

"Sit and calm down, Grace. I will explain everything," I said as I motioned the steward to bring two glasses of whisky. I remained silent until the drinks arrived and downed mine in one gulp. *This is going to be much harder than I thought. I didn't expect her to be angry.*

Grace looked at her glass with distaste.

"I don't drink whisky. It's vile tasting."

I smiled indulgently.

"You've never had MY whisky. Or maybe you just don't know how to drink it. However, that lesson can wait." I picked up her glass and downed the contents also. *I'm going to need it.*

"To begin, the presence of immortals in Hightower is a not very well-kept secret. In reality, Hightower was our fortress long before mortals discovered the peace and safety of our protection. The prosperity of this town is the direct result of our policing. At one time, this place was lawless. As the only access to the other kingdoms in the Known World, Hightower was constantly overrun with opposing armies hoping to control the passes for military purposes. It is why Hightower House looks so much like a fortress. It was and can be again if necessary. The first immortal king of the Middle Kingdom raised a formidable army and restored peace to the area. After the others were denied access to trade routes for a period of time, it was easy to negotiate treaties that benefited all parties."

"Hightower remained a military installation for centuries. Eventually, mortals discovered the safety of life under the protection of the immortals, and local business began to develop. The newcomers built permanent shops, and the town began to flourish, and the market at Hightower became the place to buy and sell a wide variety of goods. The mortal population grew, and a city emerged. Of course, the immortals benefited also. We did not have to travel far for food."

"Unfortunately, no society is without its problems. Not everyone prospered. Some families had more children than they could support. Unwanted female children were often turned out to fend for themselves. Those were the fortunate ones. Others were kept and abused by their male relatives."

"As you may remember from reading the book – which my sire and I authored by the way – vampires rely on blood to thrive. Rather than allow the discarded or abused women to live in poverty, the immortals in Hightower provided a place for them to come and live comfortable lives. In exchange, the females would provide a safe blood supply. At first, the women were skeptical. After a short while, they realized that we offered a much better life than they could possibly expect elsewhere, and all it cost them was a little blood, which they could easily give and never miss. Very few stayed longer than a couple years, and there were always others willing to take their places. If the women requested, the immortals found jobs or husbands for them in other parts of the kingdom. The women who are here now have chosen to remain here. You are the only one who was brought here against your will, and I have tried to protect you from our way of life until we could decide how to help you. You were never supposed to know about us. Jayne's little stunt changed that, and she has suffered the consequences of her betrayal."

Grace shook her head as she finally heard the subtext in what I was saying.

"You said we. You also?"

"I could not run this establishment otherwise. The patrons would not trust me. I'm sorry I didn't just tell you from the beginning but you were so fragile. I was afraid another shock would undo you."

Grace was not yet willing to give up her righteous indignation and ignored my apology.

"You make this all sound like some kind of benevolent operation," she said sarcastically. "You can't convince me that anyone would willingly be bitten by a vampire."

"Look around you, Grace. The reality is staring you in the face. Do these women look abused or unhappy?" Just then, female laughter punctuated my question. "In fact, they appear to be enjoying the experience. They will feel a little sluggish tomorrow and will take the day to stay in bed and recover. It is not unlike what you experienced from accidental blood loss but without the head injury. You seem fine now. These women are only allowed to be available donors once a week."

"But doesn't it hurt? You are sinking your teeth in their flesh!" She was still indignant.

"Our blood has the ability to numb the area affected, so the donor doesn't feel anything but a slight pull as the vampire feeds."

"Then why are they moaning if they are not hurt?"

I smirked slightly before I answered. Honestly, I was pleased at her question.

"I must assume you have never taken a lover or you would not need to ask."

Grace blushed.

"Of course I haven't!" she said. "I lived a very sheltered life until now. My father was certainly not going to tell me about the way things are between a man and a woman, and I had little opportunity to discuss it with other women. I guess Father thought my husband would take care of educating me," she admitted with a sigh. "You're right. I've no experience with such things."

"You should speak with your friends here. They are now permitted to tell you about the more intimate aspects of their job. Understand that no one is forced to do anything they do not wish to do."

"But the book said your kind could influence mortals. Isn't that the same thing?"

"That is forbidden here. If I find out about any immortal using their influence to seduce one of the courtesans, they will not be allowed to return. We have to be intentional about using our influence."

I could tell that Grace was becoming uncomfortable with the conversation and the environment.

"I think that is enough for tonight. You are still recovering from your ordeal. We will continue with your education tomorrow evening."

"Here?" she asked hesitantly.

"Yes. Although your services are not required as a donor, you need to become comfortable with the activities that take place here, so that you don't stare every time you need to come into the salon. That is, if you decide you still want to stay. You always had the choice to leave. But now that you know everything, it is a good time to carefully consider your options."

Chapter 31
Grace

For the next week, I spent my days going about my normal duties. The evenings were spent in the corner of the salon with Gabriel. The subject matter was much less alarming than the first night. To fully understand this place, he provided a much-needed overview of its unique history.

I learned that besides being the crossroads for travel and commerce, Hightower was the political capital for the immortal world. At the center of the Known World, Hightower is the home of the Vampire Council and remains neutral in all conflicts. The Council's role is to mediate disputes between the kingdoms avoiding unwanted conflict and bloodshed. If either of the parties involved refuses to negotiate in good faith, the other may be given permission to cross the border of the Middle Kingdom in a military campaign. The Council tries to avoid these types of conflicts. A battle between immortals, besides being a bloody affair which costs the lives of vampires and mortals alike, draws unwanted attention to our presence. On rare occasions, both parties chose to take out their frustration on the Middle Kingdom, the Council, or both, so Hightower maintains a secret military presence as well as several very efficient and well-trained assassins. It is the Council that decreed the Middle Kingdom would never have another immortal king, a guarantee of its neutrality.

I also learned the real purpose of the Hightower House nightly gatherings. The salon was not just a place to spend an enjoyable evening. Now that I was a frequent visitor, I realized things were not what they seemed. With its proximity to the Council chambers, the salon attracted those who wanted to conduct more informal diplomatic discussions. As a result, many decisions were foregone conclusions before they ever reached the Council chambers. The real work of government took place in the salon at Hightower House, and Gabriel Ross was in the center of it. His importance was much greater than he led me to believe. There were always small groups of very powerful immortals determining the fate of whole groups of unsuspecting mortals. Important alliances were formed and others broken during these evening gatherings. Humans were never included in the negotiations, but their lives were certainly affected. I thought it sounded much like a chess game but with the lives of real pawns at stake. Vampires, it seemed, didn't have much regard for their food source.

Gabriel was an excellent teacher, and I came to appreciate the large amount of time he was devoting to me, but by the end of the week I decided I had absorbed all the immortal history I could take. The insight helped me get over my initial aversion to having a vampire for an employer. It seemed as if vampire society was not much different from that of humans. Gabriel would contend it was because vampires were the architects of human society. In many ways, it seemed the vampires were more civilized, certainly more advanced. Gabriel's patience with my endless questions was admirable. In fact, he seemed to enjoy having a student who indulged in a little verbal sparring. I smiled as I recalled a debate about the morality of drinking human blood. Gabriel pointed out that while a vampire could feed without permanently damaging the victim, mortals killed to provide meat for their consumption. He proposed that the chicken or pig might prefer his way. He also pointed out that some mortals still practiced cannibalism. He could not think of one instance in which one vampire devoured another. I found his logic hard to refute.

As Gabriel had suggested, I also spent a great deal of time considering my options if I chose to leave Hightower House. I could not come up with any that were as appealing as staying. I just needed to investigate the one aspect which still bothered me. I needed to talk to Aubry.

Chapter 32

Grace

I had never really understood why the activities in the salon would result in so many "personal days" taken by the courtesans. It was extremely inconvenient since it frequently required a complete revision to the staffing schedule. My talks with Gabriel shed light on why. I waited until one of those days to seek Aubry out. I was sure the two of us could talk uninterrupted while Aubry recovered from the previous night. Aubry was thrilled to see me.

"I hate that I'm so tired the next day. I'm stuck in this bed all day with nothing to do. It's so boring! I can only sleep so long. I can't tell you how glad I am that you know about us. I hated keeping secrets from you. Now you can visit me on my rest days."

"Well, that's what I want to talk about." I began. I was embarrassed and not really sure how to initiate the conversation. "I know it's kind of personal, but I didn't have a female relative when the subject became relevant. I took care of my father, so I didn't really have female friends. There is a lot I don't know about…"

Aubry cut me off.

"You've never been with a man! I knew it!"

"Please don't make me feel any more like an old maid than I already do. It wasn't my choice. But it's not just that. I want to know what it feels like when you let them take your blood. It seems like you actually enjoy it, and maybe it leads to… more?"

"All right, even though you are older than me, I guess I'll have to play the part of your mother. This talk will be a bit different than the one you would have gotten, but here goes. My first experiences with men were not good. I ran away from an abusive husband who believed I was barren and therefore useless. He didn't care

109

about me except as a way to satisfy his lust or prove his manhood by making babies. As far as he was concerned, I failed him, and he was brutal in showing his displeasure."

"When I came here I discovered that things could be different. Men still have the upper hand, but since it is not all about having children or proving themselves to their peers, the immortals seem to get pleasure from making me happy. Of course, they benefit also but that was a real eye-opener for me. When my vampire patron takes my blood, I want to let him have his way with me. It feels wonderful. It is much better than anything I ever felt with a mortal. Before you think me a whore, I have only one partner, and he only feeds from me. That is not the case with all of the girls, but I'm not much in demand, so I'm quite happy with the arrangement. As you can imagine, Jayne was very much in demand, and she had many partners. I think it was a badge of honor for her. She said she would get bored with the same man every time. She did have her preferences, but she tolerated the attention of others if they could do something for her."

"I think there has to be some attraction for the kind of reaction I have with my partner. I suppose feeding does not always lead to an erotic experience, but it's best to assume it will and be prepared before you let anyone feed from you."

"So this place really is a brothel for vampires," I stated in my disappointment. I had hoped otherwise.

"Not really," Aubry was quick to respond. "The men don't pay for our company, and we get to choose who we entertain. We might get gifts from appreciative partners, but not always. I really don't know how to describe this place. It's more like a refuge from a horrible existence and an opportunity to make our lives better. Most of us were misued by men before we came here. Now we have the company of gentlemen who treat us well. What we provide is nothing compared to what we receive. Our circumstances are much improved over our previous lives. I have no desire to leave. Mr. Ross has offered to find suitable husbands if we want to leave and live what we were raised to believe is a 'normal life.' I don't really know what a normal life is, and there is no guarantee that a husband will not turn out to be a monster. I'll take my chances with the monsters I know any day."

"Do you have feelings for your partner when you are not together?"

"You mean, do I have romantic thoughts about him when he's not around?" Aubry thought a moment. "No. Not really. I would never run away with him to be his mistress, and I don't think he would ask me. He is pleasant company for the evening, but that is all. I do enjoy it when I am with him though. That is one of the things this place has taught me. You can enjoy being with a man without feeling guilty. Please remember that, Grace. If you are lucky enough to find someone, don't let anyone make you feel ashamed for enjoying their attention, no matter how far it goes."

"Thank you for that, Aubry. I will try to remember. It's not exactly what our society teaches us. Shaming seems to be a tool for keeping women in their place. But now that you've given me permission to enjoy it, I need to know how IT is done."

So Aubry spent the afternoon explaining the facts of life to me in great detail. It was embarrassing how little I knew but VERY enlightening and a little intriguing. I wondered if I would ever have the opportunity to experience it.

Chapter 33
Gabriel

I was dreading the day that Grace announced her decision. After considering her other options, I was reasonably sure that she would choose to stay at Hightower House. However, she needed the space to come to that conclusion on her own without any influence from me. I had to admit, reluctantly, that it would probably be better for both of us if she decided to leave.

To say that I would miss her was gross understatement. My feelings for her were becoming hard to conceal. After she retired for the night, I would follow her scent – lemon and rosemary – around the house to see where she had been and imagine what she had been doing during the day. I would not let anyone sit in the chair she had occupied the previous week, so they could not cover her scent. I was behaving like a love-sick adolescent. No immortal my age should act that way. I wondered if it would affect Grace's decision if she knew.

It was on one of these nocturnal excursions that I discovered something rather shocking. She had found the armory and training grounds. But it was not just her scent I detected. There were numerous others. The scent of perfume was too strong to be just one or two. *What the f…was going on?* I wondered if they were planning some kind of rebellion, but why? The vampires who visited the salon would certainly not stand for an assault on their person. No matter how hard the women tried they would never best an immortal, so they would die. I had to address the situation immediately and find out what they were up to. I would not stand for bloodshed in my house.

The following evening, I called the entire staff together in the refectory.

"I have been to the armory. Apparently, so have many of you. I need to speak with all of you who have been there. The rest can go to work." I pinned the group with a hard stare. "There is no point denying it if you have been there. You know I will find out, and it will not go well for you."

More than half of the women remained. The number was much larger than I expected. Most of them hung their heads waiting some severe punishment.

I softened my tone and said, "You don't need to be fearful. I only want to know what is going on. Are you unhappy here? You know you can leave any time you wish. Have you been threatened by someone here so that you feel the need to protect yourselves? Please tell me so that I can help."

I was met with silence as I looked around at the group of apprehensive faces. Finally, one of the older women spoke up.

"Mr. Ross. We don't mean you or the patrons any disrespect or harm. Most of us would be dead by now if you hadn't given us a safe place. That's just the thing, though. It is safe enough here, but we can't stay forever. Most of us know firsthand what we can expect outside these walls. When one of the girls found the armory, we thought it would be a good way to prepare us to live OUT THERE. If we could just be able to defend ourselves, we wouldn't have to be victims, at the mercy of whatever a man wanted to do with us. You don't understand what it is like to have your entire life controlled by someone else. You are male. It's not the same for you. Even young boys have more freedom than we do, and they're allowed to fight back."

"I do understand, up to a point," I responded. "I did not choose to become what I am. That was forced on me by another. Now I am at the top of the food chain so to speak. Oh, you don't find that amusing. I thought it rather funny myself." I was disappointed my attempt at lightening the mood went unappreciated. I realized they might believe I was not taking them seriously, so I continued, "I understand the longing to be independent, but it's not as desirable as it may sound. There is a price to be paid. Now you are protected and receive everything you need for survival. You don't have to make hard decisions about who lives and who dies. You don't have to worry about whether there will be enough food to last a hard winter. And yet, we all long to be our own master. That, I understand."

"I am not angry that you found a way to protect yourselves. That shows a great deal of resourcefulness. I just wish you had asked me, so that you could do it right. Who is teaching you?"

"We're kind of imitating what we have seen." The spokeswoman responded. "Some of us were camp followers with the army. We learned a bit that way."

"Having a weapon in your hand may make you feel invincible," I said. "But it is the most dangerous thing you can do. Unless you are very skilled, you have just given your assailant something to use against you. Are you willing to accept some guidance on this? I don't want to turn a group of unskilled, sword wielding, not to mention angry, females loose on the male population – myself included. Forgive me if it seems like I am making light of this. I am dead serious. I want to help you."

"What do you suggest then?" Grace asked. I finally noticed with alarm she had remained in the back of the room obscured from my view.

"First, I would like to see you concentrate on hand to hand combat. It will improve your strength and agility. If you learn the proper defensive moves, there are ways to escape an assailant without much risk to yourself. After you have mastered defending yourself, you can learn to be the aggressor if you must. I wouldn't recommend it though. I have several mortals who work for me as day guards. Any one of them would be able to teach you effective defensive moves. They can also schedule your training during the day, so you don't have to sneak around the house at night."

"I know some of you grew up on the streets and are quite proficient with a knife. It is a good weapon for a woman, lightweight and easy to conceal. You can depend on each other for the basics. Your instructor can build on what you already know. There are blunt practice knives in the armory for you to use. I'd prefer you weren't carving one another up with the kitchen knives. If and when your instructor determines you have the strength and skill, you are welcome to try the swords. Some may be light enough for a woman. You can't walk around carrying one, so I doubt it would be helpful unless you find yourself in the middle of a military conflict. In that case, you're safer playing the helpless female. Insulting, yes, but safer."

"You would really do this for us, Mr. Ross?" asked another of the women hopefully.

I gave a thin smile and responded, "In case you haven't noticed, you're doing it already. I just want to see you do it correctly so no one dies."

I closed the door on my way out and leaned tiredly against it. *What did I just do?* I wondered.

Chapter 34
Gabriel

There was another problem for me to address. This one would require much more delicacy.

As the result of Grace's unfortunate accident in the salon, she had generated a great deal of interest, and her place in the household was the topic of much speculation among the guests. It was clear that I considered her "my human" and under my protection, but I had not "claimed" her or fed from her. Therefore, it was unclear if she could be requested as a companion for the evening. Several of the immortals had taken a sample of the blood left behind when she hit her cheek and were very anxious to take a larger drink.

It was becoming harder and harder to put the insistent requests aside. Although I explained that it was not part of her job, those who desired her felt if she was in the room, she was fair game — unless of course there was a prior claim on her. I considered there was, but by vampire protocol, there was not. I wondered if her scent was as compelling to them as it was to me. If so, her admirers would be very hard to discourage. I had made a serious mistake by meeting with her in the salon. I thought monopolizing her attention would be enough to establish my claim. Again, I was wrong. Vampire custom required that I declare my claim and then drink from her. The other interested parties would not back off until I had fulfilled that requirement. How was I going to explain this to Grace without sounding self-serving and manipulative? There was no point in putting it off any longer. It would not get easier, so I arranged to meet Grace in the library that evening.

Grace was already in her favorite chair reading one of my philosophy books when I finally arrived. I had rehearsed this conversation numerous times and still wasn't satisfied. I finally gave up and decided to let it take its own course. Since I could avoid it no longer, I took a deep but unnecessary breath and entered the library.

Grace looked up from her book and smiled at me. I heard her heartbeat speed up slightly and wondered if she was apprehensive about the meeting. I hoped she would still be smiling by the end of our conversation. I sat in the chair across from her. Her smile faded when she noticed my concerned look.

"Is something wrong?" she asked. "You don't look your usually composed self this evening."

"Not wrong, exactly. There's just a little complication."

"Since I'm here, I guess it involves me."

"Perceptive as usual, it's one of the things I love about you." Again, I noticed her increased pulse. I hoped it wasn't because of ... Oh! I had said it out loud.

"So?" she asked me.

"There are several interested parties in the salon who are requesting some of your time. I suspect they sampled the blood left behind after your accident, so their interest is more than casual. They have been very insistent. I mistakenly assumed that by monopolizing your attention in the salon, they would respect my claim on you."

"Your claim on me?!" Grace asked indignantly. "Just what does that mean?"

"I'm afraid there is still much for you to learn about the relationship between mortals and vampires. Unfortunately, the book is not complete, and we did not get to that subject. Many vampires consider any humans under their protection their property. As such, they have an exclusive claim on them. Because of what we do here, my claim on you is ambiguous, even though you are under my protection."

"But why is it even a problem? You said any woman can politely refuse to offer anything other than companionship and conversation. I think I can handle that."

"You do not understand how convincing we can be when we are craving a particular human's blood. All we have to do is make a flesh to flesh contact, and we can compel our prey to do whatever we like. Make no mistake, you are viewed as prey when a vampire is in pursuit. It is our nature. The influence can be so subtle you would not even realize the idea was not your own, and no one would see that you were being influenced."

"I thought that was not allowed here. Besides, in this dress, how would they find any exposed skin to touch?"

"Do not take this lightly, Grace. A mere touch of the fingertips can establish a connection. You would have to be extremely careful. I know the three who are interested, and I don't trust their motives. Attractive as you are, I think there is more going on. I'm against you going back in the salon under any circumstances."

"I think I have to do this, so they are clear about my lack of interest. That should solve the problem. All I have to do is remain resolute and say no."

I was dubious, but Grace seemed determined. I think she saw it as a test of her ability to handle immortals, maybe even me. She just might be sending me a message.

I responded reluctantly, "Don't be so sure that they will accept a simple no, but if you are determined to do this, I can't stop you."

"What will it feel like if they try to use influence on me? Would I be able to recognize it in time to break the connection?"

I rose from my chair and held my hand out to her. As soon as we made contact I thought *kiss me*. She took my face in her hands and brushed my lips with hers. I wanted more but against every instinct, I managed to pull myself away.

"Could you have stopped that?" I asked.

"I have to try," was her somewhat dazed response.

Grace

Later in the evening, I entered the salon. Gabriel had described the three vampires who had requested my company. As I made my way through the room greeting the guests, I came to the table where one of them sat. He was alone and motioned me to the chair opposite him.

"We finally meet. What a pleasant surprise. I didn't think Gabriel would let you out of his sight," he quipped.

"In case you haven't noticed, I'm still in his sight. But, yes, he has loosened the tether a bit," I replied with a gleam in my eye.

"We've not been formally introduced. I'm Richard Owen. Lord Richard Owen," he said as he rose from his seat and offered his hand. I noticed the look of disappointment on his face as I extended my gloved one for the handshake.

"I'm Grace Pryce, your lordship. I apologize for the gloves, but I have been working in the garden and seem to have developed a rash which I don't care to share with the guests." Then I continued, "I understand you are one of the members of the Council."

"I see Gabriel has schooled you well. I am indeed," he replied puffing up his chest.

I sat in the proffered chair, and for the next hour Lord Owen made small talk. He recounted, at length, his many virtues hoping unsuccessfully to impress me. Finally, he got around to asking about me. I stifled a yawn and politely excused myself. I was not about to reveal any of my story to him.

Gabriel met me at the door as I left the salon.

"Nicely done."

I smiled.

"Thanks for the tip about the gloves. Worked like a charm."

Chapter 35

Grace

For the next two weeks, I divided my attention among the three immortals. I played my part brilliantly, if I do say so myself. I was so successful at charming my admirers that I began to receive invitations from others. One of these was a young vampire named Emil.

Emil was from the South Kingdom and was visiting Hightower with his sire on a diplomatic errand. Since his sire did not require the services of his young secretary that evening, Emil was free to enjoy the hospitality of the salon. When I entered, he was leaning against the wall next to the door with a glass of wine in both hands hoping to intercept me. He handed one of the glasses to me and asked if I would join him. I was more than happy to have a break from the three persistent vampires, so I nodded my assent. He guided me to a quiet corner of the room, ignoring the angry looks he received.

"Nice body armor," Emil began as he looked me over. At my confused expression, he continued, "Neck and wrists covered, and the gloves are a nice touch. You needn't worry about me. I am more interested in Gabriel. He's quite a catch. Too bad he's not interested." He leaned in closer and continued. "I'm going to keep my voice low since the other immortals in the room can hear everything we say in a normal voice. I would suggest you do the same. No matter what I say, don't react although you can laugh if you wish. I actually find what I have to share rather amusing."

"Get on with it," I said quietly but testily. "I find these evenings are becoming rather tiresome."

"Well, this will give you a little break from the vultures. As much as I can appreciate your appeal, I'm reasonably sure your admirers are more interested in challenging Gabriel. You are being used. In addition, they are betting on which one will finally seduce you and draw blood. The winner stands to gain a great deal of money in addition to enjoying your considerable charms. No matter what they promise you, don't believe a word of it. The real loser in this will be you."

"During my recent visits to the salon I notice the more successful you appear entertaining the guests, the more irritable Gabriel becomes. This seems odd since you are only doing what he expects from his other employees. However, he is acting more like a jealous lover than your protector. I expect your admirers have observed his interest, which accounts for their avid pursuit. You need to work this out with Gabriel. He is the real prize in this game, and you stand to lose more than you can imagine."

Emil saw the tears in my eyes as I stood abruptly.

"Please excuse me. I'm feeling rather unwell, and we certainly don't want a repeat of my previous adventure. Thank you, Emil. This conversation has been most enlightening. I hope I can consider you a friend."

As I left the room, I heard him say, "You can count on it, Grace. I may be doing you a bigger favor than you know."

Before leaving I looked around and noticed that Gabriel was not there. Once outside, I leaned against the door and sighed. Was it true? Was I missing something? Did he really feel something more than friendship for me? I had to talk to him.

Higgins saw me and approached.

"Is something wrong? You seem distressed. Did someone hurt you?"

"Do you know where he is, Higgins?" I asked.

"I assume you mean Gabriel. I'm trying to stay out of his way" he replied. "He's been uncommonly grumpy these past weeks. You might try the armory. Sometimes he goes there to let off steam. I saw him heading that direction with Dr. Sheng. Try to cheer him up. We're all walking on eggshells around him."

"I'm afraid I may be the cause of his irritation."

Chapter 36
Yi

Gabriel was distracted. Under most circumstances, I could not best him in our sparring, but today was different. I had never seen him with so little focus, and I was determined to take advantage of it. It would make what I had to say much easier if he could see the results for himself.

He had been trained as a soldier before he became a vampire, so those finely honed skills only became more advanced after his rebirth. He knew how to fight. I, on the other hand, was trained as a physician. Granted, all vampires learn how to fight and defend ourselves, but I was no match for Gabriel's military training. I did know enough about the body to attack the points that were most vulnerable and would cause the most pain. Disabling an opponent even for a few moments provided a strategic advantage. Vampires heal quickly, so it is not as ruthless as it sounds.

Today I had the advantage. I landed a kick to Gabriel's head, which he should have been able to block. This was not like him at all, and I was pretty sure I knew why. I was sympathetic, but I was also enjoying my advantage and delivered a blow to his kidney. Still, he could not stop thinking about her. Maybe another well-placed kick in the head would bring his attention where it should be, but as the blood splattered from his split lip, I could see it was no use. Sparring was not what he needed today.

I knew him well enough to see the signs that he was fighting another opponent. He could not reconcile himself to the idea that Grace was his mate. He was like a moth drawn to a flame, and there was nothing he could do about it. The pull was too strong, even for him. She shed light into the dark places of his life. She was the balance he craved. His instincts and desires were battling against what he thought was best for her. Affirming their mutual attraction would not be easy for either one of them and could actually be dangerous for her, but I could see in Gabriel's reaction to Grace entertaining in the salon that he could never let her go. I had never experienced the instinct to mate, so I had no idea how compelling it could be. From the look on my friend's face, it must be intense. I actually felt sorry for him as I landed what would have been a crippling jab for a mortal. He groaned in pain and shook it off.

He was also distracted enough that he did not sense Grace's presence outside in the corridor. I knew she was hesitating, trying to determine the proper moment to interrupt our sparring. The door to the room was ajar, so I knew she could hear us. Now seemed like a good time to enlighten them both.

Grace

I took my time walking to the armory. For my own sanity, I needed to end this. I understood Gabriel's anger. I had insisted I could handle the situation with the three immortals and I had – to a point. I assumed they would get tired of rejection and leave me alone. On the contrary, my refusals only seemed to make them more persistent. And then there were the bets. I'd had enough of being a prize in some immature vampire game.

My thoughts were making me angry. I knew taking it out on Gabriel would not be productive. This was not his game, and he didn't deserve my anger. It was my own stupidity that was making me irritable. I stood at the door of the armory trying to calm myself before I went in. My hand was on the door when the conversation taking place inside stopped me in my tracks.

"Come on Gabriel. You're too distracted. You're supposed to be the most feared immortal in the Known World and a weaker opponent is besting you. Why won't you just get it over with and admit that you are in love with Grace? You've been unbearable ever since she started entertaining those three in the salon. Put an end to it, and make your claim on her."

I heard the sound of flesh meeting flesh and Gabriel groaned, "Shut up, old man. It's none of your business. We'll work this out our way."

"Old man," Yi scoffed. "I'm not the one who's over 500 years old." *Now there is an interesting piece of information,* I thought.

"Well you were older when you were turned so you're still the old man even if you're a younger immortal."

"And I'm still beating the pants off you right now so focus. I should have your full attention, not her and how you intend to work this out. Your lack of concentration could get you killed."

"You're just better at this Eastern style of hand to hand combat. That's all it is. I am not distracted."

I heard the heavy thud of a body hitting the mat and then a loud laugh from Yi. "And down he goes. Another point for the little guy!"

I heard Gabriel moan dejectedly, "I don't think she wants me to claim her. She appears to be enjoying herself."

That was it! I couldn't believe he thought I was having fun! It was time to put an end to that train of thought. I knocked on the door and entered when Gabriel yelled, "Come."

Yi bowed to Gabriel indicating an end to their sparring session and then bowed to me and winked.

"I believe you two have much to discuss. Only you can fix this."

Gabriel looked at my angry expression and asked, "So is this to be my second sparring session tonight?"

I was shocked. Gabriel looked awful. There was blood on his lips from several cuts and self-inflicted bites. A large bruise was beginning to close one eye and he was favoring his left side. It looked like he had dislocated his shoulder as well. He had taken quite a beating, and I was afraid it was because of me.

I dropped to my knees on the mat beside him and dissolved in tears. I knew Gabriel hated it when women cried, but I couldn't help it. The past weeks had been too much and to see him looking like this was the last straw. He turned to face me and took my hands. I was still wearing the gloves I wore in the salon, and he began to take them off but I pulled away from him.

"I know what you are trying to do. Don't." I pleaded. "I don't need to have you calm me down. Yi is right we need to talk about this. Please don't think I'm mad at you. I'm the over-confident fool who thought I could keep three vampire pursuers at arm's length. How can we end this? If I have to listen and laugh politely at one more self-aggrandizing anecdote, I'll go mad. Why won't they just go away? Do you know they're even betting on who will bite me first? How juvenile can they be?!"

I could see by his expression this was not what Gabriel expected to hear, and he was having trouble concealing his smile. He pasted on his impassive face and listened to me rant. The longer I went on, the more even I could see the absurdity of the situation. I finally got myself under control, and we enjoyed a brief moment of levity. But Gabriel had a look that said this conversation was just the beginning.

"I'm sorry my sparring clothes don't have pockets, so I can't offer you a handkerchief." He then removed his shirt and handed it to me. "Here, you can use this."

I held the cloth away from me with two fingers expecting it to be sweaty, forgetting that vampires don't sweat. Nonetheless it was still soaked with his blood, and I looked dubiously at Gabriel.

"Really?"

He shrugged.

"It's the best I can do under the circumstances. But be careful. Until the blood dissolves, you might get a little numbness where it meets your skin. Surely there are places which are relatively clean, so you can dry your eyes."

"It does give me an opportunity to appreciate your finely chiseled chest." (I didn't think I'd ever get my encounter with the statue in the garden out of my mind.) "I guess that's not too high a price to pay for the view," I teased.

Gabriel's expression sobered.

"Now that we're both in a better frame of mind, we need to discuss the situation from a vampire point of view. Things are not as simple as you think."

"I'm finished with your shirt, so could you get dressed first? I don't think I can have a serious conversation with a half-naked immortal. Maybe we could move some place more comfortable too."

Gabriel debated for a moment. He took my hand and led me into a dead-ended corridor. I couldn't see why we would come here to have a conversation, but it was secluded and no one was around to overhear us. Sensing my hesitation he assured me that we were going somewhere safe, and he would guide me back when the time came.

Gabriel

I led her into this particular part of the house for good reason. Sensing the area to make certain no one was around, I pushed on a panel at the end of the hall and a concealed door opened. Grace hesitated but followed me inside.

The concealed access led to a tunnel hewn out of the mountain. To the right and left of the man-made corridor were doors leading to tastefully appointed suites of rooms, each with its own unique style. This was the immortals' section of the complex.

"I don't think I should be here." Grace said anxiously. "These rooms are for immortals aren't they? They will surely sense my presence."

"You're perfectly safe as long as you are with me, but at the moment I am the only one occupying this wing, so there is no chance we will be interrupted. The other suites are for Council members when they are required to reside here. Each member is assigned a room, and as you can see they are free to make it their own."

"What about Lord Owen? He's here. Won't he be using his room?" Grace was still apprehensive about her presence in this part of the complex.

"Since he is from Hightower; he has a house in town. He has no need to stay here."

"Emil and his sire?" She continued.

"These rooms are for Council members only. Emil's sire is a diplomat and friend of Lord Owen. He and his entourage stay with Owen when they are in town. I would not bring you here if it was not safe."

I could tell when she finally relaxed and gave in to her curiosity. She began to peek in the open rooms.

"As you can see, each suite reflects the style of the kingdom the immortal represents, as well as their personal tastes. As far as they know, these rooms can only be accessed from the other end of this tunnel, which originates at the Council chambers. It is necessary to have accommodations that meet the security requirements for the younger immortals who must have protection during their day rest. Higgins and I, and now you, are the only ones who know that there is an entrance into Hightower House, so you needn't worry about immortals entering unannounced from this direction."

"Since your rooms are here, does that mean you're a Council member? I thought you hated politics." Grace hesitated. "But now that I think about it, you are often called into discussions of a political nature. The Council members seem to value your opinion. "

"No, I am not a member, but I serve a very important function for them. Besides," I said wryly, "this is my house, so they can't very well kick me out. Can you tell from the décor, which rooms are mine?"

Grace pointed to the first door on the left.

"It has to be this one. It is decorated in the same style as the rest of the house."

As usual, she was very perceptive and correct. These rooms did indeed reflect my personal tastes. The colors were mostly muted shades of gray and cream with maroon accents. The combination reminded me of the dress Grace was wearing – minus the lace. I had never thought of it before.

We had entered a large sitting room which took up most of the space. It was a comfortable area with several locked cabinets along three walls. The cases in this room contained my personal journals and other books and rare manuscripts that might indicate my age or origins. I was not willing to share those details with any but my most trusted friends, a very small list to which Grace had now been added. The stone walls above the waist-high cases were adorned with a collection of original paintings representing many different places. The brightly colored sunlit landscapes added much-needed color and warmth to the stone walls. Grace wandered from painting to painting looking carefully at several which attracted her attention.

"This collection is impressive. It must have taken years to collect. Are they all places you have been?" Grace inquired.

I could see when the realization hit her.

"Of course they are!" she exclaimed. "This is how you're able to see the places you have visited in the daylight. More than anything, besides your books of course, these give the most insight into your life. Thank you for sharing them with me."

I was pleased that she appreciated art. Bringing her here had revealed another aspect of her that I had not seen before. I smiled as I recalled she did seem to appreciate sculpture. However, this was not why we were here.

A small fireplace was cut into the fourth wall. It was unnecessary for my physical comfort, but it added to the ambiance of the room and reminded me of my humanity. I could enjoy a fire even if I didn't need it for warmth. I saw Grace shiver and realized the room was a little chilly for a mortal, so I went over and lit the tinder, which was carefully laid in the grate and then added several logs.

I knew I was stalling, so I quickly pointed out the bathing room. Water from the hot spring had been channeled into this wing. It was, like the fireplace, an unnecessary indulgence, but I could not imagine eternity without relaxing in a hot bath on occasion. Grace eyed the room with envy and said it would be heaven to have hot water in her room. I invited her to take advantage of the facilities to wash up before we got down to the business at hand. She gratefully accepted. I suspect she was stalling also.

The final room was behind a locked door – not just a locked door, but a **heavily** locked door. I gestured toward it.

"I suppose you can guess what is behind that door. I would show you, but it seems highly inappropriate to show a single woman my bedroom. If you will excuse me, I will clean up a little and join you. Would you like something to drink while you wait?"

Grace shook her head and settled into a particularly inviting gray leather chair to wait for me.

In no time at all, I was clean and fully clothed. Grace jokingly expressed mixed feelings about the clothed part. Her innocent flirting was beginning to affect me. Holding a glass of whisky, I settled into one of the chairs across from her.

"Are you sure you don't want anything?"

Grace thought a moment and asked, "Is this going to be a difficult discussion?"

"I'm afraid so," I responded gravely.

"Then, I'll have what you're having," she replied.

I got another glass for her, refilled mine and returned to my chair before beginning what Grace referred to as my vampire anthropology lessons.

"Unfortunately, my sire and I did not complete *The Truth About Vampires*. It would be helpful if you had been able to read an important chapter that remained unfinished. It discusses the relationship between immortals and humans. It may be hard for you to accept, but at one time, immortals outnumbered humans. In fact, vampires bred humans for food, so that we did not have to depend upon large animals. Unless absolutely necessary, we did not feed on anything that would die as a result of blood loss. But we found that we were much stronger and did not have to feed as often if we drank from humans. It was the result of our cultivation that human societies developed. Because of our history, immortals still think of your kind as nothing more than food or property or both. Since mortals are weaker, once we accept one into our care, we feel a responsibility to protect them. We need humans to thrive, but we also resent that need."

"Eventually, as humans became educated and more sophisticated, many of us found enjoyment in human company. We cultivated relationships, both platonic and romantic. We found humans capable of creating great things in the area of art, music, literature, philosophy, and religion to name a few. Some of the greatest mortal artists and thinkers were blissfully unaware that they had vampire mentors and patrons. Until the enlightened age, vampires were thought to be gods sent to help mankind flourish, and they were grateful. When that belief died, we lost a great deal of our influence and began to retreat from active engagement with human society. Our lack of involvement finally consigned us to human mythology and the belief that we had never existed at all."

"I know our attitude toward mortals may sound demeaning to you. But you need to understand the mindset of the vampire to understand why it is going to be very difficult to just walk away from your current predicament. The immortals who have been pursuing you feel entitled to drink from you. You are food and entertainment to them. At this point, there is no reason for you to deny them. They will soon tire of this game they are playing, and someone will demand satisfaction."

"Emil said as much," Grace said dejectedly. "But you said I would not have to accommodate anyone."

"That was before you spilled blood in the salon and got their attention. I suspect they even tasted it."

"I could handle the blood drinking. It's the 'entertainment' I object to. Aubry says that feeding can excite passion in both the donor and the recipient. I'm not ready to allow myself to be used by someone I don't even like. And what did Emil mean by claiming?"

"The 'entertainment' to which you refer does not create any special bond. The only one who can claim a human is the vampire who protects them."

"What if you claim me, will they have to leave me alone?"

"That is where things get tricky. One, there are the bets. If I claim you now I can be accused of interfering with their sport. After all, from their perspective you are part of the service we provide here. In theory, you are entitled to refuse to be a donor, but very few do. I don't allow unwilling women in the salon. It is bad for business. So they might think that you were there under false pretenses. It's obvious to me that Jayne hoped to put you in an untenable position by luring you into the salon. I don't think that will matter to them though. Despite the fact that this isn't your fault, we still have to deal with the consequences."

"But agreeing to go along with it was my fault. I could have stayed out of the salon and this never would have happened. I guess a part of me wanted to know what went on. I felt excluded."

I ignored Grace's comment. There would be time to deal with that later. I continued, "Second; in case you haven't noticed, I have become very protective of you and rather possessive. My feelings for you go beyond a friendly affection. It seems everyone realized it before I did, and these three are now using it against me with you caught in the middle."

"Why didn't you tell me how you felt?" Grace's surprise was evident.

I threw up my hands and replied with a frustrated sigh.

"Because I don't know how I feel! I haven't felt this way about anyone in a very long time. No, that's not true. I have never felt this way about anyone. I didn't tell you because it is wrong for me to take advantage of you that way. I vowed never to have a relationship with one of my employees. No matter how immortal tradition tries to diminish relationships between immortals and humans, I believe you are my intended partner, and that terrifies me. I can't imagine the instinct to mate would be any stronger if you were an immortal. If I take your blood and we give in to the resulting desire, we will be mated by vampire custom. You haven't shown any indication that you share my feelings, so are you willing to bind yourself to me for life just to avoid a casual biting and a little embarrassment?"

"That doesn't answer my question. Why didn't you tell me?" Grace demanded. "You make the excuse that it is wrong, but I don't believe that's the real reason. Are you really that afraid to be happy?"

Grace sat for a long time with her head in her hands. I knew she was trying hard not to cry. But an occasional sniff escaped giving her away. Once she regained her composure she looked up at me.

"I've put you in a very awkward position, haven't I? I'm so sorry. I thought I knew what I was doing. I thought you had given me enough information about immortals to navigate the culture. I was so stupid!"

"Yes," I replied. "A little knowledge can be a dangerous thing, but you were not stupid — just not adequately informed, and perhaps a little over-confident of your abilities," I added with a small smile.

"I guess that makes two of us who were not adequately informed then," Grace replied. "How can you be so sure I don't share your feelings?"

It was my turn to be surprised.

"Do you?"

"Everyone else seemed able to see it. Why couldn't you? I've loved you since we started reading together in the library. No one ever took me seriously the way you have. I love that I can have a discussion in which my opinion is not dismissed just because I am a woman. Or have a debate in which my views are not taken as irrational just because they come from a feminine point of view. I love you because you have never treated me as a lesser being for being mortal. I love you because when I allowed you to demonstrate your ability to influence me you only asked for a kiss. I love that you respect me enough to try to protect me from the life you live. I know it is risky, but I love you, Gabriel Ross, and the idea of sharing the rest of my life with you doesn't terrify me a bit."

I stood, momentarily at a loss for words. This incredible woman returned my feelings and had for some time. Was I really that blind? How much time had I wasted thinking I was keeping her safe? Grace didn't want to be safe; she wanted to be mine. I went to where she was sitting and knelt in front of her. I took her face in my hands and gently kissed her. She returned my kiss with a passion not unlike our kiss after the evening in the garden. A voice inside my head warned that there were still things which must be said before I gave in to my overwhelming need for her. We had time, and I was determined to do this right.

Grace moaned as I pulled away from her.

"What is wrong now?" she asked.

"We need to talk first," I said as I pulled her over to the couch, and we sat together. I wanted my arms around her as I explained the rest.

I knew that the next few hours would be the most important in my immortal life, and I was completely at a loss. Because of my obligation to the Council, I had avoided romantic entanglements. Truth be told, I found most women frivolous and shallow – the mortal ones anyhow. That I would be attracted to one astounded me. I was totally unprepared for the next step.

The woman I held in my arms said she loved me. She said she was willing to bind herself to me for the rest of her natural life. A part of me knew I should tell her every downside of being united to a vampire. She had no idea how possessive I would be once we were mated. The pragmatic side of me understood no one could anticipate what a relationship held in store. But at the most, mortal relationships only lasted 30 years if the couple was lucky enough to live into old age. This one could last an eternity if she decided to… It was too soon to even contemplate that possibility.

Grace

I could tell Gabriel was struggling with how to proceed.

"You have a house full of female employees, but you don't know much about women do you?" I teased.

Gabriel looked a little sheepish as he kissed me on the cheek and replied, "I never imagined I would meet a woman who would capture my heart, so I didn't try very hard to understand them. You have to admit that the ones here, beautiful as they are, provided little to entice me. It was the bookworm with the scar who beguiled me."

"Well, some mortals like to make informed decisions about their lives when given the chance. I happen to be one of them even though most of my recent life-changing events have been out of my control. So, what exactly are we to do about our mutual attraction and the three immortals in the salon? To be clear, you are telling me that becoming your mate – or whatever you immortals call it – will not keep us from having to perform some degrading vampire ritual in front of your associates in the salon. From what you have said, they will be able to tell we are already mated as soon as they see us together, so anything more seems totally unnecessary."

"I'm afraid nothing else will satisfy them under the circumstances. But it doesn't have to be the spectacle they want. I think we can avoid that if we know what to expect first."

"What would that be?"

Gabriel sighed.

"Every instinct in me is compelling me to make my claim on you right now. Your scent and the music of your blood are becoming irresistible, and I don't know how long I can keep from tasting both. I am dangerously close to completing the ritual with or without your consent. You need to be sure this is what you want.

Once I feed from you, we will be mated. And once we are mated, I will be the most possessive, protective immortal around. Is that what you want?"

"You make it sound so appealing," I replied with a slight smile. "This is turning out to be the most uninviting marriage proposal in history."

"It's not exactly marriage we're talking about. It's a much stronger bond than mortal marriage."

"Maybe you vampires call it mating but it is essentially the same thing. So we're not having a big formal ceremony. Are we not making a life-long commitment to each other? I don't know how you could consider it anything else."

Gabriel looked at me with longing.

"Are you sure, Grace? This will change your life forever. I don't want you to do this for the wrong reasons. "

"I was sure when I told you I loved you, Gabriel. You are the one who seems to be conflicted."

Gabriel got up and walked to the door of the bedroom. He unlocked the door and extended his hand to me.

"Join me then?"

Chapter 37
Grace

Gabriel's sleeping chamber lacked the comfort of the sitting room. The room could only be considered a "bedroom" because it was dominated by a large bed. The bed itself lacked much of anything besides a bare mattress which might make it comfortable. I eyed it dubiously.

"This room lacks a female touch."

"You'll be happy to know that is because a female has never been in here until now. This is where I sleep when necessary. Since I am literally 'dead to the world,' this room provides the protection I need. The bed is for appearances, even if it lacks appeal. Still its presence makes me feel a little more human. Perhaps we should find someplace else to spend the night."

"Don't apologize," I hurried to say. "We will make due. There has to be clean bedding somewhere in here."

I set about making up the large bed with the small supply of items I found in a cupboard. I took considerable time making it look just right and realized my puttering was a form of nesting. I derived a certain satisfaction in preparing the bed in which I would become Gabriel's mate.

In the meantime, Gabriel had stripped down to nothing but the pair of tight leather breeches he was wearing. I realized it was now my turn. Gabriel approached me cautiously.

"Can I be of some assistance?"

"I suppose I could use some help. The fastenings on this dress can be uncooperative."

Gabriel

The slow pace of her disrobing was driving me mad. I wanted desperately to rip off the stubborn dress and throw her on the bed. Finally, she was dressed only in a linen shift. I could see the contours of her body through the lightweight fabric, and Grace blushed as I stood back to appreciate the view. I was sure she didn't know how alluring she was, but I was mesmerized by her.

I drew her to me in a gentle embrace. We stood together a few moments as our bodies became accustomed to one another. We were again surprised by how well we fit together. I was first to withdraw. I took a step back in order to cup her face in my hands and then lowered my lips to hers in a gentle kiss. When Grace responded, my kiss became more demanding, and my arm came around her waist. I pulled her hard against me. She moaned softly as my tongue teased her parted lips and entered her mouth. Again, I pulled away only to pick her up and take her to the bed. I tore back the sheets and blankets Grace had so carefully placed there.

"I don't think we will need these for a while," I rasped as I placed her on the bed. I turned away from her long enough to remove my breeches and then climbed in next to her.

As I resumed kissing her, my hand strayed to her breast and caressed her through the thin fabric of her shift. This time it was Grace's turn to draw away. She pulled the shift up to her waist then sat and pulled it off over her head tossing it on the floor.

"I don't think I need that," she said breathlessly.

I nodded in agreement, unable to speak as I admired her naked body.

"I ask you again, Grace. Are you sure? We don't have to do this if you're not comfortable. There has to be another way out of this."

"Now is a fine time to consider options! I thought you wanted this. Now you are the one who has doubts. I know there are definite disadvantages to having a human partner. You are so perfect. As you can plainly see, I am not. I also know that you will constantly have to be careful with me. I will always be the weak one and a liability to you."

"It's not that at all, Grace. I have desired you since I first met you. Thoughts of having you have consumed me. I tried to ignore my feelings, but I couldn't. I only ask because once we start, I will not be able to stop, even if you ask me to. The first time can be frightening, and you are unprepared."

"Please, Gabriel. Don't start with talk about wanting my first time to be perfect for me. We both know that is romantic nonsense. Just be gentle with me. I'm sure instinct will take care of the rest; otherwise there would never be children."

I sighed. I could not argue with her logic. Besides, the reality was, I was past the point of no return and had been as soon as I decided to take her to my chambers. How was it that this inexperienced mortal understood the situation better than I did? I would take my time and let nature take its course as she suggested.

I took her in my arms, and I could feel a tingle wherever our bodies met. I could tell she felt it too when she accused, "Are you trying to use influence on me? You promised you wouldn't."

"Just the opposite" I said. "I'm trying to restrain myself, so I don't hurt you. That takes a little energy on my part. I can't allow myself to give in completely."

I stopped any further discussion with another lengthy kiss, which left Grace gasping for air. My lips left her mouth and travelled downward. She tensed as I nuzzled her neck but I continued on without biting her. I knew that many women merely endured the attentions of their husbands or mates. I wanted Grace to anticipate our time together, so I patiently worked to inflame her desire. My lips traveled to her breast.

Grace

So this was what the fuss was all about. Gabriel's careful attention to my mouth and breasts was having the desired result. I arched my back in pleasure inviting him to continue. Meanwhile, the hand which lay on my belly moved down to my thighs. Gabriel moved his leg over mine and gently urged my legs apart giving him access to another part of my anatomy that was begging for attention. As he touched me, I was overwhelmed with desire. I ached to feel Gabriel inside me. He seemed to sense my building need and determined I was as ready as I would ever be. He positioned himself over me, and I anticipated what was to come. I had been told that this first time might be a little unpleasant, and I wondered what perverse creator would design it that way. I gasped and then whimpered as he thrust into me but the discomfort quickly gave way to other more pleasurable sensations, and our bodies moved together in an instinctive rhythm until we reached the limit of our restraint and collapsed in release. I could tell he wanted to ask me if I was alright, but my contented hum answered his question better than any verbal assurances I could give.

As we lay together, still joined, I had to ask, "Why didn't you bite me? I thought that was part of it."

"I wanted to prove that we desire one another without taking your blood. I can't bite you every time we make love, and I intend enjoy the pleasure often – like now," he said as he rolled me on top of him. He couldn't seem to stop touching me. He cupped my bottom and then ran his fingers lightly up and down my spine. When

I wriggled, he learned something about me I would rather he didn't know. I was ticklish. I was sure he would use it against me at some later time. Playfully, of course, but it could render me totally helpless.

The friction of my wriggling was having an unexpected effect as another wave of desire swept over us both. Gabriel's tight grip on my hips ensured that our grinding together would have the maximum effect. I raised myself up so that I could look into his eyes then lowered myself giving him access to my exposed neck. Still he refrained from biting me. Instead he kissed both breasts and then buried his head between them. I was too aroused at that point to question why.

Gabriel

It was time. Grace had tensed the first time I kissed her neck. I didn't want her to know it was coming. Her pleasure would be much greater if she was relaxed. I almost lost my resolve when she offered her neck to me, but I held fast and kissed her breasts instead. She would never anticipate that was my target all along. I never told her it was customary for mated vampires to take the blood closer to the heart. I licked the soft skin of her left breast to numb the area and then bit. She tried to pull back in surprise, but I moved with her not letting go of my connection to her. It didn't take long before she threw back her head. Her voice was husky when she moaned out my name as she climaxed. Only then did I remove my mouth from her breast and utter her name as I allowed my own release. Afterward we lay together in silence, content to explore each other's bodies in intimate caresses.

Grace finally broke the spell.

"There is still something I don't understand. It's about the blood. Why is taking my blood such an important part of our mating? In a mortal marriage, consummation is sufficient."

I sighed.

"Do you really want to do this now? Conversation at this point is a mood killer."

"Now," Grace stated emphatically. "It won't change anything but I want to know. Although the experience was extraordinary, the whole idea of being bitten is a still a mood killer for me."

I laughed and tucked her into my side.

"I suppose it is. I hadn't thought about it from your perspective. I hoped your response to it would eliminate the need for explanation." Then I tried to explain.

"In a mated relationship, sharing blood is the most intimate thing a couple can do. Blood carries our life force. By willingly giving our blood to our mate we are offering our very essence. There can be no secrets between us because we will know each other better than we know ourselves. Our very souls are bared; our hopes and dreams, our fears and nightmares, even those things we cannot admit to ourselves are open to our mates. It is the ultimate act of submission."

"Then that means I need to take your blood also."

"I'm afraid it does not work that way. A mortal cannot ingest vampire blood without unfortunate consequences. A small amount would make them sick. A large amount would initiate a transition. Without the proper preparation, the mortal would eventually die. While in that in-between state the mortal's body would not be able to digest food, nor could they obtain any benefit from their mate's blood. They would eventually starve to death."

"So as a mortal mate, I have to submit to you but you cannot do the same to me. You will know all my secrets, but I will still know only what you wish to reveal to me. It seems unfair," Grace pouted.

"Trust me. You do not want to know my secrets. It would be dangerous, not to mention giving you nightmares. Sometimes ignorance really is bliss. I only took enough of your blood to establish the relationship. Such a small amount can only reveal recent memories. I will never violate your trust by taking something from you that is not freely offered."

"And this is why your kind will consider us married but not mated. We are not equally matched. As a mortal, I cannot participate fully in the mated relationship."

"It will be enough. They will accept it, even if they don't like it."

"As far as I am concerned, we belong together. I am just trying to understand my place in this new world. It is difficult to accept, but I suppose it is no different than my place in the mortal world. As a female, my life has never been my own to control. You have offered me much more freedom to determine my future than I would have had. Even so, my choices are limited by the expectations of both our cultures. It may not be fair, but you are the best option I have."

I wanted to tell her that it didn't have to be this way forever. Instead I said:

"Now who is being unromantic?"

Chapter 38
Gabriel

All eyes were on us as we entered the salon. It was evident that we had finally affirmed our relationship.

"It is time to end this ridiculous competition," I stated. "Yes, I know about it. I also know that none of you three vied for Grace with good intentions. But since you forced the issue by demanding that she make a decision, she has done so. She has chosen me, and we were mated last night. Grace is now my wife."

Lord Owen stood and shouted indignantly.

"Foul play! She was just toying with us!" Then he continued with a wicked smile. "By the gods, it's about time!"

"What?" Grace and I exclaimed together. "You're happy about this? What about your bet? You lost. Exactly who was toying with whom?"

"Well, you were misinformed about the wager. It was actually a pool. We were betting on when exactly you would finally admit you and Grace shared a mutual attraction and act on it. We were tired of watching you two gaze longingly at each other when you thought no one was looking, so we thought a little healthy competition would move things along. I only lost because I thought it would happen much sooner. I commend you on your restraint, Gabriel. Considering the prize, I can't believe you waited this long. And you, Grace, I can't believe you didn't beg him to take you just to avoid spending any more time with us. We tried to be as annoying and self-absorbed as possible. But you patiently tolerated us much longer than I anticipated. You two deserve each other. It was Emil who finally came up with the idea of revealing the bet to see if that would affect your resolve. It seems to have worked."

I just stared at Richard Owen in disbelief. I caught Grace's arm before she could follow through with the slap she intended to place on Owen's cheek.

"Don't Grace. You will only hurt yourself. Besides, I think the privilege is mine," I said as my fist met Owen's jaw and sent him sprawling on the floor. I then helped him to his feet and said, "I guess I should thank you also. I did not find out about your little wager until Grace told me last evening. I suppose the competition for her helped me realize that I was hopelessly in love with her, so I must thank you all for giving me the incentive to make an honorable if not romantic proposal. Well then, just how many of you were involved in this little wager of yours to nudge us together? I feel like a pawn in a chess match. More importantly, who won?"

Owen pulled a slip of paper from his vest and looked it over. "Well it seems there were two of us that chose yesterday, so they will have to split the winnings."

"How long do you plan to prolong the suspense?" We demanded. "Who won?!"

"It seems your friend Yi knows you pretty well. He is one, and the other is Emil over there in the corner. Maybe the three of you planned this, or was it Grace?"

I was insulted.

"As I said, I didn't find out about the pool until after Grace and I mated," I lied. "So I had nothing to do with this and she was truly offended by it all. However," I said with a wry smile, "I will say that in your little chess game, the pawn took the queen, and she is a much greater prize than money."

Yi Sheng stood and addressed the room.

"I believe we need to toast the bride and groom. Since I predicted when Gabriel would finally come to his senses, I'm buying." He lifted a glass and said, "Congratulations, my friend. It's about time. *Hu jing hu ai!*"

"That's very generous doctor," Owen said as he lifted his glass, "but the drinks are free."

Yi merely smiled.

It was several hours before Grace and I could get away from all the well-wishers.

Exhausted, Grace excused herself and retired. As I made to follow, Owen took me aside.

"I'm personally very happy for you but you know the Council will not be pleased. You should prepare yourself for repercussions. I will do what I can to smooth things over, but you should still be on your guard. There's not really much they can do except give you a slap on the wrist for not consulting them first but they might try to make life difficult for a while. They might even try to use Grace."

Grace

Tired as I was, I could not go to sleep. *What was keeping Gabriel?* It was only our second night together, and surely he wasn't bored with me already. I was relieved when the door to our suite finally opened, and Gabriel strode in. He was trying unsuccessfully to hide his agitation.

"What is wrong?" I asked. "I thought we won that one."

"We did. It is something else. Owen suspects the Council will try to make trouble for us. I can't think of anything they could possibly do that would cause any real problem for us. There is no such thing as 'un-mating,' but there could be other demands."

"So, it's because of me?"

"I know I keep saying this, but because of the nature of the work I do for them, they think I should be unattached. I'm powerful enough that very few would think of taking me on directly. Until now, my enemies had no other option. By taking a mate, especially a mortal one, I have given them something to use against me, and as such, against the Council. If an enemy could get their hands on you, your mind would be an open book to them and anything I ever told you would be available to them."

"But you haven't told me anything. I would be useless."

"Perhaps, but you would also make a useful hostage even if you didn't have any secrets to reveal."

"So I am now a liability to you, and the Council won't like it. What can they do?"

"There's not much they can do. I suppose they will make a big deal out of reminding me of my responsibilities and that the greater good comes before my personal life; although, I have certainly earned one. They will just try to embarrass me in front of my peers. That is, if the Council decides to acknowledge it at all."

"Will they?"

"It depends on how threatened they feel. We'll have to wait and see what they come up with. Please don't worry. I've faced much worse. Now move over. I need to spend some time with my new wife."

Gabriel

But I was worried. The Council could demand that Grace become an immortal, so she would not present as much of liability. They could claim it was for her own good, and they would be correct. Still I didn't think they would force the issue if she resisted. My real concern was that if harried enough, Grace would agree in order to protect me, and I might not have a say in the matter.

Chapter 39

Grace

Gabriel was away for several days, and I was at loose ends. Since our mating, he allowed me to resume my duties as chatelaine of the house, but it was awkward. Everyone treated me differently now. Those who were friendly before were wary and even a little suspicious. Did they think I was Gabriel's spy? I was grateful that Aubry, Higgins, and Mrs. Miller still treated me in the same way. It made my new role at Hightower House more bearable. An unexpected ally was Dr. Yi Sheng. It seemed Gabriel had designated his friend my protector in his absence. I was curious to know more about him.

One evening, as I was delivering more wine to the salon, Dr. Sheng caught my eye. He motioned me over and invited me to sit with him. He smiled and said, "As you probably guessed, your mate has asked me to look after you while he is away. I am happy to do so. It gives me an opportunity to get to know the woman who stole my best friend's heart. How are you finding life with Gabriel?"

I blushed and replied, "It's not what I expected. I don't think anything can prepare a human for a relationship with an immortal." I hesitated, looked at the floor and said sadly. "Sometimes I wish he didn't have to be so careful with me."

"We could change that. I'm sure you've considered it. Have you discussed it with Gabe? Of course he would need to find the right sire. It couldn't be him, but I suppose he's told you all that."

"Hold on!" I exclaimed. "It is way too soon for that discussion. Let me get used to being married first."

I decided to try Gabriel's favorite tactic and redirect the course of our conversation.

"Since you are Gabriel's best friend, I would like to get to know you. I know your kind don't like to reveal much about themselves. But, will you tell me your story and how you know Gabriel?"

"I suppose that's fair. Gabriel has told me a great deal about you and how you came to be here, so I have an advantage. It is considered bad form for one vampire to tell another's story, so Gabriel would never tell you mine. Since you know next to nothing about me, I will be happy to enlighten you."

Yi Sheng

As you can discern from my features, I was born in the East Kingdom. I was taken from my mortal family when I was young. Precocious male children went to live in communities set apart from the rest of society and the influence of their families. I would call it monastic except there was no god worshipped there. Our god was knowledge and the pursuit of it. Our mentors believed this was the highest calling. Many of the men never left the community. They chose to spend their entire lives studying and passing their accumulated knowledge on to the young prodigies who were brought there.

Even as a young man, I had a fascination for the body and how it worked. I desired to understand how illness and injury could end a human life. Natural healers were rare at that time. Most of what we call medicine today was practiced by individuals who were no better than witch doctors, and their services came with a high price. The elders were happy to cultivate my interests in the hopes that I would become a true physician and serve all people regardless of their ability to pay. They provided me with a supply of cadavers to study, and soon I could identify major organs, bones, and systems. My first test as a healer came when one of the young students broke his leg. The elders asked me to set the injury, so the boy might walk again. It was a compound fracture, and the end of the bone protruded from a large tear in the leg. For a student my age, the task appeared impossible.

The youth was pale and in great pain. Still he looked up at me hopefully.
"You can fix me, can't you?"

I nodded. I wanted him to have faith in my ability, but I could not assure him that he would not have lasting effects from the injury. He could well be crippled for the rest of his life. I also knew that he would experience excruciating pain while I did what I could for him. I wasn't sure I could work while he writhed in pain. One of the most difficult things a healer faces is separating himself from the emotional attachment with the patient. I knew if I gave in to my empathy, I would never be able to do what needed to be done. I took my time gathering the instruments I would need to reposition and set the bone. I needed to find the quiet place where I could focus on the ordeal ahead without distraction. Finally, I gave the young man a leather strap to bite, so that he did not inadvertently bite his tongue. I steadied myself and instructed several of the stronger students to hold him still. I was ready.

Just then, an old man I had never seen before entered. The elders in the room folded their hands in front of them and bowed to him deferentially. They cleared a path to where I was about to set the boy's leg, and the old one moved to stand beside me.

"Hold." He said, "There is no need for him to suffer." Then he took the boy's hand, and my patient fell into a deep sleep. "You may proceed. He will feel nothing," the old man said.

The man remained holding the boy's hand while I worked. I repositioned the bone and prepared to repair the tissue damage surrounding it. The old one stopped me. I watched him pierce his lip with sharp fangs. He leaned over the gaping wound and let his blood fall. As soon as the blood touched the bone, the ends began to fuse. The damaged tissue surrounding the bone was also restored. I was dumbfounded. The old man told me to hold the edges of the wound together. He let more of his blood drop onto the leg and the wound was healed. That was my first encounter with Immortal Kim, the community's vampire patron and protector.

From that day on, Immortal Kim showed great interest in me. He was always present when I had to perform any kind of medical procedure, presumably to keep the patient asleep while I worked. However, I could tell he was focused on my every move. I began to sense that his scrutiny had a purpose. An invitation for tea to discuss my studies became a weekly occurrence. Eventually, he began to talk about himself, and I was drawn more deeply into the realities of immortal life.

After several years, I had become a competent physician and surgeon, and Immortal Kim got to the point of all this attention. I was too gifted to lose. I had reached the limit of my mortal abilities, but I could be so much more. He intended to sire me. I knew what he was, but I never imagined that life for myself. I did not go to my rebirth willingly.

"You mean he turned you without your consent?" I interrupted his story.
"I'm afraid so,"Yi went to continue, but I interrupted again.
"Do you regret it?"
"I did for a while," He replied and then continued with this story.

The first year was torture being around all those mortals. I often had to be confined, so I would not drain one of the students. I was given all the animal blood I could stomach, but it didn't satisfy in the same way. Immortal Kim was my only companion in that first year. He eventually taught me to control by bloodlust and endure my heightened senses, so I could be a part of the community again. But there was no going back. The rest of the community was wary of me, and I had no one to confide in. The elders finally convinced Immortal Kim it was selfish of the community to keep me there. I needed to be out in the world where I could be useful. Other humans needed me. Immortal Kim saw through their attempt at manipulation but had to agree that my abilities were wasted there, so he sent me out. That's when I met Gabriel.

After leaving the community, I was rather inept at survival skills. I was franticly looking for a place to rest before the sun came up, and Gabriel came to my rescue. He sensed that I was newly sired and didn't see me as a threat, so he helped me. He was taking a few decades off from his Council duties – meaning he was hiding from them. He had established a comfortable little cave complex outfitted with everything he needed. He allowed me to stay with him while I continued to adapt to my new life. I was extremely grateful, and we grew to enjoy each other's company.

There was a village in the valley below Gabriel's home. The residents were aware of his presence, but since he had eradicated all violent crime from the area, they were happy to accept his presence. We never fed from the residents, so they did not fear us. In fact, after I saved the child of the mayor, we became minor celebrities. They occasionally sent willing girls to us in payment, but we always refused. We needed to procure our own food. I don't know if Gabriel told you that we are hunters by nature. We love the chase. There was plenty of wild game in the mountains to keep us exercised and fed. It was a rather idyllic life.

But all good things must come to an end. After about 50 years, the Council found Gabriel's hideout and dragged him back. I think he was ready, so he didn't require much convincing. He invited me to come along, but I chose to stay and provide medical attention to the village. I grew bored after a while and left to travel and serve where I was needed. There were always plenty of patients. But it was a lonely life. I had always had people around me and although I was surrounded by humanity, I didn't belong. I also missed Gabriel. He was really my only friend. So, I came to Hightower, and here I have remained."

"If you live here, why do I rarely see you?" I inquired.

"As you probably know, the resident immortals have separate quarters and other means of entertainment. If the humans here knew just how many of us there are right under their noses, they would panic. If they understood how many immortal invaders we keep at bay, they would be grateful. We prefer that they know neither."

"So, Hightower House really is a fortress. That's a little disturbing. It makes me wonder what the Council has Gabriel doing,"

"He'll have to answer that question, my dear. You are looking a little fatigued. You don't sleep well when he is away, do you?" Yi asked changing the subject. He had learned from Gabriel as well, or maybe all vampires were adept at deflecting questions they did not choose to answer.

"No. I don't. Not without Gabriel beside me. I still find all this a little overwhelming, and your last revelation is not exactly reassuring. It's hard to feel safe when he isn't here to protect me."

Yi patted my hand.

"I owe Gabriel a great deal. Protecting his mate while he is away is the least I can do. Now go to bed, and sleep well."

For the first time in a week I did just that.

Chapter 40

Grace

I joined Yi Sheng in the salon again the following night.

"I enjoyed our conversation last evening. Thank you for being so forthcoming. Gabriel is rather tight-lipped." I was struggling for a tactful way to ask the question that still haunted me. I cleared my throat and asked quietly, "Does he ever talk to you about me? Like why did he choose me?"

"Gabriel is not one to share his feelings openly. Of course, you know that. He has had to protect the hard shell that has kept him alive this long, but I don't think he would mind my sharing what he has told me. In a way, I think he would welcome it."

"Gabe said the first time he saw you your blood sang to him. The song he heard was sad and filled with loneliness. It almost broke his heart to hear it because it reflected similar music in him. I think I am the only one who has ever seen his vulnerable side. His responsibilities to the Council have forced him to remain aloof. Of course, the fact that he can manipulate fire and burn his enemies to a crisp might have something to do with it also. It's a scary thing to cozy up to a flamethrower."

I suspect my eyes were as big as saucers.

"He can do that?"

"You didn't hear it from me," Yi laughed. "Do you like music?" he asked, abruptly changing the subject. Now I was convinced diversion was a common tactic among immortals when they did not want to continue an uncomfortable conversation.

"I love music. I am, or was, a very accomplished musician. I haven't had an opportunity lately. My father loved to hear me play the piano. But I loved the cello and oboe even more. Playing allowed me to release some of the sadness and disappointment I felt over not having a husband or children. I know my father needed me, but sometimes I hate him for being so selfish."

"Then I think you and Gabriel found something in each other that neither of you let anyone else see. Your souls were laid bare in your songs. Could you hear his? I lack the ability. Very few have it."

"I don't hear it. I wish I could," I said wistfully. "Maybe only the heightened senses of an immortal allow one to actually hear the music of another's soul. Or maybe there has to be a deep connection."

"He says that your song has developed since you've been here. He detects themes of hope flirting with happiness."

"My, you have a way with words, Dr. Sheng."

"They're not my words, but Gabriel's. He wants desperately to believe that it is because of him. He also hears your song creating a counterpoint to his. He says the harmony is comforting, I think that more than anything else finally convinced him that you were intended for him. That is why he chose you."

"I didn't realize he had such a poetic spirit. It seems I still have much to learn about my husband."

"I believe you bring out the person Gabriel was intended to be. I hope you can encourage him to let go of the one he thinks he needs to be. He needs your influence to be whole."

Chapter 41

When Gabriel returned two nights later, he heard an unfamiliar but not unwelcome sound as he entered the salon looking for Grace. It was the sound of someone playing the piano. Odd; he didn't remember a piano in the salon. Yi stopped him on the way in.

"Isn't she wonderful? Did you know she could play like that? I hope you don't mind that you bought a grand piano while you were away. I couldn't resist – on your behalf of course – once I discovered how much she missed it."

Gabriel worked his way through the crowd gathered around the new instrument and sat on the bench next to Grace. While she finished the piece she was playing, he rummaged through the stack of scores. Finding what he was looking for, he placed a piece for four hands on the piano.

"Care to try this one?" he whispered in her ear.

The crowd gathered around the piano yelled their encouragement as Gabriel placed his fingers on the keys. Grace indicated a tempo, and they began to play together. It took a few measures for Gabriel to lighten his touch on the keys to match Grace's more delicate one, but then the music they created together was exquisite. While they continued, oblivious to everything but the simple joy of creating something together, Yi looked for another piece for four hands. As soon as they finished the first, he placed the second one on the piano. The two of them continued playing until they had exhausted the supply of music. She chose several of her favorites to play alone, and he did the same. The end of the impromptu concert came, and the crowd expressed their approval with thunderous applause.

Grace was exhausted, and Gabriel was anxious to continue with their reunion, so they made their excuses and turned to leave.

"The cello and oboe should arrive tomorrow," Yi said before they cleared the door. "Did you know she played those as well?"

~~~~~~~~~~~~~~~~~~~~~~~~~~~~~~~~

As soon as the salon door closed behind them, Gabriel picked Grace up and whisked her to their rooms. His speed took her breath away. She wondered if she would ever get used to it, but it did have its advantages. It took no time at all until they were alone.

"I've missed you," he whispered as he nuzzled her neck.

Grace watched amused as Gabriel began to tear his clothes off. She sat on the bed and slowly began to remove her shoes and stockings. By the time she reached behind her neck to unbutton the dress, Gabriel was completely naked and staring at her impatiently.

"Turn around," he growled. "Let me help." Gabriel grew increasingly frustrated with the fastenings on the dress. "Who designed this thing?" he muttered. "It's impossible."

Grace looked at him and replied sweetly, "You did. You said you didn't want anything exposed that would tempt a vampire."

"I didn't mean me! We're going to have to change your style or have more dresses made. I'm ready to tear this one off."

"Patience, my love, we have all night."

Chapter 42

Gabriel rolled over and found the bed next to him empty. He knew Grace would not sleep all day, but it was early afternoon, and he had kept her up most of the night. He had hoped to find her cuddled up next to him when he woke.

The door to their room opened, and Grace peeked in. She was carrying two packages.

"I wanted to get back before you woke. The instruments arrived. I was so excited, I couldn't wait. I wanted to wake you with my favorite cello piece. But since you are up, you can help me unpack them. There may be some assembly required."

Grace tore into the larger box and revealed a beautiful *viola da gamba*. As she anticipated, it was badly in need of tuning.

"Can you tune it while I unpack the oboe?" she asked hopefully. She loved the early cello-like instrument, but hated the constant adjustments it required to keep it in tune. "Besides, your ear is probably better than mine. I'll bet you even have absolute pitch."

She handed the instrument over to Gabriel and opened the oboe.

"Oh, my!" Grace exclaimed. "How did Yi know to get an *oboe d'amore?*"

"Although I enjoy the piano, these two instruments are my favorites," Gabriel responded. "I suppose Yi thought we could play duets since your piano skills are so good. No doubt, they cost me a small fortune. Yi loves to spend my money. At least this time he's spending it on us."

Gabriel picked up the bow and began to play the viola, which was nestled between his legs. It was a beautiful melody – a little sad and full of longing.

"What is it?" Grace enquired. "It's absolutely beautiful."

"I do a little composing when I have the time and inspiration."

"That's amazing. You have quite a talent for it. Does it have a name?"

The corner of Gabriel's mouth was raised in a sly half-smile.

"It's called 'Come back to bed my love, and leave the instruments for later.'"

"You are incorrigible," Grace said as she slapped him lightly on the shoulder then continued sheepishly. "I would but there's a small problem with that. I'm currently indisposed and will be for several days."

"Damn! I thought there was something different about you today. I learned to tolerate that scent early on, otherwise it would have driven me crazy with all the human females around here. Even though the scent of discarded blood is not as appealing, it is still a distraction. Fortunately, biology helped. It seems that when females live in proximity their reproductive cycles synchronize. It is a way to level the playing field if all the available females are fertile at the same time. It also means that I don't have to deal with a constant assault on my senses. It is easy to forget that even though you are my mate, you are still a mortal. I will have to get used to dealing with 'female problems.'"

"It's not a problem," Grace said a little defensively. "It's a fact of life – a normal part of procreation." Grace felt horrible when she saw the expression on Gabriel's face. "I'm so sorry. I didn't think. I know you can't father children, and we won't have a normal family."

"Do you regret it?" he asked. "Do you resent me for dragging you into my world?"

"No. You don't get to ask me that question. I regret nothing. I love you, and this is not **your** world, it's **our** world. There is more than one way to have children and create a family – even here."

Gabriel began to play again. Grace listened to the sad song for a moment and rose to her feet. She took the *viola da gamba* from him and laid it carefully aside. She took his hand and led him over to the bed.

"We can, at least, hold each other for a while."

She nestled into his side and said mischievously, "You know, I've never seen a naked man play the cello before. Having that thing between your legs gives a whole new meaning to phallic symbol. It's quite a sight."

Gabriel slapped her playfully on the behind and said, "Now who's incorrigible?"

Later that evening, Grace turned to Gabriel.

"I need to eat something. I'm feeling a little light-headed. I think I'll go down to the kitchen." Gabriel took one look at her and jumped out of bed. He began to pull on breeches and a shirt. "I'll bring you something. You look pale. Does this happen every month, or is this cause for concern?"

"I hadn't considered the possibility that anything could be wrong. I have lost a little more blood than usual," she said, "but I'm not concerned. In addition, I didn't sleep well when you were gone, and I haven't gotten much since your return. I'm probably tired as well."

"From the looks of you, you didn't eat well either. I'll have to speak to Mrs. Miller about that – after she puts some supper together for you. I'll bring some wine also. I just saw you wince. Cramps?"

"For someone who claims to know nothing about 'female problems,' you are very perceptive. Yes. Thank you. Wine would be appreciated."

Grace was just coming out of the bathing room when Gabriel entered with a large plate of food and a bottle of wine. They sat at the table to enjoy their supper. Grace reached for the bottle of wine.

"May I pour you some?" Gabriel smacked his forehead. "I forgot the glasses. I'll be right back."

"No need," said Grace. "I don't think anyone will object if we just drink from the bottle."

Grace

Over dinner, I caught Gabriel up on events at Hightower House while he was away. He was happy to hear that things had been quiet in his absence.

Finally, I said, "I spent a lot of time with your friend Yi Sheng. I hope you don't mind."

"Of course it is fine with me. I told him to stick to you like glue. He was entrusted with your welfare while I was away. You may not have noticed since he hides it well, but Yi is not interested in women. If he is attracted to anyone, it is me. It has made our friendship awkward at times, but we've learned to deal with it. He is still my best friend."

"Well, he was very chatty about some things and raised some questions. Then he refused to answer them. He told me I had to talk to you. It was infuriating."

Gabriel laughed.

"That sounds like him. So, what do you want to know? We have plenty of time. Ask away."

"Tell me about the music."

"The music?"

"He said my blood sang to you. You could hear it from the first time you met me. How could you hear it? Yi said very few have that ability."

"That is a good question, Grace. Unfortunately, I can't satisfy you with a definitive answer. No one really understands it. My best guess is that it was intended to lead me to my mate. I never had it happen before – only with you."

"But what is it?"

"Vampire mythology suggests that this world was sung into existence. No one knows where the music or the singer came from, they just were. It also proposes that every created thing has a part of that song in them. If anyone had the ability to hear all the pieces at once, it would be so overwhelming, it would destroy them. Some can hear several pieces, but most hear none at all. I can hear my own piece of the cosmic song and now yours. I suppose if I ever sired a child, I would be able to hear theirs also. I don't know that I would want more than that."

"Yi said that you could hear my song change."

"Yes, the song that we are given at creation or birth is not static. It changes as we are changed by our life experiences. Every event in our lives adds another note or phrase to the melody. Your song, when we first met, was lonely and sad, but also angry. It was a confusing mix but understandable considering your story. I began to wonder if you might be intended for me when your song reflected more contentment and optimism the more time we spent together. I fancied I might have had something to do with that. I could sense there was a physical attraction for both of us, but the music went much deeper than that. And then your song insinuated itself into mine. It was the most astounding thing I ever experienced. Spiritual."

"I wish I could share the experience with you. It must be profound. Can you duplicate it? Play it for me?"

"I don't know. It can be very elusive. It's like a dream that you want to remember when you wake up, but the more you try to remember the details, the more it slips away. I hesitate to try. I don't want to chance losing it."

"I understand." But I didn't. Not really. It felt like he was withholding something precious from me, and I didn't know what to make of that. Maybe he didn't trust me, yet. It was time to test the limits of his trust.

"Yi told me his story and the part you played in it. He said you were the only one who could tell your own. Will you tell me?"

Gabriel let out a big sigh.

"I guess it is time," he said and began…

Chapter 43
Gabriel

I was a soldier in my mortal life – one of the best. That defined me to such an extent that I really don't remember life before the military. Life as a soldier is difficult. When not fighting an external enemy, there was a great deal of in-fighting. I suppose it is our nature to want to best our opponents whether hostile or friendly. And our superiors were invested in keeping us angry and aggressive. Now, I'm embarrassed to admit that I was the one of the most angry and aggressive of them all.

My sire was a very old immortal – maybe one of the first. He would never say. He was bored with the political gamesmanship of vampire society, so he had retreated to a remote area in the mountains. He did enjoy watching a good battle though. It was his idea of entertainment. In those years, there was plenty to watch. During one such battle, I came to his attention. He told me much later that he enjoyed observing the way my mind worked as I engaged my enemy. He could tell that I was not just a brute or bully, but an intelligent strategist. Word got out that no one person would ever best me in a fight so during one of our many battles, I was set upon by several opponents. I held my own for quite some time, but I was finally mortally wounded. My sire could not bear the thought that my talents would be wasted, so he decided to turn me.

After my demise, the battle moved away from where I lay. It was then possible for him to claim my badly wounded body and take what was left of me back to his dwelling. He first healed my wounds, so that I was unmarred and then drained what little blood I had left. I don't really have any memory of this, but I trust his recounting of the event.

The following night, I woke as an immortal. I was sure that this was the afterlife that some religious groups believe exists. I knew I had been mortally wounded, so I was certain I was dead. But I was confused. Everything hurt, but it was not the nonexistent wounds from the battle. My skin hurt. Every sight and sound was overwhelming. And I was hungry – actually ravenous. It seemed as if reason had left me, and all that remained was the instinct to kill and survive. In those first days, I imagine I behaved much like a wild animal.

My sire had the ability to control wind. This made it possible for him to fly us into the enemy camp unseen and drop from the sky in their midst. My sire took me into a small outpost of the army I had just battled. There, I was able to satisfy my bloodlust and take revenge on the enemy who had defeated me. I'm sure they thought we were gods. To some extent, I suppose we were. Being newly turned, I was insatiable. The two of us accomplished what my army could not. The gods who demanded a blood sacrifice drove the enemy from the area never to return. They were convinced these mountains were cursed.

I spent several years with my sire while he taught me how to control my urges and endure my heightened senses. With the lack of humans, we turned to hunting the plentiful wildlife in the area. He taught me to hunt only large animals and feed so that I did not kill them. He explained that was more desirable than depleting the available sources of food.

The relationship between a new vampire and their sire is not always pleasant. We were often at odds over my behavior. I was still angry and aggressive. Immortality had not changed that. During a particularly contentious altercation, I began to get very hot. The energy in the air was drawn to me and flames erupted at my fingertips. I was mesmerized. My sire had spoken with awe of immortals that could control fire. It seemed I was now one of them.

What I didn't realize at the time was that he was genuinely terrified of me. A newly turned vampire with a volatile temper was a danger to everyone around him, and fire was one of the few things that could kill us. He carefully talked me down from my temper tantrum, and the flames receded. While I was elated that I possessed a formidable weapon, he was considering what to do with me. He could not bear the thought of killing his only child, even if that was the customary remedy. But he could not risk keeping me with him. He decided to let the situation take care of itself.

Until vampires learn to master their element, they are a threat even to themselves. This is especially true for fire. More often than not, fire vampires manage to incinerate themselves in their first year. My sire chose to turn me out in the hopes that I would do the same without taking anyone with me – especially him. Of course, he made it sound like he was doing me a favor. It was time for me to choose my own destiny instead of remaining under his supervision. I needed to be free to make my own decisions. He had taught me everything I needed to survive.

It sounded better than the reality. Fortunately, my strict military discipline allowed me to eventually master the element that threatened to consume me. Giving in to the heady feeling the flames covering my body elicited was not an option if I wanted to live. And I wanted desperately to live. (It was also difficult to find new clothes to replace the ones I burned off.)

I was desperately lonely. As stated in the book, we are social creatures. I had not been in society for some time, and I was craving companionship. While in the army, I was constantly surrounded by others, often in close quarters. After my siring, I was still never alone. This was a new and unsettling experience, but I did not know how to seek out or approach others of my own kind. As it turned out, others found me.

It was in a large town in the West Kingdom where I had my first encounter. I believed that I could be inconspicuous in such a large place with so many humans. But all those humans presented a problem. I had not encountered such a plentiful blood supply, and my restraint was sorely tested. I failed. I got careless. My indiscretions caught up with me when several young women began telling of the "god" who came to them at night and lay with them while drinking their blood. I had not learned how to erase the memory of the encounter, and it is never good for us to draw attention to our presence in human communities. The resident immortals were concerned. They did not know me or where I came from. They did not want unnecessary attention, so they sent an enforcer to seek me out and destroy me. When he found me, I knew that only one of us would survive the encounter. He never returned to his friends. Before he died, I managed to find out where the rest of the group resided, and I found them.

I presented myself to them and requested their help. Several in the clan were ready to kill me on sight, but the more pragmatic ones pointed out that they needed a replacement for their enforcer, and I would be a good candidate. Fortunately for me, my supporters won the argument. It was decided that they would "civilize me." Frankly, I needed it. My sire had taught me the basics, but they advanced my education and taught me to read and write in several languages. I was astounded to discover how easily I learned things as an immortal. I loved it. That was also where I developed my love for music. While I enjoyed the piano, like you, I preferred solo instruments like the oboe and cello. And I discovered I could sing! I think I drove them mad with my incessant singing. But music kept me calm, so they tolerated it.

I remained with them for several years, absorbing as much knowledge as they were able to feed me. Only one problem remained: I was still angry and had a volatile temper. My new friends decided that I needed another calming influence. I was introduced to Guillanna. It was Guillanna who taught me everything I know about satisfying a woman. She brought out a side of me that I didn't know existed. I was a little disappointed to discover that she was being paid for her services to me, but it made sense. I didn't need any permanent attachments to distract me from my education. She made no demands on me, and I liked it that way.

"Maybe now you understand why I have no problem with employing the women here. Some consider it exploitation, but I can see the benefit for both parties. It does not offend my moral code. What does offend me are those who physically abuse others who are weaker than them, regardless of gender. Most of the women in my employ were brought or came here voluntarily to escape those kinds of situations. They can leave at any time with my blessing. Abusers rarely give that option. But back to my story."

When my friends decided I was civilized enough, they brought me to Hightower to be made known to the Council. It was my coming out so to speak. I was no longer a rogue vampire who could pose a threat to the immortal world. My introduction was especially important since mature fire vampires are rare. The Council was impressed with me and proposed I leave my current company and become one of their negotiators. The job description essentially meant, 'if you can't convince them to behave, kill them.' I proved to be very effective. So, long story short, here I am.

"Are you really over 500 years old?" Grace asked.

"Five-hundred years is an ambiguous phrase for vampires. It could mean, literally, 500 years, or so long ago that I don't remember or don't choose to say."

"I notice that is a non-answer."

I smiled indulgently.

"It's alright for you to ask me that question, and someday I'll even answer it, but never ask another immortal. In our culture, it is impolite. There are two, possibly three things which determine the power of an immortal. The first is the power of their sire. The second is the longevity of the vampire him or herself. If the immortal is mated and shares blood with their partner, the strength of their mate can also affect the vampire's strength. That information is closely guarded since it can give an advantage to an enemy, and it is not freely offered."

Grace filed that information away for a later time.

"Nevertheless," she persisted. "In all that time, you never found a mate?"

"The short answer is no. That is not to say that there were no women in my life from time to time, but nothing I wanted to continue for a long period. That is until I met you."

Grace could see that I was beginning to succumb to the coming of dawn. The telling of my tale had been emotionally exhausting, even for a vampire.

"I think that is enough for today. Let us just enjoy each other's company until you go to sleep," she suggested.

I agreed wholeheartedly.

Chapter 44
Grace

I still felt that there was much I needed to learn about the life I would be sharing with an immortal husband. I also suspected that Gabriel wanted me to know he just wasn't sure how to go about telling me. His need for secrecy throughout his long life made it difficult for him to confide even in me. Though I understood his reluctance, it still hurt a little. I realize we were still learning to know and trust each other, and he was not the only one with trust issues. It was too bad that he and his sire had not finished *The Truth About Vampires*. But since we wouldn't be engaged in any intimate activities for the next night or two, my incessant questioning provided a good distraction, and I was determined to take advantage of the opportunity and move onto my next pressing question.

"You mentioned vampires controlling the elements. What is that all about?"

Gabriel began, "There is much even we don't understand. We know that because of our heightened instincts we are able to utilize one or more of the elements which are present in all of us, including mortals. The four elements; earth, water, air, and fire are the stuff of which we are made. We have bodies which are mostly water and humus (earth, ergo human), and we breathe air. Fire as an element is much harder to explain. Somehow, those of us who are able can call it forth and manipulate it, but we don't understand why or really how, and we don't create fire. It seems to have something to do with anger, but everyone gets angry. Not everyone erupts in flame."

"Then there is the fifth element, the force which animates all life. Some call it the spirit, some the soul, and some just acknowledge it as the element that unites all the others and makes us whole. It is also the force which allows us to control our instincts so that we are more than just animals."

"As I said, we have all the elements present within us and our heightened awareness allows us to recognize them and utilize them. Since all but the original immortals were human first, we have the same characteristics we possessed before we were reborn. You seem to be well grounded and have a love for all growing things. If you became an immortal, I suspect you would control earth. But you also have a love of water. I have seen you stare at a fountain as a form of meditation. You might also have an affinity for water. Either would make you a good complement for a fire vampire. When I was reborn, I was an angry, aggressive young man with a quick temper. All those traits are desirable for a soldier. It could also be why I manifested an affinity for fire."

"Earth and water vampires tend to remain in one place for long periods of time and demonstrate more pack behavior than air and fire vampires. They also tend to sire more children, much like human farming and fishing families. Large families are desirable to divide the workload. Immortals that control air are flighty. You can never tell where they will turn up or when they will disappear. They are very solitary and may never sire a child since they would be required to tend to them until their offspring could control themselves – a process that can last many years."

"What about fire?" I interrupted. "You have been alone for a long time. Are your kind also solitary?"

"Not by choice." Gabriel said quietly. "It is very lonely being what I am. I am feared because I have the ability to control the one element that can destroy us. That is why even our sires often kill us, but it is also why I am such an asset to the Council. It is very unusual for a fire vampire to live to become as old and powerful as I have become. I am their weapon of choice."

"So, it's true; you are their assassin?"

"One of them, but we prefer the title 'negotiator.' The job doesn't really require my talents, but the threat makes me highly effective. Having a reputation can be a powerful deterrent in this line of work. It usually removes the necessity of using the power I control, so assassin may be an overstatement."

I thought for a moment.

"Is that why you chose me, a mortal? I didn't have enough sense to be afraid of you?"

"You know that I didn't choose you. Some force I don't understand brought us together. I tried to resist it because of what it would mean for you. The instinct to take you as my mate was stronger than my desire to protect you from what I am. Love finally won out. I can't say I'm sorry, but I am concerned for you."

"I'm not sorry either, and I'm not afraid, but I do want to understand. You said earlier something about my 'becoming' what you are. Is that what you desire?"

"I would never ask that of you. That is a choice you will have to make on your own. It should not be made lightly. It most definitely should not be made as a way to prove your love for me."

"You said you were turned against your will. It didn't turn out so badly for you."

"It was not exactly against my will. True, I was beyond the point where I could make my choice known, but my sire could tell from the way I fought my enemies that I was not prepared to die."

"Did it hurt?" I asked tentatively.

Gabriel laughed.

"I don't suppose it hurt any more than the lance and sword gashes I'd already endured. But, yes, it hurt. It is not a pleasant transition from dead to undead. Grace, you mustn't even consider this right now. There is no need. I only mentioned it in relation to natural affinities. I'm not suggesting that you should join me as an immortal."

"Just out of curiosity, how would an earth or water vampire be a good complement to you?"

"Well, if I flame up over some stupid thing you could always douse me with water or throw dirt on me to put out the flames. It could be quite handy. Now, is there anything else you want to know?"

"Well, yes. Did you write it? I know you said you and your sire did, but the writing looks a lot like yours and the paper is too new to be that old. Did you?"

Gabriel looked puzzled and then responded.

"I assume you are referring to *The Truth*. The answer is yes and no."

"What is that supposed to mean?"

Gabriel settled back in his chair for what looked like the telling of a long story and began.

"It was dictated to me by my sire. It was part of my early training to transcribe his lessons on the subject as way of teaching me the basics of reading and writing in the common tongue. The version we read is a copy I have been working on for years. I made changes and rewrote it as the original deteriorated. Not to mention that the original looked like it had been written by a child. In some respects, I suppose it was. The purpose of the writing exercise was twofold. First, it forced me to sit quietly and listen without question or comment. Second, he was one of the ancients and wanted to ensure that the truth did not become overshadowed by ridiculous myths."

"But why force you to discipline yourself to such an extent?" I asked.

"You will recall that I was trained as a soldier. Uncontrolled rage was encouraged. I was a disciplined soldier, but I lacked the kind of self-control that would enable me to master my fire element and survive. By this time, my sire had decided that I could be useful, but only if I could be judicious in the demonstration of my abilities. The fewer immortals that were aware of my talent the longer I would live."

I interrupted again, "If your sire was an ancient, then you must be a very powerful vampire even without the fire thing."

"The ancients had agreed not to make children indiscriminately. I should not have been turned. Between the powerful blood of my sire and my affinity for fire, I was a threat."

"Where is your sire now?"

"Gone," Gabriel said sadly.

"Did you kill him?"

"No, but I watched him cease to exist. One of the things that makes our long existence bearable is to take a mate. Someone with whom we can be completely honest about who we are. He never did and I believe I was created to fill that gap in my sire's life. But it was not the same, and it was not enough. He sought me out before he ended his life. The following day, he chose to walk into the rising sun and let its destructive rays consume him. I offered a quicker option when I realized he would not be deterred. He refused. He didn't want his death on my conscience. He did want a witness to his passing. I'm still not sure which was worse."

"It was a gruesome affair. He was ancient, so he could tolerate the sun to a point which meant it would take time for the end to come. I watched as he slowly burned away layer by layer. Toward the end, he could not refrain from screaming in agony. That sound still haunts my nightmares. I continued to watch as he finally turned to ash and blew away. At the end, all that remained was a single pure blue-white flame which ascended and disappeared. That is what feeds my hope that we still exist after this life. I believe his essence returned to his maker. Maybe that was his final gift to me, hope."

"You'd think I would be over it by now but the loss of your sire is profound," he said sadly. "Not as bad as losing a mate, but it leaves a void in you that nothing else can fill."

I put my arms around him and held him until the sadness receded.

"He must have been extraordinary," I whispered.

"He was."

"I don't think I have any more questions at the moment," I said. "This is more than enough to think about for now. But I'm certain I'll pester you incessantly the longer we are together."

"Well, I have a question for you," Gabriel countered. "I've read about an ancient culture in the North Kingdom that worshipped in oak groves and was attuned to the natural order. They were called Terrans because of their harmony with the earth. It is believed that they will play an important role in some future event. You are from the north. Is there any chance that you are a descendant? It could explain some of your grounded nature."

I was a little taken aback. The question seemed to have nothing to do with our previous discussion.

"Does it matter? I'm not even sure how to find out. The only one who might know is dead."

"It could. That bloodline is very powerful and thought to be extinct. The author of the ancient text believed otherwise. It could be relevant. It might also explain some things about our attraction to one another. I'm convinced that our coming together was not random. I just can't figure out why."

Chapter 45
Gabriel

Married life took a little adjustment. While I craved Grace's company and certainly enjoyed our time in bed, it was different than being alone. I understood why the Council wanted me to stay unattached. Each time I had to leave her was more difficult than the last. I began to dwell on what my life would be like when she was gone. I knew of immortals who felt such overwhelming grief at the loss of their partner that like my sire they simply chose to end their suffering. Would it be like that for me?

Grace and I had avoided any discussion of her joining me in immortality. It was not a decision she should make lightly. She needed to be sure we were really meant for one another first. Did we have any secrets which could potentially tear us apart? I most certainly did. Would she regret not being a mother and eventually resent me for it? There were many questions that had no immediate answers, so I would have to give her the space to make up her mind in her own time. I would not press her. However, I feared others would.

Chapter 46
Gabriel

The Council had set a date for their next meeting and immortals from all over were descending on Hightower House. There was a rumor that I was to be called to task for actions against the will of the Council. Curiosity about the charges ensured that this would be one of the best attended Council sessions any could remember. There was even speculation that the chambers would not be able to accommodate the demand for spectator seats. Since I had not defied the Council in any way, the list of imagined offenses was so much worse than the reality. The Council and I both knew that there were no real grounds for disciplinary action. It was merely a way for my enemies to publicly harass me without fear of repercussions. It wasn't the first time and wouldn't be the last. After all these years, I was used to providing an outlet for those who wished to vent frustration or try to increase their influence with their peers by attacking me. I had learned to handle it without demonstrating my temper. What I could not abide was that this time Grace would be a part of it. She was my weakness, and my enemies sensed it. By attacking her, they just might be able to provoke me into doing something rash. Something we would all regret.

The obvious charge concerned my mating a mortal. It would be alleged that this relationship was a liability since I must be constantly protecting my wife while still trying to perform my duty to the Council. I had to concede the validity of their concern. I was aware, therefore, that some would pressure me to compel her to turn against our wishes. I was afraid there would be support for this, even among my friends. Most frightening of all was that Grace would recognize the logic in their argument and make the sacrifice for me. I didn't want her coerced into it. I wanted her to become immortal because she truly wanted to be with me forever. To be honest, my ego demanded it.

However, there were rumors of another charge – this one against Grace herself. Pyotr, the king in the North Kingdom, was up to something. The Council knew it. They just couldn't prove it. A small group of Council members alleged that since Grace was from Pyotr's kingdom, he might have sent her here as a spy. By getting close to me, she would have access to information that could be helpful to the ambitious king and upset the fragile balance in the Council. Furthermore, they had knowledge that Grace was the sister-in-law of Pyotr's mortal mistress and suspected her as a fellow conspirator. This charge carried a death sentence if proved to be true.

I pulled Higgins aside.

"Have you found him yet, Higgins? I think time is running out. The Council is coming together soon, and I'm relatively certain that my marriage will be on the agenda. Worse than that, I need to make sure that I can defend Grace against any charges concerning her ties to Pyotr. There is increasing unrest in the north, and she is from there. My enemies are trying to accuse her of being a spy. There are some on the Council that have a vested interest in keeping me from any attachments that might interfere with my job. My taking a wife is, at the very least, inconvenient. Removing said wife would make them very happy."

"My brother can be slippery as an eel if he doesn't want to be found. I have reliable information that he might go to the sister-in-law for more money. We have sent men to intercept him in the north," Higgins replied.

"Well, I hope he shows up soon, and we get to him before he has a chance to approach her. If my suspicions are correct, Lilith will kill him on sight. He is a dangerous loose end for her. Of course, she doesn't know that Grace is here at Hightower. That information could buy him some time."

"We can always hope that he goes to the brother instead. That would be the best-case scenario. With Ethan's help, we might be able to disrupt Pyotr and Lilith's plans whatever they are."

The North Kingdom

Chapter 47

Pyotr was the immortal king in the North Kingdom. He had been growing restless for years and was spoiling for a fight. He didn't have anything against the other kingdoms except that they existed. The war he was planning to initiate was just a diversion from the boredom of his very long life. He was aware that there would be a tremendous loss of life. The mortals were expendable, of course. In a practical sense, the growing population was a potential threat. Culling the herd would be a welcome by-product of any conflict. He knew of a few immortals he would like to see in the front lines as well.

He was elated when he discovered a willing human ally in Lilith. When they happened to meet, Pyotr was immediately attracted to her. Besides being a very alluring woman, he perceived that she had a cold, calculating side that he could exploit. She was more than willing to entertain him when she could get away from her boring husband. From her perspective, this relationship was an opportunity for access to a power she would never acquire in the mortal realm. Their pillow talk soon evolved into planning a war.

Chapter 48

While Lilith was away dallying with Pyotr on some pretext of visiting an ailing relative, Arthur saw his opportunity to approach Ethan Pryce. Lilith told Arthur when she hired him to get rid of Grace, that she would kill him if she ever saw him again. Arthur had no reason to doubt she meant it. But he needed money and thought he might take a chance with Lilith's husband instead. He would take a different approach than simple extortion. Maybe if Arthur gave Grace's brother the welcome information that his sister was alive, Ethan would see fit to offer a reward. It was not necessary to tell him everything about Arthur's involvement. If that didn't work Arthur would issue the warning. While he was awaiting the opportunity to talk to Ethan, he had followed Lilith's activities. He knew she was in bed with Pyotr, and that did not bode well for Ethan.

Arthur was finally able to intercept Ethan as he was walking to the village one afternoon.

"Sir, could I speak with you? I have information about your sister Grace."

Ethan was dumbfounded. After all this time there was finally news of her.

"Is she well?" Ethan asked hopefully.

"I think we should go somewhere you can sit down. Her story may come as a bit of a shock."

Ethan pointed to an establishment across the street.

"We're almost to the pub. We can have a pint, and you can tell me about her."

As predicted, the story took most of the afternoon and several pints to dull its impact. Of course, the narrative was constantly interrupted by Ethan's questions. When Arthur was finished, Ethan just sat there shaking his head in disbelief. He couldn't fully comprehend what he had just heard, and Arthur was aware he did not look like the most reputable source. At first, he was not sure Ethan even believed him. But despite Ethan's reservations about the messenger, he could see how Lilith had carefully crafted Grace's demise. A part of him had always suspected Lilith's treachery, but he didn't want his comfortable life disrupted by confronting her. Like most of the young men of his time who grew up rich and never had to work, he was indolent. Not only was he too lazy to work, but he was too lazy to think for himself. Wasn't that why he married? He had someone to handle all the irritating petty details of life while he spent time with other men of privilege doing the things that men like them did.

Arthur could tell that Ethan was considering the information and sensed when Ethan began to accept the truth of it. Arthur was relieved that Ethan didn't seem to hold a grudge for his part in Lilith's plan. He had been very deliberate about telling mostly the parts where he helped Grace, but the response from Ethan was not the enthusiastic thanks and cash reward Arthur desired so he continued with the bad news, "I'm afraid there's more."

Ethan shook his head. *More? How could it get any worse?* He was still trying to imagine the confrontation with Lilith when she returned home. How should he handle it? Maybe he wouldn't. He could just go and collect Grace and be done with it. Peace restored. His preoccupation was shattered by Arthur's next revelation. Ethan put his head in his hands. Indeed, things could get worse.

"Do you really know where your wife is right now?" Arthur asked.

"From the tone of your question, I have to assume it's not where she said she was going," Ethan replied dejectedly.

"Have you checked your accounts lately?"

"Get to the point man!" Ethan exclaimed. "As you may have surmised, I am not a brave man. I don't know how much more of this I can take"

It was at that point in the conversation that Gabriel's men intervened. Two of the men dragged Arthur outside while another took his place at the table with Ethan.

"What Arthur was preparing to tell you is that your wife is currently in bed with the vampire King of the North plotting a war and financing it with your money. Her trips to 'visit sick relatives' have been visits to influential men in the area. She has been very successful at seducing them and gaining financial support for Pyotr's cause. Of course, she is not above a little extortion if they don't comply with the first request. Were you aware of your wife's activities?"

Ethan shook his head sadly. This was all too much.

"I hope you will believe I had no idea. I knew Lilith only married me for my title and money. My father tried to warn me, but I was so flattered that a woman like her would want me that I wouldn't listen. Now I find out that she tried to have my sister sold into slavery and is currently whoring around the countryside to get support for a vampire king. It's all more than I can take."

"Now that you know, what do you intend to do?" the stranger asked.

"I'll have to confront her, I suppose," Ethan replied.

"We think that would be very unwise. I don't know how long she intends to keep you around, but disrupting her plans right now could mean your death. You need to go along. Right now, you provide a good cover for her. You humans have no idea she plots to embroil you in a conflict that is just the whim of a bored immortal. People will die – lots of them. We can only stop this if she has no idea that you are on to her."

"What do you mean, you humans! Are you trying to tell me the legends are true? Father was not just making this stuff up? This just keeps getting better and better – but back to the other matter. I'm no actor. I don't think I can pretend I'm unaware of Lilith's activities," Ethan replied.

"Even if your life depends on it?" the mysterious stranger asked.

Ethan shrugged.

"I can only try."

Arthur was outside fuming.

"You idiots dragged me out before I could get my reward."

"Your reward is that we aren't going to kill you. Lucky for you, your presence is required in Hightower. You need to help your friend Grace. I'm sure her husband will be very generous if you cooperate."

Arthur smiled. Grace. He always hoped he would see her again. He had developed a major crush on her. A part of him hoped she would end up in a brothel he could afford, so he could visit her. The nobler part of him had won out when he placed her in his brother's care. It seemed that she had done well there. She was married. Arthur wondered to whom.

"Who's her husband?" he inquired. "More important, how generous can he afford to be?"

"Very generous if you come willingly," the man who appeared to be in charge replied, "and very lethal if you decline. He's someone you really don't want to piss off. She's married to Gabriel Ross."

"The fire vamp? That's surprising. I thought he was a confirmed bachelor."

"So did Gabriel. I'm sure it came as a surprise to him as well, but you have to admit, Grace is quite lovely."

"I do indeed. You don't need to worry about me. I'll come just knowing that it's to help Grace. If I'm rewarded, that would not be unwelcome though." Arthur smiled. "Grace."

"Your brother thought you had a soft spot for her. But we're wasting time. We need to leave now. There is some urgency."

As they departed, Gabriel's men explained the gravity of Grace's circumstances. How could Arthur refuse? Not only would he help Grace, but he could get back at that bitch, Lilith. It was a win-win as far as he was concerned.

Chapter 49

Ethan had taken a lover. Lilith could smell her when he finally came to bed. No matter. Lilith had not bothered to disguise her growing distain for her husband. She was relieved that she did not have to put up with his inept and unimaginative attempts at lovemaking. She was sure he was aware of her indiscretions also. If he hadn't still been useful to her, she might have disposed of him as she had her previous husbands and lovers. Pyotr still needed the funds Ethan could provide, and she didn't want to raise suspicions by eliminating him yet. Soon enough, she would sit next to the powerful vampire king and rule with him. She had finally found someone worthy of her.

For her part, Lilith was too consumed with delusions of grandeur to see that there was something bothering Ethan. She had always mistaken his laziness for stupidity and constantly underestimated him. As he predicted, he was not a very good actor. The mistress was a good cover.

When Lilith announced that she needed to make a trip to see another sick relative (*How many could she possibly have?*) and the visit could last several months, Ethan did not protest. He almost packed her bags for her in his haste to get rid of her. Lilith was sure that she could talk Pyotr into taking her with his delegation when they went to the Council meeting in Hightower. If she was successful, she would be gone for quite some time. She didn't expect to see Ethan again.

Chapter 50

Pyotr hadn't intended to take part in the Vampire Council meeting. He was well into plans for his little war and didn't relish the thought of any further delays. He opened the summons out of curiosity and immediately changed his mind. This was just too tempting to pass up. The first item on the agenda read: *Gabriel Ross – To answer charges of dereliction of duty*. Pyotr had to wonder what the golden boy of the Council had done to deserve a public trial, but it must have been good. He had always envied the man and thought his value to the immortal world was vastly overrated. Perhaps Pyotr was also a just a little jealous. Controlling fire would have made him possibly the most powerful immortal in the Known World. That was a title he coveted. To see Gabriel Ross brought down a peg or two would make the trip worth it. After all, what were a couple months of delayed gratification to a vampire? He could pursue his lofty ambitions when he returned – perhaps with one less obstacle.

Pyotr's history with Gabriel Ross was complicated. They had been reluctant companions long ago. As trained soldiers, they had a lot in common. When they were not otherwise engaged, they both liked the boxing ring. Fighting was a popular sport for unemployed soldiers. They discovered each other when they both entered a contest at one of the many arenas in the West Kingdom. It was not particularly wise for vampires to fight in human competitions, and two of them could be a problem. It would be very easy to give themselves away, but both Gabriel and Pyotr had learned the restraint necessary to blend in. On this occasion, they both made it to the final round – no surprise there. The contest was brutal. Since the mortals could not tell just how hard the jabs, punches, and kicks were neither held back. They learned a couple things that day; they could earn a lot of money by determining the winner each time they fought and placing bets accordingly (a good thing), and they healed too quickly from their injuries (a not so good thing).

Depriving themselves of blood several days before a match ensured that they could limit their strength against mortal opponents and keep the injuries, slowing the healing process. After each bout, they fed voraciously. It took Gabriel a little longer to be satisfied because he refused to drain his victims. Pyotr had no such difficulties. Pyotr could have exploited Gabriel's weakness then, but they were making too much money to stop. Thankfully no one took notice of the increased death rate whenever they were in town, and the two immortals did not stick around long enough for questions.

Eventually Pyotr realized that his only real competition in the immortal world was Gabriel Ross, and things between them changed. He began to pay more attention to any weakness in Gabriel's fighting style and learn how to use it against him. From the calculating look in Gabriel's eyes when they fought, Pyotr was certain Gabriel was doing the same. The bouts became more intense, and the mortals were beginning to wonder. The brutality of the last matches gave rise to the rumors of their hatred of one another. Not entirely true. Pyotr did not hate Gabriel, but he did resent him. He should have been the one to control fire. Gabriel had too many scruples to be a good leader. Pyotr, on the other hand, had the desire and the ruthlessness to be a great king. In his mind, it was a shame really that they were both so competitive. Together, they could have taken over the world, if only Gabriel was willing to be Pyotr's tool and not his partner. Gabriel's refusal was his salvation because Pyotr would never share. After he got what he wanted, one of them would have to die.

But Gabriel Ross was not Pyotr's immediate concern. Let the Council take care of him. The king was not pleased with Lilith's demand that she accompany him to the meeting in Hightower. He was growing tired of her sharp tongue and constant demands. She needed to learn her place. Pyotr was looking forward to traveling without her. There was plenty of sport in Hightower of a more agreeable and less demanding nature. She had a point however. Most of his human entourage was there because of her skills at seduction and manipulation. He didn't understand it, but then, they were human without his keen sense of the kind of woman she truly was. When he was being truly honest with himself, she had bewitched him in the beginning also. He should have recognized how much like him she was, even if she was a woman. It was likely that her opinion of all things male matched Pyotr's opinion of all things female. He could sire her, of course. That was probably her ultimate goal in allying herself to him. She was ruthless and craved power. She would make a formidable vampire, and together, they might be unstoppable. But she was not his mate, and Pyotr was already finding her company tedious. No, it would not do to create an immortal that would be an eternal thorn in his side.

Lilith's expectations about this trip were worse than Pyotr feared. He was a king, so that meant the two of them had to travel in a style befitting their station. She ordered the building of a new coach. In addition, she would need a completely new wardrobe so that he wouldn't be embarrassed by her shabby attire. She hadn't actually approached him about any of this. He became aware of her extravagances when the scribe came to him with the pile of bills. Pyotr put his head in his hands and groaned. This had to stop. When Pyotr called Lilith in to account for the expenses, she pointed out that it was actually her husband's money that was paying the bills. He couldn't argue with that even though he had better uses for the funds. Fortunately, they would leave in two days, and that would put an end to it.

The trip to Hightower took a little less than two weeks. By the time they arrived, Pyotr was in a foul mood. Two weeks confined in a coach, no matter how luxurious, with Lilith was enough to try anyone's patience. He was grateful that mortals were not permitted into the Council's chambers under any circumstances and hoped the proceedings would be lengthy, so he could avoid spending any more time than necessary with her. Pyotr didn't even enjoy her company in bed anymore. She was an inventive and adventurous lover, but even that was overshadowed by her obnoxious personality. He decided when he left Hightower, it would be without Lilith.

Hightower

Chapter 51

Gabriel opened his summons to the Vampire Council with as much enthusiasm as Pyotr had opened his. He scanned the formal diplomatic language and got quickly to the part which concerned him. He was answerable for dereliction of duty. He shook his head and had to laugh. What a load of crap! He knew there was no justification for the charge and knew he could counter any accusations they made, but the second item on the agenda was more troubling. It made reference to mortals aiding plans to start a conflict among the four kingdoms. There were no names or specific charges. Gabriel wasn't even sure that mortals fell under the jurisdiction of the Council. To him, it sounded like an excuse to go fishing for information, and there was only one mortal he could think of who was worth the trouble – Grace. He sincerely hoped that was not the case. He was not sure how he would respond if they came after her with unsubstantiated charges, which could result in her death. Since mortals were not allowed in chambers, she could not even defend herself. He thought it best not to tell her about any of this.

The opening night of the Vampire Council was dedicated to ceremony and political posturing. It was an incredible waste of time as far as both Gabriel and Pyotr were concerned. The two vampires were seated across the chamber from each other, so they had to acknowledge one another. They nodded cordially, but their expressions were anything but. Pyotr lounged in his seat and looked bored with a smirk on his face. Gabriel fidgeted in his and looked tense. He was anxious and not concealing it very well. Yi sat next to him and tried to distract him, but it was a lost cause. Finally, the night came to a close, and everyone went to rest and prepare for the next night's session.

Grace was waiting anxiously for Gabriel's return. She knew he was more concerned about the proceedings than he was willing to admit. Something was wrong. Something he wasn't telling her. When she saw his face all thoughts of confronting him left her and all she could think to do was console him. He looked terrible. She wrapped her arms around him and held him until he calmed down.

"Come to bed," she whispered. "You need to rest. Tomorrow will take care of itself."

He let her undress him. He was so distracted he almost didn't realize what she was doing until she gently pushed him on to the bed and got in next to him. He buried his head in her neck and breathed in her comforting scent.

"Do you need to feed?" Grace asked.

"Not like this," he groaned. "Never like this."

Gabriel was still not himself when he rose later in the afternoon. He wished that he was still young enough that he slept through the entire day, so there were fewer hours for him to worry. He rarely dreamed when he slept, but today had been an exception. The dreams were not pleasant ones. Grace finally insisted that they play some duets. He reluctantly agreed and eventually lost himself in the music he and Grace made together. Too soon, it was over, and he had to leave for the first trial.

Chapter 52

Lilith paced the corridor outside the Council chambers. Pyotr had not informed her that as a mortal she would not be permitted in the chamber with him, so she raged when the guards turned her away at the door. *Don't they understand just how important she is to him?* She added a few more names to the growing list of people who would suffer when she was queen.

Lilith was shocked to find Grace sitting on a bench outside the chamber door. What on earth was she doing here in Hightower? Lilith never should have trusted that idiot Arthur. She knew he was too stupid to follow her instructions. This was not at all what Lilith had planned for Grace. But it no longer mattered. Lilith was mistress to the most powerful being in the Known World. At least, that is what he told her. She was certain that she would become his queen when the conquest of the other kingdoms was accomplished. She could even be immortal. She could afford to be gracious.

Meanwhile, Grace was caught up in her own world of worry and seemed not to notice Lilith's presence in the hall. Lilith preferred to keep it that way. There would be plenty of time to gloat later, so she quickly retreated down the hall.

However, Lilith was curious. Information was power, and she lacked the information she needed. She went to Pyotr's entourage of mortals to see what they knew. Pyotr had been irritatingly vague about details when she asked about the Council's proceedings. She suspected that he was so caught up in his own intrigues that he didn't even know what was going on. Rumor had it, they confided, that Lilith's sister-in-law, Grace, was now married to the Council's foremost assassin. *Grace married to an immortal? That's surprising to say the least.* Had they been on friendlier terms, Lilith would have loved a little tête-à-tête to find out just how she had managed that. What was even more surprising was that Grace and Gabriel happened to be in the center of the current controversy.

She was disappointed that she would not be allowed in the chambers when Grace and her vampire were brought to task. That was something she wanted to see. She was not aware that her presence in Hightower figured into the accusation against Grace.

Chapter 53

Grace

I sat down, stunned while Gabriel paced the floor of our sitting room.

"How could they think such a thing? Have I given any indication that I'm passing secrets? Why would they suspect me?"

"You're from the North Kingdom, and Lilith is your sister-in-law," Gabriel explained patiently.

"Who tried to kill me or, at the least, sell me into slavery!" Grace interjected.

"They won't know that until you testify. From their perspective, it makes sense. But we've located Arthur, and he is willing to verify your story. We just need to get him here in time."

"How will that help since mortals are not allowed in the Council chamber even to defend themselves?"

"If you are willing, I will insist that the Council Presider interview you. I believe he will be fair and not abuse your willingness to cooperate. It does mean that he can compel you to be completely honest in your answers. I can understand if you will not agree, but he can determine if you are telling the truth, so he can advocate for you. That is the only way the Council will believe it. I cannot defend you in this. Be warned, there is no way to prevent him from asking about other things that have no bearing on this particular case."

"You mean anything you might have told me in confidence. I'm afraid he will be disappointed. You haven't revealed much. There is nothing in your story which could damage you. Can you be there when he interviews me, so you can stop any unwarranted invasion of my thoughts?"

"To be fair, I will request that both your accuser and I are present. I don't see how anyone could object to that."

"Will they do the same to Arthur?"

"If he will allow it, I imagine they will. It may not be necessary for your defense. It won't look too good for Lilith though. I expect they will want to talk to her also. Pyotr will regret the day he allowed that woman into his life."

Chapter 54

With all of the immortals at the Council session, the women at Hightower House had time on their hands. They took the opportunity to pursue other occupations since there were no guests to entertain, and many found themselves in the training room.

Under the tutelage of Gabriel's chief of security, the women had progressed at a rapid pace. All had mastered basic self-defense skills, and many had progressed to weaponry under his watchful eye. He was skeptical at first. The chief (coincidentally, his name really was Chief) could not imagine why Gabriel thought it necessary to use his impressive talents training women. In Chief's opinion, women were meant to stay home and take care of their husbands and family. The idea of a group of fighting women was laughable. He learned, however, that women with enough incentive, skill, and adrenaline were not to be underestimated. He began to think of them proudly as his personal army.

Soon, sparring with one another was not enough for his more advanced trainees.

"I'm truly impressed by your capabilities," Chief admitted. "I never would have guessed you could come so far. But you will not have to defend yourselves against other women. Your assailants will most likely be much larger than you, and you need to be prepared. I am inviting some of my men to assist with your training."

When Chief began to employ other members of his security force in the sessions, they too shared his initial disdain for the task, but after one of the more diminutive women managed to disarm and throw a much larger opponent to the floor, they began to see the value. The downside of allowing the women to work out in this manner was that some of them were spoiling for a fight. Those who had been rescued from abusive situations wanted to employ their new abilities not only to defend themselves but be the antagonist. They were thrilled to be able to take out their aggressions against someone who looked more like their abusers. During the course of the training, both groups came to a grudging respect for one another. Chief had to admit that he would be happy to have any one of these women on this security team.

Chapter 55

Pyotr was not sure how much the Council knew about his activities, so he took the precaution of bringing twice the usual number of personal guards. Half of them were disguised as a trading delegation, so no one would suspect anything out of the ordinary. It was not unusual for merchants to accompany their immortals to Hightower. Travel was much safer in their company.

In his own strange way, Pyotr could be a generous man. His disdain for mortals was thinly disguised, but he saw the benefit in rewarding them, so they entertained the notion of being valued. Since all the immortals brought their own personal guards, he suspected that Hightower House would have minimal protection. After all, who would waste guards on a bunch of women? They were easy to replace. He suggested to his men that while all the immortals were occupied, they might take advantage of the hospitality of the renowned salon of the immortals. Under no other circumstances would their kind be allowed access. This was their opportunity to see how their betters lived. Pyotr saw little problem with this plan. He had twice as many men as he needed, so if some were apprehended, they were expendable. If not, he would be the hero to his men securing their undying loyalty. For Pyotr, it was a way to strike at Gabriel Ross in his own home. Since the assault would not involve any immortals, Pyotr could claim ignorance. He would allow the men disguised as traders to go first so that the association to him would be even harder to prove. He was pleased with his plan and couldn't wait to set the pieces in motion. One way or another, he was going to damage Gabriel Ross.

Chapter 56
Higgins

There was loud shouting and pounding at the door to Hightower House. I could not imagine what was going on. The salon was closed. The immortals were all in Council this evening, so why was anyone looking for entrance? When I cracked the door open, I was overrun by a large group of drunk and rowdy Northmen. Pyotr had given them the night off, and they were going to take his advice about where to spend their free time they informed me. They knew Hightower House salon was off-limits to mortals, so there was an added element of excitement to be doing something forbidden, especially when it involved little risk.

The men pushed past me and broke into the salon. They were disappointed to find it empty of the women they were promised.

"Where are they?" they demanded as one of the Northmen held me up off the ground. "We were told there were women."

I struggled to answer since the lout was holding me up by my collar, and I was choking.

"Let him down you idiot. Can't you see he couldn't answer if he wanted to. He can't even breathe, let alone talk. Put him down."

I knew where the women were, but I needed some way to warn them without raising the suspicions of Pyotr's men.

"Since all the potential patrons are in the Council meeting, they, like you, were given the night off," I managed to choke out as soon as I could speak. "I'm sure you can understand. It will take a little time to assemble them, but you can make yourselves comfortable in the salon while I inform them that their services are needed after all. You may help yourselves to the bar while you wait."

I hurried down the corridor followed by several of the Northmen. Rather than take a short-cut, I made sure to pass the kitchen, which distracted my pursuers. They abandoned me, lured by the aromas of Mrs. Miller's cooking. I knew she could keep them busy and buy me a little more time.

I stopped first at the bathing house, a favorite gathering place for the women who were not working. My persistent banging on the door was finally answered by a very irate female in a towel.

"What do you want Higgins? We have the night off."

"You need to get out of here and hide. We've been overrun by a group of Northmen who are demanding to be entertained. Right now, they are entertaining themselves in the salon, but you are vulnerable here if they get bored and decide to explore. I'm going to fetch the group in the practice room. It looks like they will finally have an opportunity to utilize all that training."

The woman smiled.

"I think I'll get dressed. I've got to be part of this."

I was not sure that was a good idea, but who was I to refuse more willing hands?

I proceeded to the practice room. I was breathing heavily when I arrived, and my anxious expression got the attention of the group as I explained the situation. The women stood in stunned silence. Someone would invade Gabriel Ross's establishment? This could not be tolerated. I urged them to gather their weapons of choice. They all needed a quick dip to wash off the sweat from their workout, and then they would dress. I could not contain my amusement as I watched them grab any weapons which could be concealed under a skirt or in a boot. I could imagine lethal knives strapped onto the thighs of the otherwise elegant and fragile-looking women. The men in the salon were in for a surprise they would never forget – if they lived to (or chose to) tell about it. From the angry looks on some faces, I doubted the men would emerge from the encounter unscathed.

"Be careful and remember your training," I shot back at them as I left and returned to the salon.

In no time at all, 13 women – literally dressed to kill – entered the salon. The room was already in a shambles from the drunken brawls that had erupted while the men waited for their promised entertainment. They had consumed every bit of Gabriel's expensive alcohol and were rummaging around for more. They were about to look for the wine cellar when the ladies entered the room.

Pyotr's men were awestruck. The north lacked the sophistication of the Middle Kingdom, so they had never had access to this many beautiful women, and it was overwhelming. They began to fight again over who would get first choice.

Aubry took charge of the situation.

"Calm down, you will draw lots. That is the only fair way to resolve this without further bloodshed. Besides," she said coyly. "You need to conserve your energy for other pursuits."

That brought them up short. Why waste energy on pointless arguments when something much better awaited them? *They have no idea,* I thought.

Soon all the men were paired with one of the house's courtesans. The men were still a little unsure how to act with a sophisticated woman, so they did what they knew best – grab and grope. That put the unsuspecting men close enough for the women to react. The women utilized a divide and conquer strategy keeping the men separated, so they could not assist one another once they realized what was happening. The encounter was over before it really began. The men were so surprised at being attacked by a woman that they reacted slowly losing possession of their weapons and control of the situation. Some of the women never even had to draw their own weapons but that didn't make them any less deadly. Several unfortunate men lay on the floor clutching their groins. *They would think twice about underestimating women. As would I!*

Two of Pyotr's more competent guards managed to disarm their female assailants and turn their own knives on them. The women employed the techniques they learned from Chief to escape and sought help. So focused were the frustrated guards on pursuing their intended victims that they never saw the knife to their neck as two of the other women slit their respective throats severing the carotid artery. Their eyes were wide with disbelief as they bled out on the expensive carpet.

"Do you think Mr. Ross will take that out of my salary?" the first said.

"Oh, who cares. It was worth it," said the other. "Besides, those bastards deserved it!"

The remaining men suffered a variety of non-lethal injuries. The victorious women herded their captives into the center of the room where any remaining weapons were collected at sword point. In order to ensure that they were not concealing anything else, the men were ordered to disrobe. They had expected to do that anyhow but just not under these circumstances.

One of the younger women giggled and said, "I guess the wild red hair goes all the way down."

The women looked at one another and then at me.

"What do we do with them now?"

At this point I took charge.

"We will keep them locked up until we can contact Mr. Ross. He can decide on an appropriate punishment." Then I sent a messenger to the Council chamber with the news of the attack on Hightower House. Gabriel could find out the details when he arrived. Rather than risk losing anyone if they tried to move them to another location, the women secured the salon and left their captives to contemplate their mortality and await Gabriel's return.

A messenger was admitted to the chamber and delivered the news of the attack on Hightower House. Gabriel was understandably frightened and angered.

"Was anyone injured? Killed? I need to leave at once," he stated as he rushed from the room where he was meeting with the Council Presider.

Pyotr saw the messenger come to the door and was waiting outside in the hall where he heard the message as it was delivered. He knew what the content would be but acted as if he was shocked and said loudly enough for anyone in the vicinity to hear him, "If someone would dare to attack Gabriel Ross's home right under his nose, then we are all in danger. I need to give new instructions to my personal guard. Who knows who will be the next target?"

He quickly departed before anyone could see the satisfied smile on his face.

Chapter 57

Pyotr gathered the remaining guards in his suite.

"What do you know about this? They were only supposed to screw a few women to let off a little steam. What the fuck happened?"

"We haven't heard anything from them, so we only know rumors. We don't know which of our men started it but the guys were pretty drunk when they left to go there. The rumor among the other guards is that it was a bloodbath."

"Well, I can't risk acknowledging them as mine, so they are on their own. I never said they should kill anyone."

"You misunderstand. It was our men that suffered the casualties. After they tore up Ross's salon, they went for the women. We heard the women got the drop on them."

Pyotr's shock was followed by disgust.

"Beaten by women? That's what they get for going over there drunk. I can't have such incompetence in my ranks. Once they are released, you know what to do. I don't want anyone alive who can point a finger at me."

This was an unexpected turn of events. Pyotr knew that at least one of his guards would be interviewed by an immortal. He could not help but reveal the association with Pyotr and that Pyotr had sent them to Hightower House for a little fun at Gabriel Ross's expense. Pyotr would probably have to admit to it and take the consequences. No one could hide the truth from a vampire inquisitor. No worries. He would explain that he only wanted to prove that Ross was not as invincible as everyone thought. Nothing was supposed to come of it.

Pyotr began to suspect that the lure of seeing Gabriel Ross brought down off his high horse might have been a ploy to get him to the Council meeting. Not much else could have drawn him away from his other plans. It was too tempting, and he had come to resent Gabriel with a passion, so he came. He had to ask himself, *Why?* Why did they want him here badly enough to potentially damage the reputation of their most accomplished assassin – oh sorry, negotiator? What, exactly did they know or suspect? It was not possible to wage a war on the scale he intended without someone spilling the beans. It was nothing for an inebriated soldier to brag that someone would "get theirs" when Pyotr won the war. Or some petty lord might promise his mistress that he would get rid of his wife when the North Kingdom ruled the Known World. The rules would change in their favor when they were the victors. There were many ways in which rumors could leak out. He was just too arrogant to admit that it would matter. But now he had to accept that he had made a mistake coming to Hightower and it was high time to leave.

There was only one other task remaining before he departed.

Pyotr left the meeting in a foul mood. He didn't need any of this. The Council proceedings had not gone as he expected. The reckoning he expected for Gabriel had been blown out of proportion. He was now certain the rumors had been exaggerated in order to ensure his presence. Again, he had to wonder why. In addition, the Council demanded to interview Lilith in order to either convict or exonerate her sister-in-law, Grace. He doubted he would be able to use his considerable influence to keep Lilith out of their hands, and he had no idea how far they might go in order to get information on his plans. It had been a mistake to bring her. She knew too much about his plans and the names of all his fellow conspirators. This was a disaster.

Lilith was pacing the hall still aggravated that mortals were not permitted in the Council chambers. She wanted desperately to see Grace condemned and executed. It still galled her that Grace had escaped the fate Lilith so carefully planned for her. Now Grace had the status in the immortal community Lilith had unsuccessfully worked so hard to gain. Grace was married to one of the most powerful vampires in the Known World while Lilith remained a mistress. Where did it go wrong? She suspected that idiot Arthur had a hand in it.

Lilith intercepted Pyotr as he left the chamber. He brushed past her, but she hurried after him. She could see that he was not pleased, and she was anxious to find out why.

"What happened?" she inquired. "Did things not go as you expected?"

She was several steps behind him, so she did not see the contemptuous look on Pyotr's face. He regained his composure and turned to face her.

"It was a curious proceeding." Pyotr replied impassively. "It appears that Gabriel did nothing punishable. Of course, the Council is not pleased that he married a mortal, but it is no crime. It seems that someone has an axe to grind and was using the Council to get their revenge for some perceived slight."

"I'm sorry you won't have the opportunity to gloat over his downfall. It seems he proved himself untouchable once again."

Pyotr hid his irritation at Lilith's assessment of his interest in the proceedings against Gabriel.

"The Council's allegations against Grace are causing quite a stir though. Your name came up."

"Me? Why?" Lilith asked.

"It seems that there is a witness who can confirm Grace's story that she has nothing to do with us. The council now wants to hear your version, which is fine, as long as Grace is the extent of their questioning. The council might use the opportunity to expand the scope of their inquiry to include your activities on my behalf. Some of my allies are worried."

"I can handle them. I'm a very convincing liar," Lilith scoffed. "As you are well aware."

"I have the greatest confidence in you, or you wouldn't be here" Pyotr lied.

As usual Lilith overestimated her abilities and importance Pyotr thought. He motioned her to the stairs. "Let's discuss this somewhere a little more private."

Pyotr put his arm around Lilith, and they ascended the stairs. She leaned into him. She felt safe with him as her protector. He would not let the Council compel her to do anything she didn't want to do. She had never had a problem controlling the men in her life, and Pyotr was no exception.

They arrived at the balcony on the second floor and Pyotr stopped. He turned to look out at the lobby sensing for listening ears.

"This will do. We can see anyone coming from here." He faced Lilith and took her face in his hands. She looked into his eyes in expectation of the kiss which would follow. *Men are so predictable,* she thought. *Get them alone and all they can think about is satisfying their lust.*

She couldn't quite read the expression on his face as he leaned in to her. He bypassed her lips to whisper in her ear, "goodbye Lilith," as he twisted her head and snapped her neck.

Pyotr carried Lilith's lifeless body to the head of the staircase and dropped her. No one would know that she was dead before her body tumbled down the stairs. They would assume that her neck was broken when she fell. It was just an unfortunate accident. He knew the Council would be suspicious. The "accident" was a little too convenient even though Pyotr had torn the hem of her dress to make it look as if she had caught her heel causing the fall. It's a shame Ross wasn't around. Pyotr could have implicated him. Oh well. Let them try to prove it was anything more than a tragic occurrence. There was no way the conniving mortal woman would ruin his plans now.

Chapter 58
Gabriel

I barged through the door of Hightower House and ran into Higgins.

"What happened here?"

I dreaded the answer but was surprised to see Higgins grin.

"Oh, Mr. Ross, you will be so proud of them"

That was not the response I was expecting. I'm sure I looked puzzled.

"Proud of whom?"

"See for yourself," Higgins replied as he opened the door to the salon.

I couldn't believe my eyes. I expected to see the damage done to the furnishings in the salon, but nothing could have prepared me for the rest of it. Surrounding a group of injured not to mention naked Northmen were the Hightower House women holding knives and swords. On the floor lay the bodies of two men who did not survive the melee.

One of the women whose fine dress was covered in blood grinned at me and said, "Thanks for the self-defense lessons boss. They paid off. These oafs never had a chance. That will be the last time they underestimate a woman."

"Once this gets out, it may kill business," I mused out loud. "On the other hand, my associates will feel well protected in these walls with you bloodthirsty lot around. Well done, ladies. Now will someone explain exactly what happened here?"

The women told the story from their perspective. Most of it matched what I had already been told. They were forced to admit that they may have used more force than was absolutely necessary in some cases, but the need to demonstrate they were no longer victims won out over restraint. It felt good.

"All right, please go and clean up. There is something disturbing about being confronted with 13 blood-spattered women with weapons. I will handle things from here. Oh, and if you are going to act like soldiers you might as well learn the rest of the responsibilities. Make sure those knives and swords are cleaned and returned to the armory."

Pyotr's men breathed a sigh of relief as soon as the last of the women left the room.

"Those bitches are nuts!" one of them exclaimed. "You must be crazy to live around that lot."

"I'll thank you to refrain from unkind comments about my employees. They were trained to protect the house in my absence, and that is exactly what they did. You just had the misfortune to try to gain unauthorized access. What gave you the idea that you could invade my premises? You know that this salon is reserved for immortals only. I'd say you got off easy. If you had surprised any of my immortal guards, you would be dead."

"Pyotr gave us permission," the Northman said. "He said we could be here since there would be no vampires around to stop us."

"Pyotr." I snorted in disgust "That's all I needed to know. I doubt your king will back you up on that claim. I also doubt he will appreciate you implicating him in this fiasco. If he lets you live, I think you had better look for other employment. You will be safe for a little while. The local magistrate is arranging accommodations for you. He and his deputies will be here soon. I suggest you don't give them any trouble, or he may seek the assistance of some of my people."

Later that night, I sat in the library with Higgins and Yi. We were discussing the events of the day over a glass of scotch and a cigar.

"Was I wrong to let them learn to defend themselves? If Pyotr's men had not been so drunk and overconfident, the outcome could have been very different. I don't want one success to go to their heads."

Yi shook his head and replied, "If they were men you would not feel that way, Gabriel. We all had to prove ourselves at some time. Look at all the young lives wasted in unnecessary wars. Most of those boys were not prepared, and they died. There were times in our history when women fought alongside their men. Certainly, immortal women can be fierce fighters. Face it. After all proof to the contrary, you still underestimate them. The women you rescue have been forged in fires much fiercer that most men. They survived, and now you have given them the tools to overcome the circumstances of both birth and abuse. Now they can truly enjoy their lives. You should be proud."

I was still trying to process the events of the evening and my employees' part in them. "It is my nature to want to protect that which I value. You know I appreciate women, even if it did take forever for me to find the right one. I have put my life on the line for them over and over again. I want them to have the lives they deserve – husbands, children, safety. Is that wrong?"

"That version of life may be right for many women but not all. Why shouldn't a skilled woman be a warrior? From what I have seen tonight, the ranks of your day guards could be enhanced by the addition of a couple of the women here. Their skills are wasted in the salon. They have some anger issues to overcome but then, so did you. At least they don't catch fire when they are angry."

I raised my hands in surrender.

"Point taken. I'll admit I still have very traditional views on women. I congratulated myself on being progressive when I admitted that how a woman chose to use her body was up to her. Those who take the moral high ground would rather see a woman starve than turn to prostitution. But men are still stronger, and we should protect women not take advantage of them."

"You'll get no argument from me on that count," Yi responded, "but I do challenge your statement that women are weaker. You should ask Pyotr's guards if that assumption is valid. Several of those men were subdued without the use of any weapons at all or were relieved of their weapons before they were kneed in the balls. I doubt they will ever underestimate the strength or skill of a woman again."

"I'll have to give the security issue some thought and see how Chief feels about it. After all, he trained them. If he is comfortable, I'm willing to give it a try. As for the others, I don't want them to think that they're ready to fight a war on the basis of one victory. Overconfidence can get them killed, and I could never forgive myself for having a role in that."

Yi raised his glass for a refill.

"Enough of this. We should be celebrating. Your ladies saved the day. Pyotr looks like the unconscionable scoundrel he is. Grace will probably be exonerated after she meets with the chairman tomorrow night, especially now. Oh, by the way, there is a rumor that Lilith had an unfortunate tumble down the stairs and broke her neck. She won't be available to meet with the Presider and tell her version of events – how wonderfully convenient for Pyotr. We have much to celebrate."

I could see that Higgins' mind was preoccupied with visions of restoring the ruined salon but managed to join in the toast with a half-hearted, "Slainte."

Chapter 59
Grace

"So, is that it?" I asked hopefully after we returned to our chambers. "I don't have to testify for the Council?"

"It doesn't appear so. When Lilith had her unfortunate 'accident,' and Pyotr left in a hurry it confirmed what we all thought was going on. Pyotr is definitely planning something."

I was relieved. I was not looking forward to an immortal other than my husband having access to my thoughts. I was still concerned that I might reveal something which could cause Gabriel problems, even if he claimed otherwise.

As I thought about it, there were several things which were now resolved, not the least of which was Lilith. I was pleased that my brother would now be free from her influence. As much as I hated to see anyone die, Lilith deserved it. There had been speculation about the number of husbands she had lost. There were far too many for mere coincidence. Lilith's reputation as a "black widow" seemed to be well-earned, but Ethan had ignored all that and married her anyhow. At the time, I was sure he had ruined my life with his foolhardy marriage, but now I had to admit it had given me the best gift of my life – Gabriel. Now maybe I could relax and enjoy him.

Gabriel

It was clear from its disastrous condition the salon would not be open for business in the near future. Yi Sheng pulled me aside.

"You know you and Grace have not had a honeymoon. Perhaps now would be a good time. I can't imagine the Council would deny your request after the farce they just put you through. They owe you both. Besides, it will take Pyotr some time to regroup, so I can't think of a better time for you to disappear for a while."

I sighed.

"You're right. There are things Grace and I need to find out about each other, things that can't be learned here. She needs to see what I am like in a less civilized environment and acknowledge the hard choices I must make to survive. She needs to see me hunt and feed and, yes, kill. These are all things she will face if she decides to join me in this life. I don't want her to make a decision based on some romantic idea as a newlywed."

"I'd go slowly," Yi advised. "You could lose her."

"I don't fear losing her nearly as much as I fear the resentment and possible hate she might feel toward me if she thinks I misled her about the consequences. I would rather have a loving wife for a short time than be in love with a woman who can't stand the sight of me for an eternity. Unfortunately, we don't have time to take things slowly."

"You are both considering this then? Just be gentle with her, Gabriel. I rather like her and, as you know, I don't like many of her gender."

"As usual, you will handle things in my absence. Ah – Speaking of your dislike of females, I have a rather large favor to ask of you. Would you …?"

Yi shook his head in dismay.

"Oh, Gabriel please don't ask me. I would do almost anything for you, but you know how we feel about each other."

"She is perfect, and it can't be just anyone. Unless you can think of a better option it has to be her," Gabriel insisted.

"You know she would do it for you. Why don't you ask her yourself?"

"I don't have time to track her down. You know how flighty she is. I need to spend what little time I have with Grace. I will supply you with a letter making my request and my reasons for it. With luck, she will honor the invitation, even if I can't ask in person. Hopefully she can see past the messenger."

Yi threw his hands up in surrender. "You know I love you like a brother, Gabriel, but right now I don't like you very much."

I gave him a quick embrace. "I owe you, brother."

"I'm going to collect on that someday."

When I found Grace she was in our apartment playing the oboe. I did not want to interrupt her, so I stopped in the doorway to listen. She had not played in several weeks, and I was pleased she had started again. I made a note that we would have to take the instruments with us. I came around behind her and rested my head on her shoulder while she finished the piece. She put the instrument down and turned to face me.

"You know, there's not much for us to do here until the salon is restored," I said. "I think we owe ourselves a honeymoon,"

Grace was thrilled. With the Council meeting so soon after our marriage, we had never even considered getting away by ourselves. She threw her arms around my neck.

"That sounds wonderful. Will they let you go? Where will we go? I've never been anywhere but my home and here."

After disengaging her from my neck, I replied, "I have a hunting lodge in Weston. I was thinking about going there. It's very secluded with plenty of natural resources. We could stay there quite some time and never have to see anyone."

"It would just be the two of us? There would be no one else? What if there was an emergency?"

I laughed.

"You are just full of questions. Does the prospect of being totally alone with me frighten you? After all, I am a blood-sucking creature of the night. Maybe you should be afraid," I said, playfully nipping her exposed neck.

Grace stomped her foot.

"I am not afraid!" Realizing how juvenile she must look she took a deep breath and continued, "We have had so little time alone it is just a little hard to imagine. If I am honest, I suppose I am a little afraid, but not because you are a 'blood-sucking creature of the night' as you so eloquently put it. What if we run out of things to talk about?"

I laughed again and hugged her.

"I'm sure we can think of other things to do."

The West Kingdom

Chapter 60

Grace

The coach arrived at Gabriel's estate well after midnight, but it seemed as if every available light was lit in anticipation of our arrival. Gabriel warned me that he had not visited for some time, and his arrival with a wife would be cause for celebration and more than a little curiosity. Every one of the servants was lined up outside the house to greet us and get a look at his mate.

"I thought you said we were going to be entirely alone," I whispered.

"We will eventually. I thought you would appreciate some help until you become familiar with the place. We can send the servants away when you are ready. The place is rather large, and I don't want to overwhelm you. Besides some of these people are like family. I want to have the opportunity to see them, and I know they would be very disappointed if they did not have the opportunity to meet you. They never thought to see this day."

"I appreciate the thought," I said looking at the surroundings. "The house does look a little intimidating. Some help at first might be welcome. Besides, I have never done the hands-on work of running a household. I don't even know how to cook, although I suspect than won't be a problem for you."

"Don't worry. Once the staff leaves, we will be confining ourselves to just a few of the rooms. It shouldn't be too difficult to manage. We'll be fine, and I promise not to let you starve."

Gabriel introduced me to each member of the staff as he escorted me to the front door. I graciously greeted each one repeating their name.

Finally, I turned to them and said, "Please forgive me in advance. I am tired and embarrassed to admit that I will probably never remember everyone's name. I don't want to insult anyone. I don't have Mr. Ross's gift of memory. Please just remind me who you are and what you do, and I will try to do better the next time I see you."

Gabriel seemed pleased with my response and leaned toward me.

"You're doing fine. They don't expect you to remember them all. I'm just happy that you are trying. You are right though. You are tired. It's time to get you to bed before you fall down. That would make an embarrassing first impression."

When I woke the following day, it was almost noon. Gabriel lay next to me looking like an effigy. I raised myself up on one arm and just looked at him. I never tired of looking at him and had memorized every inch of his body both by sight and feel. Today, I ran my hands over his muscular chest. I traced the faint scars underneath his pale skin and wondered again how many times he had endured near fatal injuries only to heal and do it all again. Did he remember how it felt or did the memory of the pain fade as the wound healed? I was afraid to ask.

I wondered if he knew what I did while he slept. He didn't always sleep. At his age, he didn't need to, but I also knew he welcomed the occasional oblivion of dreamless sleep. It had been some time since he had experienced the pleasure. It appeared this was one of those rare moments. I hoped I was not disturbing him, but I just couldn't stop touching him. I wanted him in a way that was almost primal. I needed him. Yet there he lay, still and unmoving. Was this going to be my life? Finally, I got out of bed and went in search of something to eat.

The vast house was quiet. I tried to remember how I got to our bedroom. I did not recall climbing any stairs, so it must be on the ground floor. I looked for anything that I might remember from last night, but everything looked unfamiliar. I don't suppose I had paid much attention.

I assumed the staff knew I was human, so there must be a kitchen. I decided to follow my nose. The aroma of baking bread finally led me to the kitchen. I was salivating by the time I got there and hoped I wouldn't embarrass myself by devouring the first thing in sight.

The cook looked up. Her manner was reserved, maybe a little frosty.

"I'm sorry, madam. We were not aware that you were awake. Can I get you something?"

"The bread smells delicious. I would love some of that. I don't remember when I last ate."

"Will Milord want something also? I can have someone bring it up to your room. We did not want to disturb you."

"He is not up yet,'" I replied. "This is the first he has really slept in a while. I would not want to wake him. The last few weeks have been difficult for him. I'll just eat here, if you don't mind."

"That will be fine. You can tell me what you would like to eat during your stay here."

"I'm not particular. Your human staff has to eat. Whatever you make for them will be fine."

"I was referring to after the staff leaves. You know Mr. Ross intends to give us all some time off, so that you can be alone. I will need to procure the supplies you need while we are gone."

Again, I detected something in her voice. Did the cook dislike me already? What about the rest of the staff? Did they all resent me for marrying Gabriel? Maybe they didn't think I was good enough for him.

"I'm sure I can make due with whatever you think I need. I'm not much of a cook, but I will figure it out." I rushed on before I lost my nerve. "Perhaps I can spend a little time with you in the mornings while Gabriel rests. That is if you can spare the time. I know it's a lot to ask. You can show me a few things. It occurs to me that I don't even know what he eats, what are his favorite things – besides that, of course. We have a cook at Hightower, and she never shared those details with me. I really want to spoil him while we are here."

"As you wish, madam."

I realized then that the cook's clipped response was that of a trained professional and was not meant to convey any animosity. I could tell that my appeal on behalf of Gabriel hit its mark, however, when the cook continued with a wink, "I would be happy to assist you any way I can. Shall we start now while you eat? Although some aspects of his diet might need to wait until you are finished with your breakfast. There's no point in wasting good bread if you have a weak stomach. Milord would be most unhappy with me if I made you ill."

At Hightower House, I was used to being one of the employees. I continued the position even after our marriage and still considered the other staff friends, so I was not accustomed to the stiff formality of the servants here. Hopefully it was the way they were trained and not that they resented the presence of their master's new wife. Either way, I was determined to modify their behavior.

A maid met me outside the kitchen as I was trying to remember how to get back to the room I shared with Gabriel.

"I was just coming to see if you needed help dressing. I thought you must be up by now."

I thought I detected a reproachful tone but decided to let it pass.

"Thank you. I might need some assistance getting unpacked and dressed. Lead the way."

"You will find that the chambermaids have already unpacked your trunk. Everything is in your dressing room. You must let us know if there is anything else you need. Your personal maids are waiting to assist you, so I will leave you in their capable hands," the woman replied.

I was nearly dressed when Gabriel walked into the dressing room looking for me. He was naked and clearly not expecting anyone else to be in the room. The maids looked away but not before they got an eyeful. They were blushing furiously and giggling behind their hands. I quickly moved to stand in front of him and block any peeking by the curious young women. I was sure this would be the topic of much conversation in the servants' quarters for the rest of the day. I also suspected this was not the first time. Gabriel had a casual attitude about nudity in his own home and was oblivious of the appreciative stares of the females in his household. Some, like the young maids, thought it was funny. To the older, more experienced women it was plain seductive. Perhaps there was just a touch of envy in their stiff attitude toward me after all. Gabriel shook his head over the giggling, looked over my shoulder and addressed the maids.

"You ladies can leave now. I will help my wife with the rest."

Before the room was cleared of the first group of gaping females, there was a light rap on the door. I opened it a crack to see one of the kitchen maids with a large tray full of food.

"You can leave it there. I will get it in a moment. Mr. Ross is – uh – indisposed at the moment." I didn't need another female in the house discussing my husband's impressive attributes.

I turned from the door and placed the tray full of food on the table in the bedroom. I looked at Gabriel. He had not made any attempt to get dressed yet.

"Please get dressed and show me how to find my way around this place, so you can send the staff away. I'm not sure I can take many mornings like this. Being waited on can be inconvenient."

"With pleasure," Gabriel replied as he quickly donned his clothes.

After a week of trying to avoid hovering servants in order to have some privacy, I was ready to send them away. He and I had chosen a small section of the house close to the kitchen which would be our home while we were there. The rest of the house was closed off. The staff rebelled against Gabriel abandoning the large master suite in favor of a smaller more intimate bedroom, but he pulled rank on them. I preferred the smaller room since it was much easier to heat. I would never get used to things on the massive scale which seemed to be normal for Gabriel. I grew up thinking Oakridge was large, but I had no idea people actually lived like this.

Finally, we were alone – completely alone. The house was silent. There was no one lurking in the shadows waiting to bring breakfast at some inopportune time or waiting to dress me. I would never get used to that.

Chapter 61
Gabriel

Now that the house was cleared of extraneous people, I was anxious to get on with Grace's education. We would not have all the time I thought was necessary, but I would make good use of what we had. How to begin was the question. Should I continue with what Grace referred to as "my lectures," or would a demonstration be in order? I finally settled on a demonstration hoping that it would help illustrate the "lectures."

It was early evening and Grace was sitting comfortably by the fire when I entered the room and announced, "We need to go out."

"But it's dark outside," Grace responded.

"You forget that is the only option for me. Besides, the hunting is better at night. After all, I am a nocturnal predator. You asked the cook about my dietary preferences. This is one of them. I need to feed, and you need to witness it."

"Oh," Grace replied. She knew this lesson was inevitable. We had discussed it, but I still wished we had more time together before she had to confront the unpleasant realities of my existence. I had already pointed out we didn't have much time to complete her education, so I hoped this excursion would not be too much too soon. "I will grab a cloak and we can go."

I was relieved that she accepted the announcement so easily. I was afraid there would be an argument over its necessity, but once more she surprised me, and I wondered for what seemed like the hundredth time what I had done to deserve her. An insecure part of me still believed that she would eventually decide she could not accept this life and reject me. Love might not be enough.

Fortunately for Grace, it was a moonlit night, so walking into the woods was not impossible for her limited night vision. I explained I always hunted on foot. The smell of the horses, no matter how familiar would be a distraction and cover the scent of potential prey. Horses were also noisy and got spooked easily when they sensed the metamorphosis to predator. Stalking required focus and stealth, and horses inhibited both.

As we ventured into the forest, I stopped periodically to sniff the air, but so far, I scented nothing that would be worth the chase. I hadn't been to this estate in some time, so I knew that the game was not over-hunted. It was curious that there seemed to be so little to hunt. Because of Grace's slow pace in the dark, we were still fairly close to the house, and she was not exactly a quiet stalker, so that might account for the lack of wildlife. I might need to rethink this expedition, or it was going to be a long night.

Grace

I was having reservations about this excursion. I was tired and clumsy, so I was probably scaring off any potential game. I was wondering how I could salvage the situation when I heard a crashing in the undergrowth. Whatever it was seemed to be large and heading my direction. Gabriel was a little farther ahead of me when he heard the noise. Apparently, we were not the only ones out hunting tonight. He turned in time to see a large cougar heading toward me. He bared his fangs and dropped to a crouch. A vampire driven by hunger and the need to protect his mate was a terrifying thing to see. I was not certain which alarmed me the most, Gabriel or the cat. Either way, I felt like a potential meal.

With a speed which astounded me, I saw Gabriel intercept the cat before it could reach me. The two were rolling on the ground, each trying to gain the advantage and the kill. The cat tired long before the vampire, and soon Gabriel had his fangs buried in the cougar's throat. Under normal circumstances, Gabriel would only drink enough to subdue his prey, but the instinct to remove the threat to his mate was stronger than his ethical considerations. Soon the cat lay dead at his feet. I could see that he was fighting to subdue his feral instincts before he came to face me. He could be as much of a threat to me as the cougar if he did not get himself under control. He was still hungry.

Several minutes later, he rose and walked slowly toward me. He made no attempt to clean the blood from his face and hands. It was obvious that hunting was not a clean business. I suppose I needed to face that reality. I stood still as Gabriel approached, not sure what to expect since he was still battling for control. I didn't think he would hurt me, but he had warned me that instinct often overruled any other considerations where blood was concerned. If I tried to run away from him as a predator, he would be compelled to pursue, and it could end badly. So, despite the impulse to flee, I stood my ground and forced him to face me as he approached.

He appeared to be under control by the time he reached me. However, it seemed he felt the need to reinforce his point. Holding my face in his bloody hands he kissed me savagely. I could taste the metallic tang of the cat's blood on his lips, but I was determined not to cringe or back away from him and returned his kiss with trepidation.

Gabriel looked into my eyes.

"This is what it is like, Grace. This is what I am. Can you accept that?"

"I accepted it a long time ago in the salon. I will admit, the less-refined manner of feeding is a little bit disturbing, but I think I can handle it."

"This is how it usually is. The salon is a unique place. Very few immortals have the luxury to feed like that. But we still need to hunt. We revel in the exhilaration of the chase. Can you truly accept that?"

"I don't understand why you continue to seek reassurance. How many times do I have to tell you?" I said in exasperation. "YES! I accept what you are and what you must do. This little demonstration is not enough to scare me away, if that was your intent."

Gabriel sighed.

"This demonstration, as you call it, was not about me, Grace. Can you accept that this is what you will become and what you must do if you decide to join me in this life? That is the bigger question you must answer."

OH MY. I thought. *That is definitely something to consider.*

The following night Gabriel prepared to go out again. I hurried to get my cloak and follow.

He raised a hand to stop me.

"I have to go out alone this time. I should have sensed the danger to you last night. I realize my restricted diet has dulled my abilities."

"You need to feed on human blood then," I stated. I was afraid this day would come, but I avoided thinking about that aspect of his needs. He hadn't explained that the lack of human blood might hinder his abilities. Still, it bothered me that he might be feeding on innocent people. It bothered me even more than I wanted to admit that they might be female. Gabriel was not the only possessive one.

Gabriel hung his head refusing to meet my eyes and replied softly, "Yes."

"How? I haven't seen a soul since the staff left."

"There are villages within a reasonable distance. I can usually find some poor soul who is on death's door and will beg for a quick end to their suffering. It's not the best quality blood but it will do. If I'm lucky, I will find someone who has been terrorizing the villagers. Although it is not my preference to kill my prey, I don't mind ridding the world of those. I do not feed from innocents. You need not worry about that, and I definitely don't seduce and feed from women."

"No attractive courtesans then?" I asked only half joking. I had observed the erotic reaction of the courtesans when their patrons fed from them. I also remembered how it affected me.

"You have never seen me feed from another woman, and you never will." Gabriel responded adamantly. "But there are different kinds of feeding. It is not always about pleasure."

"Why not me then," I asked tentatively? "I am your mate. If you can take my blood without killing me, why not do so?"

"I can't take enough of your blood to make up for my abstinence. There is also the issue of my possessiveness. If I were to start feeding from you regularly, it would be impossible for me to let you go. You must be absolutely certain about us before I will risk taking your blood again. You have no idea how hard it is to refuse you. I have craved your blood from the beginning, and the desire has only gotten stronger now that we are mated, but I cannot risk it yet. We are not ready. I am not ready."

"You still doubt me," I stated shaking my head sadly. "Even though I have committed myself to you, you still fear I will reject you."

"Please don't tempt me like that again, Grace. I am haunted by the possibility that I won't be able to stop. Even so, your offer just then nearly destroyed what little resolve remains."

Then Gabriel turned abruptly and raced from the house.

Several days later I was enjoying some quiet time in the estate gardens when a messenger arrived with a letter for Gabriel. Just the night before, we had discussed the possibility that he would be called back to Hightower. I didn't think he would mind, so I broke the seal and unfolded the single sheet of stiff paper. I was surprised to find that the letter was written in code; however, I could read the signature. It was from Yi.

It was late afternoon when Gabriel finally began to wake. He was sleeping longer here since he had no real problems to deal with. Fixing broken fences and leaking roofs was nothing compared to the delicate negotiations that required his attention when he was in residence at Hightower House. It was such a relief to be able to get away if only for a little while. It was clear to me that he needed it. I worried that the letter I was about to give him would change all that. It turned out, I had reason for concern.

Gabriel read the letter several times before he threw it in the fire. It was definitely not good news.

"We need to go back," he stated. "The concerns about Pyotr are growing. We need to be prepared if he decides to go through with this insane attempt to rule the Known World. Can you be prepared to leave in a week?"

He did not mention the one part of the letter I was able to decipher. *I found her.*

Chapter 62
Gabriel

Before we left for Hightower House, there was one more revelation I needed to make. Grace had to understand the importance of the Middle Kingdom and my place in it. As we enjoyed a quiet evening before leaving the following night, I took Grace's hand and said, "There is still something we should discuss before we go back."

She sighed.

"Let's get on with it then."

"Since you are well read, you must know the history of the five kingdoms in the Known World."

"I know as much as the vampires allowed us to know. We never understood why the divisions were called kingdoms. We never knew that they, rather we, were ruled by immortal kings."

"At least I won't need to explain that to you. But you need to understand how lawless and wild the world was. Young immortal warlords with small bands of raiders devastated the countryside without a thought to the ultimate consequences of their actions. They behaved like an unruly pack of wolves and left carnage in their wake. They were also rather indiscriminate in siring children without taking responsibility for training them. Finally, a group of older and wiser immortals joined ranks and helped each other gain dominance in their own area of the continent. The four most powerful carved up the land like a pie and each took a piece."

"There was one piece of land that the new kings did not touch. It was the area which became the Middle Kingdom. Since that area provided the easiest access from one kingdom to the other the four kings were determined that it would belong to no one. It would remain neutral territory, and there would be no fifth king. This neutral territory would be governed by a council of representatives from each kingdom. This council would provide stability for the Middle Kingdom and would also negotiate disputes among kingdoms. That solved the problem for a little while until rogue vampires realized that by taking the Middle Kingdom, they could hold the others hostage."

"For several centuries, the Middle Kingdom endured numerous attacks by power hungry immortals who wanted to carve out their own piece of the pie. Since there was no one to rule the Middle Kingdom, it seemed like an easy target. The four kings anticipated that possibility and appointed a Warden to oversee the welfare of the Middle Kingdom. The existence and identity of the Warden was a carefully guarded secret. The Warden was given the task of building up the area's defenses so that it would remain a neutral territory."

"The result of the first Warden's labors was the Hightower complex. The tower itself provided a lookout post which precluded any sneak attacks, and there were numerous tunnels that provided shelter for the immortals who protected those who lived and worked there until a more permanent solution was built. Some of those same tunnels are now the chambers for the Council members. Over time, the city of Hightower grew up around the complex the Warden built."

"Does that mean the Warden rules the Middle Kingdom?" Grace interrupted.

"No never!" I exclaimed. "It would mean death to anyone who tried. The Warden protects, not rules. The Council maintains control over the area, so no one person can pose a threat to the balance of power."

Grace backed away from my overly vehement response.

"I didn't know it was such a touchy subject. Sorry! There's more to it though isn't there? It seems to hit a little too close to home."

"Hightower House is an important part of the Council's management of the Middle Kingdom. It is the place where most of the important decisions are made, not in the Council Chamber. As proprietor, it is my responsibility to provide a safe environment for those negotiations. I have to admit, I am rather invested in keeping the Middle Kingdom neutral."

Suddenly, Grace understood.

"You're the Warden."

I had hoped that she wouldn't put the pieces together, but I suspected she would.

"I can neither confirm nor deny your conclusion. If I deny it, I narrow the possible field of candidates. If I confirm it, we're both dead. You must never express your knowledge of a Warden to anyone. As it is, you pose enough of a threat just by thinking it. You are human and your mind is an open book to any immortal who is unscrupulous enough to accesses it. We are on very treacherous ground here."

"But you're the Council's negotiator and assassin and…"

"By wearing many hats, no one can pin me down to the important one. It's safer that way. Please, Grace, you must put this as far out of your mind as you can. It might be safer if I removed this from your memory. I know I said I wouldn't tamper but…."

"You know I would never do anything to endanger you, Gabriel, and everything possible to protect you. Humans can be just as protective as vampires. I would die first."

Chapter 63

The committee summoned Yi. He was sure he knew the reason for the meeting, and he was not exactly looking forward to it. This was none of his business, and he resented that they were trying to use his close friendship with Gabriel to their advantage. But he went – under protest. What else could he do?

"We need your help Dr. Sheng. You are probably the only one here who has enough influence with Gabriel to make him see reason."

"I know what you are going to ask me, and the answer is no. I cannot be a part of this, even if I do agree with you," Yi stated.

"How do you know what we want, doctor?" the Presider inquired.

"You want me to convince Gabriel to persuade Grace to become one of us. He would like nothing more. It is Grace you need to convince, and he refuses to influence her in any way. He believes it has to be her decision alone."

The Presider did not try to conceal his frustration.

"Doesn't she understand how vulnerable she is? What a liability she is to Gabriel? What a liability she is to us all? There is unrest in the north. We cannot be worried about what she might reveal to Pyotr's people if they get hold of her."

"Look," said Yi. "It isn't as if Gabriel and Grace haven't thought about it. Gabriel has even contacted a potential sire if Grace decides to become one of us. But he is adamant that she not be coerced into this. If the Council tries to force the issue, I'm afraid you will be in for a battle."

"You could help us avoid that."

Yi shook his head.

"Gabriel is one of my only real friends. I know how most of you feel about my preferences. I am tolerated because of Gabriel's friendship but without him, I would be a pariah. I will not jeopardize our relationship by participating in some plot to manipulate the situation to the Council's advantage. You will have to think of something or someone else."

"Suppose we contrived an abduction just to prove how she could be used against him. What do you think Gabriel would do?"

Yi snickered.

"You know very well what he would do. Scorched earth would be an understatement."

"Then what would you suggest. Is there anything we can do to move this along?"

"Let things run their course. Grace is a smart woman. She just needs to examine all her options. She loves Gabriel, and I'm sure she will choose to spend eternity with him — eventually."

"You say Gabriel has chosen a sire for her. Who is it, and have they accepted?"

Yi responded with a twinkle in his eye, "Gabriel is determined that Grace should be his equal. That means her sire will have to be someone with considerable power. Are you sure you want to know?"

"Stop playing games, Yi. Who is it?"

"Gabriel has contacted Sophia. He is still waiting to hear from her."

The presider' eyes opened wide.

"He doesn't fool around does he? Grace will be a formidable vampire with Sophia as her sire. She might even exceed Gabriel."

"That's true in some respects, although Gabriel will always have the edge as long as he controls fire, and it is doubtful she would have that affinity. Together they will be a force to be reckoned with. Are you still sure you want to encourage Grace to turn?"

"A mated immortal couple with that kind of power would be a tremendous asset to the Council," the Presider mused, then looked over the Council members for some sign of their frame of mind. Seeing only acceptance mixed with a little dismay, he responded, "I guess we are agreed that we will not interfere in Grace's decision. It would appear we need to keep them both on our side."

Yi sighed in relief.

"I believe that is wise. Are we done here?"

The Presider waved toward the door and excused him.

The chamber erupted as soon as the door was closed. Everyone seemed to have an opinion about the interview with Yi. Finally, the Presider held up his hand for silence, and they continued with the Council meeting.

A delegate from the North signaled his desire to speak and rose from his chair.

"Despite Dr. Sheng's cautions, I don't think we can leave a decision as important as this to chance. There has to be a way to force the issue that cannot be traced back to this body. I have had some dealings with Grace. She is not unreasonable for a mortal. I don't think it would be difficult to push – no nudge – her in the proper direction."

"I agree," said a voice from the Eastern delegation. "But even if she makes the right choice, do we think we can wait for the appearance of an immortal no one has seen for ages? We don't know if Sophia will even acknowledge Gabriel's request or how she will respond."

The room erupted again in a cacophony of questions.

"How long can we wait?"

"Just make her."

"Gabriel will thank us!"

"Are we going to let some mortal woman hold us hostage?"

The Presider waited until the grumbling subsided and spoke:

"It seems as if we agree that something must be done. It would be best if that 'something' involved as few of us as possible so that you have deniability. Do you trust me to see to it?"

The members nodded their assent much relieved that they would not have to face Gabriel's wrath if he discovered the Presider's involvement.

Chapter 64

Grace

After our marriage, I began to leave Hightower House to do some shopping at the market in town. My first visit brought back some rather unpleasant memories, and I almost left in tears. The next time was easier and then the next until the outings became more pleasurable than threatening.

Gabriel insisted I have an escort, but they rarely got in my way. Rather than guards, I usually took one or two of the other women with me. They were not at all interested in buying supplies for the house and more often than not deserted me for the stalls which sold fabrics and jewelry and more luxury items. Finally, they drew me in, and I discovered the pleasure of shopping for things other than necessities. Soon, my companions were enticing me to buy fabrics which complimented my coloring. I pointed out that I would never have an opportunity to wear anything other than my gray dress, but they were insistent. I confess I wasn't that difficult to persuade. After all, I could wear other things when I was not working. Aubry had even made me some very alluring silky nightwear. Gabriel preferred me in nothing at all, so he devised some pleasurable methods for their removal.

It was two weeks before the winter festival, and I was visiting the market with a small group of friends. My quest today was to find a gift for Gabriel. Since he could buy anything he wanted, it was no easy task. The other women were oohing and aahing over the latest shipment of silks, so I left them to investigate a booth containing items with more masculine appeal.

As I approached the tent, a familiar scent with unpleasant memories greeted me and that is all I remember until I found myself tied to a chair with a sack over my head and a splitting headache. *Here we go again!* I thought glumly. I was not particularly afraid. It was doubtful anyone would dare risk Gabriel's retribution by harming me. I did wonder what they wanted though. Gabriel's concerns about my being used as a hostage in order to control him rang in my head. The subject had come up in one of our many discussions about my becoming a vampire. Apparently, this was exactly what he feared. Well, there was nothing I could do now but play it out.

The sack over my head was loosely woven, so I was not completely blind. Although no one spoke to me, I made out the shapes of three men. They seemed to be waiting for something or probably someone. Gabriel perhaps? It was a little after sundown when a fourth figure finally arrived. He entered the room and pulled up a chair opposite me. I could not make out any features and when he spoke, I did not recognize the voice.

"Hello, Grace. I hope you are being treated well. It seems we have a little problem that I believe you can help us with. I need some information, and you are going to tell me everything I want to know."

I spoke up with a bravado I didn't actually feel.

"I don't have any information which could be of interest to you. Gabriel doesn't confide in me. But even if he did, I would not tell you anything."

"Oh, my dear," he said covering my hand. "How very wrong you are."

Several hours later the door burst open, and Gabriel stormed in. I was alone still bound to the chair in the middle of the room. He removed the sack from my head.

"Are you harmed?" He asked looking me over carefully.

I looked at him with tears in my eyes and replied simply, "We need to talk."

We returned to Hightower House far too soon. I needed time to compose myself. I would not leave anything out of my story, but I wanted to think carefully about how I would express it. As it turned out, no amount of time would have helped. I began sobbing as soon as we arrived and blurted everything out in the bluntest terms possible.

Gabriel's concern was visible.

"What did they do to you?" He demanded.

"They, or he, questioned me." I responded.

Gabriel looked relieved.

"That can't have been too bad. You don't know anything and it doesn't look like they tortured you."

"You don't understand!" I cried. "He questioned me and I had to answer him. I couldn't help myself. When it was obvious I didn't have anything to tell – at least nothing he asked about – he asked me about other things – embarrassing and very personal things, and I had to answer. He asked about us — about what gives us pleasure in bed. I'm so ashamed. He knows things nobody but us should know!"

Gabriel looked stricken. He took me in his arms and held me tight against his chest.

"I'm so sorry that you had to go through that. I could kill the bastard! He didn't really want to know any of that; he just wanted to choose the one subject that you wanted to keep private and prove he could make you reveal all the details. He was sending us both a message. You are an open book to any immortal who wants to exploit you."

"I can't do this anymore, Gabriel. It's time," I sobbed against his chest.

"Take a day to think things through, Grace, and then we will discuss it."

I knew Gabriel well enough by now to know that only the most rational argument would convince him. I had already made up my mind, and no one would ever again take control of my life or the decisions I made about it. Not even him. So, I began to list the reasons, which would support my decision. I knew very well that "because my heart tells me this is the right thing to do" would not work, even if it was exactly what I wanted to say. I hoped my preparation would allow me to take charge of the confrontation. Ultimately, the decision came down to this. Could I spend several lifetimes with a man I was still getting to know? There was so much to learn about him and his culture. I suspected there were still secrets waiting to be revealed at the worst possible moment. I know I had mine.

Gabriel said he did not want me pressured into joining his immortal world in order to protect him — as if he needed protecting! His responsibilities to the Vampire Council along with his years as a mortal soldier and a natural affinity for controlling fire had turned him into a ruthless killing tool. He was feared by most of the vampire world for good reason. Fortunately, I was acquainted with this aspect of him only through comments by others and his own very non-specific admission. He had tried to use his reputation as a way to distance himself from me when we first realized our attraction to one another. He almost succeeded.

But there was another side of him. The side he had forged for himself. He was well-educated and well-read. He concealed his fiery nature behind a façade of stuffy dignity and refinement. He could be gentle (something his detractors would never believe) and compassionate. Many saw his creation of the salon at Hightower House as a way to exploit unfortunate women, but I knew his real motive and it moved me. He loved music and art. He loved debating religion, mythology, and philosophy, but hated to lose the debate. Like any vampire, he was protective and possessive to a fault and could smother anyone who mattered to him.

I could list the pros and cons until I was exhausted, and one thing would not change. I loved him. We loved one another. I truly believed that would win out. After all, I was not without my faults. Why would he want to share eternity with me? I could be opinionated and stubborn. I was not nearly as accomplished as Gabriel in any of our mutual interests. Would he become bored with me over time? He seemed to enjoy mentoring me, and I don't think we would ever run out of things I didn't know. Maybe we would become intellectual equals, eventually. After all, we would have all the time in the world.

Still, I knew my answer before I began this fruitless process of evaluation. I loved him, and yes, I would accept eternity with him.

As we faced one another, I inquired as calmly as I could, "Don't you want to spend the rest of your life with me?"

Gabriel looked very surprised at my question.

"More than you can imagine!" he exclaimed. "It has been so difficult to keep my feelings on this to myself, but I was and still am convinced that the decision must be yours. And it must be made for the right reasons."

"And I suppose you are the judge of the 'right reasons'?" I countered.

He was struggling to maintain control but his frustration was evident. "Have you considered everything you will be giving up – children, family?"

"Why do men always assume that women want to be mothers or that we want to be the matriarch of a large family? Let's look at this from my perspective. You think keeping me mortal is protecting me? Do you know how many women die in childbirth? We risk our lives every time we get pregnant. And then there is the pain of miscarriages and children who die in infancy. Do you really think that is what every women wants? I don't honestly think I would be missing much. Let's see what else am I giving up – illness, aging. Yes, there would be some regrets either way, but life is full of them whether you are mortal or vampire. Would I miss the sun? Yes, but I have the moon which is a gentle reflection of a sun which can be brutal and relentless. And so what if our family is made up of the people we choose instead of those we breed?"

"I have thought this out thoroughly, and there are numerous rational arguments supporting my decision, but the bottom line is this: I love you. I want to protect you as you protect me, and I want to spend more than just one lifetime with you. Do I have to make some sacrifices? Of course, and I accept them gladly. I chose you when we mated. I should only have to do that once. You seem to need the reassurance of my doing it over and over again. Well, for the final time, I choose you Gabriel Ross, and I intend to become immortal, any objections?"

Gabriel sighed and pulled me into his arms.

"Screw rational, you made the only argument that really matters to me."

Chapter 65

Sophia was ancient. She was taken from a temple devoted to the pursuit of wisdom and the goddess who ruled it. She was the high priestess of the temple, and she was consulted on everything from when to plant crops to when to initiate a war. She had another gift. She had glimpses of the future, a gift she guarded ferociously. To admit to it would be disastrous for her. Her foresight was never precise and left much room for the subject to interpret the vision any way they wished and blame her when things were not as they hoped. For example, she had glimpses of Gabriel and Grace together, but no indication of the nature of their relationship. To share such information with its vague innuendos made little sense. She would know when the time was right. She was not surprised then when Yi intercepted her travels with the letter from Gabriel asking her to come to Hightower. She was already on her way.

Sophia arrived at Hightower House amid much speculation. The wind vampire was a mystery to almost everyone. Some doubted she even existed. Although she originated from the small islands in the south, she did not appear to call any place home and could show up just about anywhere at any time for no apparent reason. Of course, she knew why.

Yi was first to greet her when she arrived. The two embraced stiffly. Yi was not one of Sophia's favorite immortals. She didn't understand his preference for other men even though many males in her part of the world chose that path. However, she understood his love for Gabriel Ross and distrusted it. She feared Yi might do something rash because of his unrequited feelings. Sophia shared his feelings for Gabriel, but she had seen from the beginning that he was not meant for her. In fact, she would never mate. Sophia was probably the only one who saw the pain in Yi's eyes when he spoke of Gabriel and Grace. On some level, she shared it. Despite their feelings, on one thing they could agree: they were glad that Gabriel was finally happy.

Yi led Sophia off to find a quiet place to talk. It was difficult to speak openly around immortals with their acute hearing and anyone who noticed the strange woman with Yi was curious. Since they had not yet entered Hightower House, Sophia and Yi were free converse.

"I think I know why I am here," Sophia said. "But I want to hear it from you. Gabriel was short on details."

"You know from the letter, Sophia, that Gabriel and Grace are married. She is a mortal, and I don't know how long the Council will allow that to continue. The two of them have been away on a honeymoon of sorts, so they are not aware of how precarious is their position. There will be a lot of pressure for Gabriel to set her aside if she wishes to retain her humanity. I think that would destroy him."

"Does Grace know how badly Gabriel wants her to join him? I assume that is why I am here. He wants me to sire her, and I would be honored to do so, but only if she is absolutely sure – and worthy of him."

"It's not just that. I think he is afraid for her safety. If the worst should happen and her life is in danger he wants…"

Sophia put her finger to Yi's lips to silence him.

"I know what he wants, but I will need to speak to Grace before I agree to anything."

"You need to know there was an incident after Grace and Gabriel returned. I am almost certain Grace has made her decision. Now it is up to you."

Grace

Gabriel led me up to the woman standing with Yi.

"Grace, I would like for you to meet Sophia – Sophia, my wife Grace. Sophia has agreed to be your sire."

The meeting with my sire-to-be was awkward. Sophia was not at all what I expected, and I'm afraid my initial reaction insulted her. For one thing, the entirety of her tall frame was covered in a dark purple robe and head-covering which concealed everything but her eyes and hands. I was acutely aware of how we judge each other by what we see – facial expressions and attire – and none of that was available to me. Sophia had the advantage while I was completely exposed. I could however see her eyes and realized they conveyed much more than the more superficial things we use to define ourselves.

I could tell from her wrinkled hands that she was in her later years when she became a vampire. The rebirth could eliminate some of the effects of age, but not all, and her hands looked old. But it was her eyes that held my attention. It was impossible to miss the wisdom and compassion those warm brown eyes conveyed. She seemed to look into one's soul and empathize with what she found there. At the moment, I was the focus of her gaze, and I wondered what she saw in my eyes. Fear and apprehension perhaps?

Sophia took my hands and greeted me warmly.

"I can't tell you how surprised and pleased I am that Gabriel has finally found you. I have had glimpses of you for many years. I didn't have any idea what it meant; Gabriel, you know my visions are imprecise," she added as she saw the look of betrayal on his face. "There was no point in raising expectations. Would you be happier now if you had waited centuries in anticipation? Now, leave us. I think you have to catch up on events here, and I need to get to know your mate."

Gabriel watched as we walked arm in arm into the garden and then left.

Sophia chose a spot with two benches which faced one another. She sat and motioned me to the other. We were barely seated when I blurted out, "Gabriel has asked you to sire me, hasn't he? What other reason would there be for having you come?"

"I was on my way here before his letter reached me," Sophia replied.

"Was that due to another of the visions you spoke about earlier?" I was curious about how much she had actually seen, even though I was certain she would not tell me.

Sophia smiled. At least from the way her eyes crinkled, I guessed she was smiling. It was a little disconcerting wondering what was going on under all that fabric. Sophia sensed my discomfort and removed her head covering.

"We do not show our faces to men but since you and I are alone, I will not violate any vows by showing my face to you. After all, I am reading your expressions. It is only fair that you have the opportunity to observe mine."

As I had already guessed from the appearance of her hands, Sophia was not young. As she removed her hood, she released a mass of dark wavy hair which was streaked with gray and fell beyond her waist. She sighed with pleasure as she ran her fingers through the mass of hair and fanned it out over her shoulders. She saw my look of surprise.

"Yes, even old women can be vain about their hair. Having to keep it covered is supposed to be a sign of our humility and sets a priestess aside from the other women of our culture. I won't bore you with my feelings about the practice, but I have been doing it for so long that it is second nature. It's just something I do even though I no longer have to." Then she smiled. "But letting one's hair down on occasion is a good thing don't you agree?"

I nodded in agreement, but I was still trying to reconcile my mistaken beliefs about vampires with the reality. Somehow, I had the idea that all vampires were young and beautiful. Sophia was still beautiful. She just wasn't young. Her advanced age was both surprising and reassuring. After all wisdom came with age, didn't it?

"You seem uncomfortable, and maybe disappointed," Sophia observed.

"I apologize. It's just another misconception destroyed. I'm not disappointed at all. I find your age comforting. My mother died when I was young, so I never really got to know her as an adult. Maybe that's why Gabriel chose you as my sire."

It was then that the conversation turned uncomfortable.

"If you're looking for a mother figure, then listen to me. It is time for you to grow up and realize the risk to Gabriel if you remain as you are. I don't know you yet. I'm sure your motives are sincere, but I am here to protect him, and if you become a danger to him I will not hesitate to act regardless of your ambivalence."

I was taken aback by Sophia's vehemence.

"Well, that was blunt. I didn't realize you were in love with him too. Am I in your way?" I was becoming angry at her implication that I was not thinking about Gabriel's safety.

"Calm down, child. I am afraid I gave you the wrong impression. I love Gabriel. I am not in love with him. However, I am afraid for him. I know your honeymoon was more of a lesson in what it means to be a vampire, but I still wonder if you truly understand. Much has happened while you were gone. Pyotr is moving more quickly than anticipated. I don't want to see Gabriel distracted and brought down by a clueless human girl."

"I'll tell you what I keep telling him. I would never do anything to hurt him. If that means I need to give up my mortal life, I will do so gladly. I think I have finally convinced him it is what I truly want, but he has been alone too long. He has endured centuries of being despised by humans for what he is and by his own kind for what he can do. The Council doesn't realize what his responsibilities are doing to his soul. He doesn't believe he is worthy of my love or anyone else's for that matter."

"I can see why Yi likes you. That says a lot since he is the one who is in love with your husband. You know, they were lovers when they first met. They were both lonely and provided consolation to each other. Yi was devastated when Gabriel decided he could not embrace that kind of relationship. Yi finally decided the only way to keep Gabriel's friendship was to give up all hope of anything more. I think he gained more as a friend than he would have as a lover."

"I came here expecting to find you unworthy of my friend. My visions of you were not clear or linear. I'm not even sure that they represent your future anymore.

I see that you complement Gabriel well. You possess the feminine wisdom, which men often lack. You give him hope and provide balance. You have my blessing, and I would be honored to call you daughter when the time comes. But you must make your choice soon. You also need to know that if there is any danger to your life Gabriel intends to keep you regardless of your wishes."

Grace sighed, "I suspected as much. But as I have already said, I have made my decision and I am ready to get on with it."

Gabriel intercepted me as soon as Sophia and I parted company.

"How was your talk with Sophia? You two looked very comfortable with one another."

The look I gave him could have peeled paint off the wall.

"Appearances can be deceiving. Why didn't you tell me about her and the real reason you asked her to come – your back-up plan?"

Gabriel looked sheepish.

"She told you then. I thought this was just a visit to get to know you."

"She wasn't here to get to know me. She came to warn me. She was quite blunt and perfectly honest – unlike someone who shall remain nameless. I know you didn't want to alarm me or make me come to a decision before I was ready, but minimizing the danger was not helpful. I am well aware that I am a liability, but that is not the only reason for my decision. As I told her, I want you to believe I'm turning because I want to share your life completely not just the parts which happen after dark. But more importantly, I want you to believe that you deserve to be happy with me. I don't want to have to keep fighting the same battle for eternity. I don't think I can bear it. I may have been alive before we met, but I wasn't really living. For good or ill, you are my life now. I choose you and everything you are. Sophia was satisfied with that. Are you?"

For the first time in months, I saw Gabriel relax. Even our marriage did not fill him with the joy that my declaration and Sophia's acceptance had.

"That's it then? Have you two decided when?"

Gabriel

Sophia, Yi and I met in the nearly renovated salon. It was time to get down to specifics before I spoke with Grace again.

"How long do you think we have, Yi? You probably know more than I do at this point. When do we expect Pyotr to mobilize his army?"

Yi replied, "He lost some of his mortal allies when Lilith died and they were no longer under her spell. That set him back a little, but he is still strong, and everyone who ventures an opinion thinks it will be in the summer."

"It's early winter now so that gives us less than six months."

Sophia looked dubious. "You know Grace better than I, but will she be able to conquer her new instincts in so little time? You know she expects to fight with you Gabriel."

I was taken aback at Sophia's revelation. Although Grace trained with the courtesans at Hightower House, she was not involved in the melee with Pyotr's men. She had never mentioned fighting. Yi responded before I had a chance.

"Grace is a strong woman. She has been through a great deal. I believe she could be ready with the proper training. But does she know that you will spend most of that time apart? The Council will want you here. They are not likely to let you leave to babysit your new vampire wife. Sophia and I will have to oversee her transition. Of course, you will be able to visit her but only for short periods at a time."

"There is the other issue," Sophia continued. "Her physical training will need to be intense if she expects to fight. That means that Yi and I cannot go easy on her. If you are around, your protective instincts will just get in the way of her training. Fortunately, as an immortal, her bruises won't show and broken bones heal quickly."

I tried unsuccessfully to contain a growl.

Sophia and Yi both smiled.

"You see what we mean?"

Chapter 66

With the looming threat of war, the Council members had not returned to their homes after the meeting but remained to strategize and speculate as to where Pyotr was most likely to strike. The obvious target would be Hightower. If he could control the passes, he could cripple any attempt to thwart him. Of course, he was smart enough to know that the Council would guess this target. Surely he would not be so obvious. There had to be some other place which was as valuable. Donaldson, the King of the West, was not a strong leader. He was more likely to plan a party than mobilize an army. He would be the most vulnerable, but the West Kingdom was a long way around and would necessitate going over the mountains. None of this made sense unless Pyotr hoped to gain control of another kingdom and then attack Hightower from two different directions with a much larger army. That strategy would require a longer time frame to accomplish and presumed Pyotr was not out for an immediate victory. That was doubtful since Pyotr was impulsive and not a master of the long game.

Gabriel entered the closed session in the middle of the discussion. He sat in the chair reserved for the Warden and waited for the Presider to address him.

"I trust your sojourn in the West was profitable. Did you find out anything worth sharing?"

"My contacts were not hopeful that Donaldson would be able to hold off any attack by Pyotr. It seems that a change in leadership will be necessary if we want to depend on the West."

"That's not good news, but it was not unexpected. Is there anyone they would support to replace Donaldson?" The Presider inquired.

"There are several. The problem is choosing one of them and putting a strong leader in place before Pyotr can get there and fill the power vacuum. Things are so chaotic that I believe the people will support anyone who promises to restore the status quo, even an outsider like Pyotr."

"So you think the West Kingdom is the real target?"

"I'm not sure." Gabriel shook his head. "The possibility has merit. Pyotr has been working to destabilize the area for years, but I think Hightower is the ultimate destination. The question is which one is a diversion and which the real target, and there is no reliable intelligence to support either option. If his campaign doesn't start until summer, he will have to move quickly to finish before the snow starts. I doubt even his army will fight in the winter. If he waits and forces us to cover two fronts, he might be able to pull it off. Even with the additional time to prepare, I don't think we can muster enough troops to prevail. We barely have the resources to defend one front."

Gabriel looked around the room.

"I would like to suggest something which might shock you. You heard about the ruckus at Hightower House during the Council session."

"I assume you are referring to the battle of the courtesans," Lord Owen chuckled. "It was quite demoralizing for Pyotr's men to be defeated so quickly by a group of women. I would have given anything to be a fly on the wall for that one. Imagine their surprise."

"I would like to propose using them if we need to increase our defenses here. They are more than competent. I have even moved some of the women to my day security force. It might give us a bit of an edge if Pyotr's men have to face the women who already beat them once. Of course, mortal women would be useless against vampires, but I think they have shown they can hold their own against other mortals."

Owen nodded in agreement.

"You want to play mind games with them. How novel. It just might work though. Since Pyotr's men would not want to admit they were beaten by normal human females, I'm sure they fabricated some outrageous fantasy about Gabriel's army of supernatural women warriors who were invincible. It might scare some of the more superstitious into deserting. Maybe we should be embellishing the story also. Before we are done, those women will be legendary."

The Presider cleared his throat and turned to Gabriel.

"I think you know your military expertise is not the only reason we wanted to see to you. There is still the issue of your wife."

"You can rest easy on that count. Grace has decided to be reborn, and Sophia has agreed to sire her. She and Yi will help with the transition and train Grace, so I can attend to my duties here. She intends to fight with us when the time comes, so

I will have very little time with her before they take her away. I hope you can understand my desire to make this meeting as brief as possible."

"Do you think Sophia is the right choice? That will make Grace nearly as powerful as you. Is that wise?" Owen asked.

"As far as I am concerned, Sophia is the only choice. I want an equal at my side. Sophia has a feeling Grace will be important in this conflict. I want her as strong as possible."

"Do you have any idea what element she will control?"

Gabriel considered a moment.

"She has a love of all things growing as well as a love of water. She could possibly control both earth and water. Either would be a good balance for me. She is too grounded for air, and one can never predict fire. Now if that is all your questions, I would like to return to my wife."

Gabriel did not think the Council needed to know about his suspicion that Grace was a Terran descendant. If she was as he suspected, she could be much more powerful than anyone imagined.

Chapter 67
Grace

It was Gabriel's first visit since my rebirth. Sophia was reluctant to let him come, but I was so adamant she could not refuse. My heightened senses made me rather volatile, and I often behaved like a spoiled toddler. Sophia told me I was a reminder of why she had stopped creating children and Gabriel never had.

We were finally together for the first time in a month. While all Gabriel wanted was some quiet time in bed, I was practically bouncing off the walls with energy.

"I can hear it now," I exclaimed. "I can hear my music, your music, our music. Why didn't you tell me how wonderful it sounded? When we made love, it was the most beautiful fugue I have ever heard. I can't even begin to describe it – two separate themes flirting with one another – coming together in harmony and then diverging until the tension was too much to bear, and they had to converge again. Was your experience the same?"

Gabriel shook his head in wonder. Was I the same woman he mated? I was like a child experiencing things for the first time. Everything was new. Everything was exciting, and I couldn't wait to share it with him.

"Yes, Grace, it was the same. Now maybe you understand why I could not describe it to you before. You had to experience it for yourself."

"It feels like there is so much you withheld from me. Why?"

Gabriel shook his head sadly.

"I don't know. I just felt like you needed to know the bad things first. Don't you miss the sun?"

"I guess I will at some point, but there is so much to absorb that I haven't thought about it. Even though moonlight is only a reflection of the sun, it has a gentle beauty of its own without the sun's harshness and heat. I think I can live with that."

"Sophia says that your self-control is admirable."

"I guess that means I haven't drained the blood out of any humans yet. Not that is isn't tempting. They smell so good. Did I smell like that to you?"

"Grace, you have no idea the number of times you tested my self-control. The night you offered me your blood almost undid me."

"I'm sorry I tempted you like that. I didn't understand what it was like for you. You were so patient with my ignorance. Sometimes I wonder what I did to deserve you. I asked Sophia not to tell you too much. I wanted to tell you myself how I was doing before she gave you her evaluation."

Gabriel nuzzled my neck and said, "If we're not going to make love again, you might as well give me a progress report. Have you determined your element yet?"

I smacked him on the shoulder. I could tell from the sound that what I thought was a gentle tap was much harder. I was still coming to terms with my new strength.

"We have plenty of time for both, but to answer your question, it appears you were right about earth. Sophia says it is manifesting in a way she has not seen before. There is something different about me. I don't just push dirt around or dig holes. I make things grow or wither, depending on my mood. To be honest, it's a little frightening."

"Then it is as I suspected. You are a daughter of the Earth Mother."

"What does that mean? "

"Growing up in the North Kingdom, did you never encounter stories about the indigenous people of the north? I asked you once about this when I discovered your love of gardening. Maybe you just forgot. The Terrans were the first children of the Earth Mother."

I was surprised.

"Yes, there were stories, but everyone thought the bloodline had been exterminated. People were afraid of them. They were thought to be barbaric because they made human sacrifices."

"Nothing could be farther from the truth, but we have a propensity for killing anything we fear or don't understand," Gabriel said sadly. "However, the bloodline took care of itself. It seems that the fewer Terran descendants remained, the more powerful the blood of the existing descendants became. It's almost as if the energy was not eliminated but was redistributed to the survivors. It appears you are one of the remaining carriers."

"You make it sound like a disease."

"Some believe it is as dangerous as one. At the height of their culture, the Terrans could literally change the face of the earth. People could not see the advantages of this power. They only saw the potential for evil and set about eradicating the Terran race. Since the Terrans had always been peaceful people, they did not have the resources or skills to defend themselves."

"Well," I observed with satisfaction. "It seems they missed a few."

"At least one," Gabriel agreed. "Be very careful who you tell about this. Sophia may suspect, but I would let her figure it out on her own. No immortal has ever sired someone with Terran blood, at least not that we know of. We have no idea what effect it might have on your element or your abilities."

"One more secret to keep," I sighed. "Oh, and you were right about another thing. I seem to have an affinity for water also. Besides being able to manipulate water in pools or lakes, I can pull it from the ground to irrigate a field. It hasn't rained here in a long while, so we tried it yesterday – it was amazing. We haven't tried to make it rain, but that might be next. The possibilities are mind-boggling."

"I'm so proud of you, and if I'm honest, a little afraid for you. You have certainly exceeded all my expectations. Now," he said kissing me softly, "Let me introduce you to the greatest pleasure of mated immortals."

Gabriel grabbed me around the waist and pulled me on top of him.

"Bite me."

Gabriel

I had bad news for Grace. More of my time was required in Hightower, and this would be my last visit for a while. I hated it, but my duties as Warden required it. As I suspected, Grace was disappointed. She said she understood, but I could tell my time away from her was affecting her progress. Sophia said she was often depressed and uncooperative when I was not there to encourage her.

Grace sighed.

"I know this is necessary, but I hate it. I miss you so much. How long can you stay this time?"

I could not meet her gaze.

"Only a few days. The longer Pyotr takes to make a move, the more apprehensive the Council gets. All this anticipation is making them jumpy, and they are constantly at each other's throats. I feel like a referee. I honestly don't know what they will do if left to their own devices. The delegates from the North and West seem to have their heads together a lot and that makes the others nervous. If the two decide to become allies and exclude the others, what will that mean for the future?"

"I had no idea things had gotten that bad. Maybe that was Pyotr's plan all along. He doesn't intend to take over the West but to seed suspicion in the Council and destabilize it. Without a strong Council, he could do whatever he wanted without fear of repercussions. Then he could attack and subdue Hightower. Can you stop him if that is his real intention?"

"Without the full Council, I'm not sure. Can we talk about something else? I get enough of this at home."

Grace was adamant.

"This is important. I think we need to talk about it. What is the best hope for Hightower's defense?"

I replied reluctantly, "We have resources that few know about. We just don't know how to utilize them."

Grace was intrigued.

"More secrets? What on earth are you talking about now?"

"It goes back to the discussion on my previous visit about keeping the Middle Kingdom neutral and protecting the passes through the mountains. Since the mountains effectively divide us geographically, the Earth Mother saw the need to preserve the one place people could easily travel among the four kingdoms. The Earth Mother compelled the Terrans to create not only a means of escape for the residents of Hightower in case of an attack but a secret weapon. Some of the tunnels leading in and out of Hightower now house the Council members and provide undetected access for the immortal population, but there are others which are hidden even from us. To preserve the access points, the Earth Mother created the Guardian and Sleepers to defend Hightower if the need arose."

"But the Sleepers are the subject of myth, stone giants with great strength who protect the first children," Grace stated. "They like the Terrans no longer exist, most believe they never did."

"They do exist such as they are," I replied. "They remain locked in the mountains until they are called forth in a time of need."

"Does that mean they can be released to protect Hightower if Pyotr attacks there?"

I gave a downhearted laugh.

"In theory, yes, but we don't know how. According to my study, only a descendant of the first children can waken them." Then I looked at Grace hopefully. "That means you. But the lore is lost. I have not mentioned this possibility to anyone. I don't want to create hope where there is none."

"You say the Earth Mother anticipated a need for protecting the passes. She undoubtedly saw the near extinction of the Terrans and the loss of their knowledge, but we now know that descendants did survive, just not the lore. She must have created a way for the surviving children to release the Sleepers in the future. There has to be a way. We just have to find it. Are we sure there are no surviving records of the Terrans?"

I shook my head.

"None that I know of. One of the reasons my library contains so many books about mythology is that I have been looking for the lost lore. My interest has been purely academic until now. I never guessed there would be a need."

Then I took Grace in my arms.

"No more of this talk now. I need the kind of distraction only you can give me. There will be time for all this later. Make love to me, Grace. I need to know something in my life isn't falling apart."

"Don't be so melodramatic, Gabriel. I will gladly provide a respite from your responsibility to save the world."

I kissed her gently and began to remove the loose tunic she wore. Her normal attire still irritated her sensitive skin, so the loose, soft tunic was much more comfortable. As I slipped the garment over her head, I gasped in surprise. "When did you get a tattoo? More importantly, why?!"

Grace looked at me in surprise.

"What on earth are you talking about? I would never get a tattoo. They are unsightly. If there is something there, I didn't have a hand in it, and I don't know how anyone could have disfigured me without my knowledge... although it has been done before," she said bitterly.

I was puzzled.

"Well, you have one now, and it looks like some kind of ancient rune I don't recognize. It is very difficult to tattoo a vampire. I wonder..." As I was examining her shoulder another rune appeared next to it.

"That's impossible!" I exclaimed.

"What is impossible? Grace asked.

"There is another one. I think the Earth Mother is responding to your need."

"What do you mean?"

"Perhaps the lore of the Terrans is not lost as long as even one of the descendants still lives. You expressed a need, and the runes suddenly began to appear on your skin. Now we just need to be able to interpret them."

"Can you copy them?" Grace asked. "I'm afraid they will fade before we can analyze them. Marks don't usually stay long on a vampire's body. Look for some vellum. You should be able to read through it to trace them."

"That is an excellent idea," I agreed. "Tracing would be the most accurate way to preserve them, although I doubt they will fade. They are not the usual tattoos. I fear you may be marked for the rest of your existence. I suspect you might be the only one who can decipher their meaning and it will be impossible for you to read what is written on your back so a tracing will be helpful. Lie down. I will get the supplies we need."

"Get Sophia while you're at it. I would like to see what she thinks of this. She might be old enough to have seen these runes when they were in use and help translate them."

Grace

While Gabriel went to get Sophia and the writing supplies, I lay on my stomach and pondered the strange turns my life had taken in the last year. Could it be that I was really the best hope for the Council to keep the world from descending into chaos at the hands of a greedy king? This task should belong to someone like Sophia, not a nobody like me. Then I remembered the heroic tales I learned as a girl. It was always the little guy no one thought of who eventually saved the world. But not before all hell broke loose. What would become of everyone I loved before this was all over? In all those tales, someone important to the hero was invariably sacrificed.

Gabriel and Sophia entered the room deep in conversation putting an end to my musings.

"You have to see for yourself," Gabriel was saying to Sophia as he pointed to my back. Several more runes had appeared since he left the room. "I've never seen anything like it. Maybe you can explain it."

"I would agree that the Earth Mother is responding to some question Grace asked. But these runes look wrong somehow. I have seen similar ones in very old manuscripts, but I can't make heads or tails of these."

Sophia shook her head.

"Runes, why did it have to be runes? Runes were used extensively by almost every ancient culture in many different areas of the Known World, but especially the North. They were a primitive means of communication in most and a method of fortune telling and prophecy in a few. The runes used for casting fortunes survived because there was a perceived use for them. Others, like the runes of the Terrans were presumed lost. Still others survived in written documents and provided an esoteric form of entertainment to scholars like you, Gabriel."

"So, what are these runes?" Sophia mused aloud. "Where did they originate? That would certainly provide some clue as to their meaning. At the least it would provide a context. Some symbols are obvious and have the same meaning across cultures. Those depicting animals of some kind are the easiest to decipher, but then one has to know what the animal represented to that particular culture. There is also the problem that all of them have multiple possible meanings. The rune for horse could mean trust, faith, or companionship, depending on the context, or it could just mean horse. There is nothing straight-forward about interpreting runes." Sophia declared with dismay.

The scholar in Gabriel could not resist the urge to direct the discussion he and Sophia were having while I lay on the floor.

"We need to start with a theory which will determine the direction of our study. We can only hope that we make the correct assumption. Because of the unexpected appearance of Grace's tattoos, we can theorize that these runes belong to the Terrans' lexicon. That is problematic since their meaning has been lost. However, a comparison of the runes of several different cultures might contain similarities and give us some clue as to their meaning."

"Even if we make an educated guess as to the meaning of individual runes, what is the message?" Sophia queried. "Is it literal or open to interpretation? How on earth are we supposed to put the pieces together?"

"Hey you two. It's me down here on the cold, hard floor. Will you please just trace the symbols," I interjected. "You can argue about their meaning later. Have they stopped appearing?"

Gabriel put the paper down on my back and began the painstaking work of tracing. It was not an easy job since my back was not flat and the vellum didn't always cooperate. Finally, after more time than I would have liked, Gabriel finished.

"I hope that is all," I was in an unpleasant mood after the ordeal. "If any more appear, someone else can copy them. You are too slow."

Gabriel snorted. "That is the first time anyone has ever accused me of being slow. You are just impatient. Now let's have a look at this." And he held up the paper so that he and Sophia could read it.

I was shocked. I slowly got to my feet.

"I recognize some of these!" I said in wonder. "But I have only seen a few of the more common runes before. How could I know the meaning of these?"

Gabriel and Sophia looked incredulous.

"You can both close your mouths. It's not that impossible. I have been educated." Then I took the paper out of their hands and turned it around.

"It's written backwards!" they exclaimed together, "but how?"

"Let's see," Gabriel mused. "I watched the symbols as they formed. They were not written by anyone here. It stands to reason that they were formed from the inside so what we see through Grace's skin is the reverse image not the actual one. It appears the Earth Mother has a lot of tricks up her sleeve."

I ignored them and focused on the symbols on the paper.

"Some of these have survived and are still well-known in the north. That one," I said pointing out the first rune, "is a warning. And there is one for the Earth Mother. There is one later in the sequence, the scary looking one, which represents the Guardian you spoke of. Now we just have to figure out the other 90 percent of them. No big deal."

Sophia looked at the paper again.

"I think I can help with some of the others, but I don't know anyone who would be able to decipher the rest. We may have the information we need, but now we don't know how to interpret it."

I was frustrated. Gabriel and Sophia were still making wild guesses as to the meaning of the message and I felt totally useless.

"Could you two go argue somewhere else? I would like to be alone for a while. I need to think. There has to be something I'm missing in all this. Why give me information I can't use? Oh, and leave the paper."

I closed the door after them and just stared until the images began to blur. I was not a religious person, but I was willing to pray to any deity that existed if it would provide an answer. Mentally exhausted, I fell asleep.

Gabriel

I ran my fingers through my hair in frustration.

"I don't know what to do. I have to go back but I can't leave her like this either."

Sophia took me by the shoulders.

"You know you have to go, Gabriel. Not just for the Council but for her. Every time you insist on helping her, you undermine her self-confidence. She needs to figure this out on her own, and neither one of us is helping right now. You have your part to play and so does she. Kiss your wife goodbye and go home. She'll be fine. Will you?"

I don't know, I thought.

Grace

The following day they were both gone, and I was alone. Sophia was off on some vague errand which would take a few days and Gabriel had to return to Hightower. I felt abandoned at first, but I recognized the truth. They were giving me the space I needed.

I picked up a mirror and examined my back. It didn't appear there were any new runes, so I could now concentrate on the paper, which had consumed my thoughts for days. I had tried all kinds of techniques but still couldn't understand the Terran writing. My anxiety was beginning to immobilize me, so I tried meditating to clear my head. Sitting by the fountain in the garden I let my mind wander. Water always soothed me when I was anxious. I focused on the sound it made as it splashed into the basin out of a large jug held by some forgotten goddess. I felt the soft spray against my skin and finally began to relax. Then I heard the voice. I started and looked around to see who had spoken but could see no one. It came again. It was a clear, musical voice, not unlike the sound of the water, but I couldn't quite make out what the speaker was saying. The third time I heard it clearly. *Do not look only with your eyes.* I shook my head and yelled at no one in particular.

"Why can't anything be said plainly? Does it always have to be a riddle?"

I stomped off to my room to retrieve the paper and try again.

"Do not look only with your eyes!"

For once in my life I wished I possessed a greater supply of curse words. I could use one about now. This was frustrating.

Chapter 68

"We have discovered a little more about Pyotr's plan. He is proposing an alliance with Donaldson. It's not like Donaldson has any choice. He doesn't have the military might or support of his people to withstand an assault by the armies of the North. Maybe Donaldson doesn't realize that Pyotr's idea of an alliance means Donaldson becoming his lackey while Pyotr wields all the power. Or maybe he just doesn't care. I think he admires Pyotr and would be just as happy to lick his boots. He never had the skills to run a country, and he knows it. It would get him off the hook. And his country is in such disarray that people would accept any leader who would allow them to live out their lives in peace. No one wants a war."

"We still have concerns about his plans for the Middle Kingdom," continued the Presider. "We know why he would want it but how he intends to take it is the question. It would require a huge army to accomplish, and he would lose at least half of them. I can't imagine he would be that imprudent. He's a better strategist than that."

Gabriel had been silent during the briefing but could contain himself no longer.

"What if he knows about the tunnels? We don't have the manpower to defend both the passes and the tunnels, and he knows it. Maybe his preoccupation with the West is a ruse to further divide our forces, requiring us to deploy an additional army to defend the Western border unnecessarily."

"But the tunnels are defended, aren't they?" Owen inquired. "What about the Guardian?"

"That's just a myth, and the entrances are concealed, so I can't imagine Pyotr could access them," replied a delegate from the South.

"I'm afraid it is not a myth," Gabriel replied. "There is evidence that the

Guardian exists and can be called into action to protect the tunnels. The tunnels just have to be opened by a descendent of the Earth Mother. Once opened, the Sleepers will then respond to defend them."

"That's absurd. The Terrans were wiped out, and good riddance to them," responded another of the Council delegates.

Gabriel thought about how he wanted to reveal what he knew. He did not want to endanger his wife, but he knew there was no other way.

"Grace has discovered some ancient runes that seem to reveal the secret location of the tunnels and how to defend them." (He neglected to tell them that the symbols were on her body.) "She is working to decipher them even as we speak. Since no one has seen that language in millennia, it is not an easy task, and we can only hope that she figures it out in time."

Chapter 69
Grace

Sophia had finally returned, and I was looking forward to having another person to help with the seemingly impossible task of decoding the runes. I also needed to ask her what she thought of the cryptic message I heard at the fountain and what it might mean. I was absent-mindedly running my fingers over the vellum when Sophia entered the room. I looked up to greet her, and my finger rested on one of the runes. Immediately a picture came into my head. I drew the finger away in alarm, wondering what just happened. I tried touching another of the runes, and the same thing happened although the picture was different.

"Sophia, is there any chance that these runes represent images instead of language? I'm seeing pictures in my mind when I touch them."

Sophia thought for a moment and responded, "It would make sense. The Terrans could not have known who might need these runes or when. If their written or spoken language was lost the only way to communicate would be through images. Images that would have the same meaning to anyone at any time, a tree is a tree no matter what you might call it in your own language. I think you might have made a breakthrough."

I sighed.

"It's about time I thought I would never figure it out. It was driving me crazy. Can you help me record what I see? Then maybe we can make sense of it."

Sophia and I spent the next several hours making a record of each symbol and its meaning according to my mental images. It was exhausting work. The meaning of some of the runes was very clear, but others left us shaking our heads in frustration. By the time we were finished, we still didn't understand the content of the message – if there was one at all. We had no clue whether the placement followed a pattern or was random. It was aggravating.

"I wish there was at least one other person who could understand these. Maybe together we could make sense of the message. With my luck, it is some kind of code. Gabriel is the one who is skilled in that area, but he isn't here. I had a disturbing thought while I was grappling with this puzzle. What if Pyotr has someone like me and what if they are able to translate the runes before I can? It's hard to believe I'm the only one."

Sophia had the look of someone who was making a very difficult decision.

"I don't know how soon Gabriel will be able to get away again. Do you think you are ready to be around humans? I think you need to go back to Hightower. You and Gabriel have been sharing blood since you were turned, haven't you?"

I was embarrassed but responded, "Of course. Don't all mated immortals?"

"If you have Terran blood, and you are sharing it with Gabriel, doesn't it stand to reason that he would now possess any abilities you have also?"

"I suppose so. There were once male Terrans. I see no reason why there wouldn't be again. How else would the race be able to reestablish itself at some point? You think that together Gabriel and I will be able to make sense of all this?"

Sophia nodded.

"I do. I believe that was Her plan in bringing you two together all along."

Chapter 70

In the middle of any crisis, some have more mundane concerns. This was the case with Arthur.

He had come to Hightower House to defend Grace. Was it his fault that his testimony was not needed? Now he was stuck in the Middle Kingdom without prospects for employment either legal or illegal. He needed an advocate, and the logical choice was his brother.

Gabriel looked at Higgins and Arthur and shook his head. It was hard to believe that two so dissimilar men could be brothers, let alone twins. There had been cases where it was suspected that twins had two different fathers, but there was no way to prove or disprove that claim. Higgins admitted that their mother did have a rather loose interpretation of monogamy, so it could be possible. Or it could just be their choices as adults.

Higgins – no one seemed to know his given name and he wasn't divulging it – had carefully constructed a life that was as far from his origins as humanly possible. His father was a worthless drunk, so Higgins rarely drank. It was no wonder his mother sought solace in the beds of other men, but Higgins could not condone her choices either. He taught himself to read and write with the help of a neighbor who took pity on him. He grew up being a bit of a prig with a superior attitude, which made him a target for the less-refined boys of his age. As a result, he also learned to fight.

This unique combination of skills made Higgins a perfect candidate for the position of overseer at Hightower House. The only obstacle Gabriel could see was his ignorance of the immortals who ran and frequented the establishment, so Higgins was the first mortal to read *The Truth About Vampires*. Higgins found it a bit startling at first to realize that he had been living in the midst of vampires all his life and never realized it. Not to mention that he would be working for one if he decided to accept the position. He finally decided that if the vampires had not bothered him before, they were not likely to do so now. He accepted the position with an open mind and never found a reason to regret the decision.

Arthur, on the other hand, believed his brother's desire for education was a waste of time. Why bother learning how to make a living when you could just take what you wanted? At first, he defended his brother when the other boys picked on him but finally decided that Higgins needed to take care of himself. Arthur had other skills to perfect. He was an accomplished pick-pocket and could outsmart just about any lock ever invented. He reasoned that reading and writing were not going to be necessary for either profession. He began taking jobs for others who needed his unique skills or just didn't want to dirty their hands with petty theft. He discovered to his dismay that those same people were more than willing to turn him in to the authorities if things went badly. He developed quite a reputation in his hometown and finally had to relocate.

Over the years, the brothers occasionally ran into one another. Arthur never worked in Hightower, so he could travel freely there without fear of arrest. When he visited, he would always see his brother, usually to ask for money. Higgins did not look forward to these visits, eventually refusing to see Arthur. He would grant no more favors to his degenerate brother. Let him make his own way in the world. But now, it was he who owed the favor. Arthur had come to Grace's rescue at his employer's request and now he wanted something in return.

Arthur looked uncomfortable. He wasn't sure how to ask for what he wanted. The vampire looked rather intimidating, and Grace was not there to intervene on his behalf. Yes, he knew about vampires. He had encountered them on many occasions in his travels. They had occasionally been helpful. He was not particularly afraid of them in general but this one specifically terrified him.

Gabriel waited for him to make his request. He was mildly irritated that this poor excuse for a man would have the audacity to ask him for anything, but Arthur had braved the possibility of an interview with the Council committee to vouch for Grace. For that alone, Gabriel would grant almost anything. He just hoped Arthur didn't realize it.

The request when it came surprised him. Gabriel expected some exorbitant sum of money and he would willingly give it. What he got was a job request. Arthur was tired of his life. He admitted that constant running from the authorities and lack of consistent income were wearing on him. He was not a young man anymore. He wanted to settle down, and he wanted Gabriel to help him.

"How exactly do you propose to earn a living?" Gabriel asked skeptically. "I don't really have a need for your particular skills."

Once more, Arthur wished that Grace was there. He knew she could convince Gabriel to help him, but he had just learned that she was away learning how to be a vampire and would not be available for some time yet. Arthur was on his own.

Arthur hung his head and replied, "I can learn to do other things. You have to admit I am good with my hands." He said wiggling his fingers. "I am willing, and I'm not stupid, even though it might appear that way. I'm just asking for a chance to prove myself. If things don't work out, I'll go my way and not bother you again."

Gabriel knew that Grace was twice indebted to Arthur. He may not have saved her life this time, but he had made life a lot easier for her by verifying her claim that she did not come to Hightower as a spy for Pyotr. Lilith didn't live long enough to confirm Grace's story, so Arthur was her only witness. And if Grace owed Arthur a favor, so did her husband. Gabriel would need to figure out how to utilize Arthur, so he could repay the debt. Arthur obviously had nimble fingers. He could be trained in some craft which required a delicate touch and steady hands. There were always plenty of small items that were in need of repair and not many people who could do a satisfactory job of it. Perhaps that was the answer. Better yet, Arthur might be able to invent a lock that even he could not circumvent. Gabriel nodded to Arthur.

"You will have a place here as long as you don't cause any problems. If you last long enough, you will even see Grace again. I'm sure my wife will want to express her gratitude. That should be incentive enough to behave."

Arthur bowed.

"Thank you, sir, and congratulations on your marriage."

Chapter 71
Grace

Sophia and I managed to return to Hightower without notice. Until we spoke with Gabriel, we did not want to reveal our presence. It still remained to be seen if I could control my urges, so I needed to stay away from the human staff at the house. We snuck into the apartment through the entrance reserved for immortals where we waited until Gabriel came to retire for the day.

I was anxious and excited. I had not been with Gabriel for several weeks, so I had much to tell him. We had chosen to refrain from writing since we were not sure who might intercept our letters. I paced the floor in frustration as the hours dragged on. Finally, the door opened and a whirlwind blew into the room.

"I caught your scent in the corridor. When did you arrive?" Gabriel said as he picked me up and planted a kiss on my lips. "Should you even be here yet?"

Sophia stood and replied sarcastically, "It's good to see you too, Sophia."

Gabriel was at her side in an instant giving her a hearty hug.

"I am indeed glad to see you also. As you might imagine, Grace captured my attention first. I apologize if you felt ignored. But, I repeat, should she even be here? Can she control herself among so many humans?"

"It is a chance we had to take. We have something we need to discuss with you before anyone else finds out we are here. Grace has a theory, and it involves you."

Gabriel snickered.

"I have many theories about Grace, but I haven't come hundreds of miles to express them. What is so special about this one?"

"She can explain it. I am going to find suitable quarters before you feel inclined to celebrate your reunion. If you will both excuse me, I need to rest."

Gabriel

We waited until Sophia departed before we came together in another passionate kiss. I pulled away.

"I would take you to bed, but Sophia's statement has roused my curiosity. What about this theory of yours?"

Grace picked up the vellum with the runes inscribed on it and handed it to me.

"Sit down first if you will, and close your eyes." I did as instructed. "Now I want you to touch right here." Grace took my finger and placed it on one of the symbols. "What do you see?"

"Is this some kind of joke?" I uttered with an exasperated sigh. "How am I supposed to see anything with my eyes closed? There is a limit to the enhanced senses of a vampire. Am I supposed to guess which rune?"

"No, I just want you to relax and tell me what comes to mind when you touch it. No guessing, just tell me what pops into your head. I know it seems silly, but this is important."

I realized Grace was not playing games with me, so I did as she asked. I cleared my mind as I did when I meditated, and immediately an image of a stone pillar came to mind. It looked like some kind of milestone similar to the ones which were placed to help travelers on a road. I shared my vision with Grace.

"Now another one," she said as she moved my finger to another spot on the paper. I let my mind go blank again and a different picture came to mind. This one was much less benign.

"I see a monster made of stone," I said.

She sighed happily.

"I am right. You have it too. You can open your eyes now, and I will explain."

I was understandably confused.

"What is it that I have?"

"Let me give you a little background first by way of explanation. I was so frustrated after we discovered that the runes were backwards, and I still couldn't read them. I took some time to meditate and clear my head. During my meditation, the water in the fountain spoke to me. It said, *do not look only with your eyes.* Later, I was talking to Sophia, and I allowed my mind to wander while I was touching one of the runes. I saw a picture. I tried another and the same thing happened just as it happened to you. I reasoned that these runes do not represent a language as much as a series of images which are meant to convey the same meaning no matter what language the reader understands. That is only the first theory. That you can see the images confirms the second."

"Now you have me intrigued," I replied. "What would that theory involve?"

Grace had a mischievous look in her eyes when she asked, "What is the most intimate thing two mated immortals can do?"

I replied, "I would guess you are not talking about sex. So that leaves sharing blood." My surprise was evident as I grasped where she was going with her question. "We share blood!" I exclaimed, my excitement mounting. "What is in your blood is now in mine. We both share Terran blood! But even after we discovered the runes were backward, I couldn't read most of them."

"I couldn't either until I touched them as you just did. I also could not find a pattern in the placement of the symbols. I reasoned that they were in code. When I expressed need of another who could help break the code, the Earth Mother provided the answer, and it had been in front of me all the time. You. Having preternatural sight doesn't prevent us from occasional blindness."

"I assume you have seen each rune's meaning. Did I confirm what you already knew?"

Grace nodded her assent.

"You did, but I would like for you to look at some of the others in which the image is not as clear. Your vision might be a little different and help clarify the meaning. We also haven't looked at the ones we recognized at first. Maybe they are not intended to be taken at face value. They could be there to distract us."

She stopped then and threw her arms round my neck.

"I can't tell you how happy I am that we can do this together I was feeling as if the future of the world rested on my shoulders alone. It was horrible."

I took her in my arms again and said, "I know this is important, but I'm sure it can wait an hour or two. I missed you. When I am not so distracted, I can be more helpful."

Chapter 72
Grace

Gabriel and I entered the Council chamber. What we had to say could change everything. It could also mean we would be ostracized or even put to death for our revelation. There was still a great deal of superstition and prejudice in the world, even here. After deciphering the remaining runes and making an educated guess as to the message, we decided we could not withhold what we knew and how. Gabriel and I had discussed our decision with Sophia and Yi and given them the opportunity to distance themselves, but both declared their intention to support their two friends. They shared the belief that what we knew could prevent a war that would expose the entire immortal shadow world to the mortals we sought to protect. None of us would allow the intolerant, ignorant views of a few to jeopardize us all. So it was decided.

The Presider brought the unruly group to order, ending the rampant speculation about the reason for this meeting. Many wondered if Pyotr had made his move, plunging us all into war. There was still doubt about the immortals' ability to defend Hightower if it was the target. In their collective unconscious was the idea that there was a way to stop him, but they just couldn't put a finger on it. The assembly looked expectantly at Gabriel, and I and hoped we had the solution they were hoping for.

"This meeting of the Council will come to order," The Presider began. "Are all members present?"

All representatives, including the members from the North Kingdom responded, "Aye".

"We will dispense with further formalities and get straight to the reason for this unscheduled meeting. Gabriel, you and your mate have requested this meeting, so please explain yourselves."

Gabriel began, "As you know there was an ancient race which resided in the North Kingdom. They were the first children of the Earth Mother and called the Terrans. They were a peaceful race who concentrated primarily on understanding the forces of nature and how they could be manipulated to mankind's benefit. For this reason, it was believed that they practiced magic. One way in which they sought to appease their gods was to sacrifice one of their own virile young men each spring to ensure the Mother's blessing for the coming year, ensuring a good harvest. Their men considered it an honor to fulfill this destiny and competed for the privilege. Other cultures found the ritual barbaric, and the Terrans were viewed with suspicion and fear. Those cultures sought to eradicate the Terrans and their barbaric practices."

Gabriel was interrupted by several spectators.

"We don't need a history lesson!"

"We all know this."

"What does this have to do with us? Get to the point!"

Gabriel stood patiently while the Presider restored order and then continued.

"What this has to do with us resides in the bloodline of the Terran race. The Earth Mother knew how important the Middle Kingdom would become. For that reason, escape tunnels were created leading in and out of Hightower and then sealed. She also created the Guardian and Sleepers to protect the tunnels from invasion. The lore needed to utilize the defenses the Earth Mother put into place was entrusted to the Terrans. Until recently, we believed all of this was just a part of the creation mythology. But myth often contains an element of truth."

Again, Gabriel was interrupted.

"What do you mean until recently? What do you know that the rest of us don't?"

Gabriel leaned toward me and whispered, "Are you sure you want to do this? It's not too late to find another way."

In response, I turned my back to the Council and lowered my robe just enough to display the runes on my shoulders.

There was a collective gasp and someone shouted, "What is this magic?"

The Presider again called for order and turned to Gabriel.

"I assume you have an explanation for this?"

At this point Gabriel turned to me, "I cede the floor to my mate."

"If you will allow me, I will explain. After I became a vampire, I spent a great deal of time in meditation in order to control my new instincts and urges. You all know how difficult the time of transition can be. Because of the unsettled state of our world, I felt a need to accelerate the transition, so I could stand with my mate if there was war. During my periods of meditation, I discovered that I had a strong connection with the Earth Mother. My growing ability to manipulate both earth and water further confirmed this connection. I had been grappling with how to best serve the Middle Kingdom in this crisis, and the Mother provided clues. When Gabriel came to visit, he discovered the tattoos on my back. I was understandably confused since it is almost impossible for an immortal to retain a tattoo because of our ability to heal quickly. But the symbols continued to appear, even as he was examining the ones I already had. We expected them to disappear, so Gabriel traced the runes to preserve them and give us the opportunity to study them. Rather than go through the whole process, I will say that we discovered them to be of Terran origin. Gabriel had suspected for some time that I carried Terran blood. Those suspicions were confirmed when I was able to understand the runes. We also discovered that by sharing blood, Gabriel was now able to decipher them also. We are both part of the surviving bloodline."

Gabriel was holding my hand during the speech. He brought it to his lips and kissed my knuckles. Then we waited tensely for the chaos I had just created to settle down. The reaction was not what we expected. One after another of the spectators stood silently and exhibited similar tattoos until there were four people standing. When the room was again quiet one of the four, a delegate from the West, spoke.

"My tattoos appeared about the same time as Grace's. I could only attribute their appearance to the fact that I had Terran blood. I was terrified that someone would find out. I have witnessed cruel treatment of those suspected of being part of the bloodline. I know now that I have to come forward and stand with Grace and Gabriel."

Of those now standing one was from the West, two were from the East and one was from the South. The company numbered six, including Gabriel and I. Reluctantly one of the Council members from the North stood and revealed that she, too, was adorned with Terran runes.

The Presider addressed me.

"Do you believe you have the information necessary to protect Hightower?"

"I believe we are close," I replied, "but nothing is certain. I would like to confer with the others. I was not aware that there were others, so I have no idea if each of us carries a part of the spell – I don't really know what else to call it – or if each individual carries a complete set of instructions. We have a long way to go to understand exactly what these runes mean and determine if there is a consensus. I know we don't have the luxury, but we need time to study what we have and then we can present our findings to the Council at large. Is that acceptable?"

"You're correct. We don't have much time but this seems our best option at the moment, so we will have to give you however much time you need."

Chapter 73
Grace

While vampires are social creatures, they are not cooperative ones. When the Descendants, as we to become known, convened, it was clear that our group faced many challenges, not the least of which was our inability to agree on almost anything. Unfortunately for me, the one thing they did agree on was that no one wanted to be in charge. The consequences of failure were too intimidating, and no one wanted the blame to fall on them. So they looked to me.

"Grace, you are the one who seems to have a personal connection with the Earth Mother, so you should lead the group. Besides, you are Gabriel's mate so you have the credibility that we lack."

Their response was not unexpected. I was, after all, the one who brought the possibility of a solution to the "Pyotr problem" to the Council. If we were to accomplish anything in the limited time we had, I would have to step up and take charge. So it was decided.

I quickly discovered the group had to deal with their anxiety before we would be able to get anything done. Everyone had a story about the appearance of their tattoos and what it might mean for them. They needed to share those stories. We didn't really have the time for story-telling; however, they would not settle to the task at hand until that need was satisfied. There were so many questions. Instinctively, we all knew the source of our disfigurement but not the why. Were we being identified so that we could be sacrificed to bring an end to the current crisis? Not everyone had in the group had the luxury of another person with whom they could confide their fears. Now was the only opportunity they would get.

Finally, it appeared we were ready to get down to work, so Gabriel turned me over to my new group of associates. He had other priorities. It was his job to marshal the forces that would be required if the Descendants failed in their task. Before he abandoned me to my task, he contributed several books from his collection that might shed more light on the symbols and their meanings. I could tell by his reluctance that saving the world as we knew it won out over protecting his precious library by only a minuscule margin. We all had to make sacrifices.

I was frustrated. This was taking entirely too long, even though we were working non-stop trying to decipher the runes which adorned our bodies. The problem was not only identifying individual images and determining their meanings, but we still lacked a context, and that was something we badly needed to focus our energies. At the moment, we were all over the place. Many unanswered questions still plagued us, and it was likely the answers to those questions would determine our success or failure.

When examined, it was evident that each of us had a different set of runes. Question number one became: Did each individual possess a complete message, or did the available runes need to be combined to determine the message? More importantly, did we have everything we needed? After all, these were only six immortals. How many others had similar tattoos and were afraid to come forward? The group hadn't even considered that there might also be mortals displaying these strange symbols. After all, the blood of the first children had run in our veins when we were still mortal.

It was also evident that all of us were of a different opinion and each held steadfastly to their own interpretation. How was I, as the reluctant leader of the group, going to get them to work together? Immortals could be a stubborn lot and time had a different meaning for us. I was the youngest of the group and still remembered the meaning of urgency. Finally, I threw up my hands in frustration.

"It seems we are bogged down in meaningless details. I need some time away from this to get some perspective. The Council is breathing down our necks demanding a solution, and we can't even agree on the basics. We either cooperate or die. I doubt Pyotr will keep any of us alive if he is successful, not to mention, if we get it wrong, we could bring about the destruction of our world as we know it."

The delegate from the North shook her head sadly.

"I can't help feeling responsible. Pyotr is my king, and I never saw this coming. How did I miss the signs? Maybe I spend too much time here arguing with other Council members and not enough serving my own people.

Nevertheless, I feel compelled to stop him. I am willing to do whatever it takes to find the solution. We will continue to work on the problem and try to work together," she said as she glared at the others. "You have a connection with the Earth Mother, Grace. Maybe She can give us some direction through you. Take the time you need to seek Her wisdom."

I left the room in which we had been working and sought the solace of my favorite fountain. Maybe the delegate was right. We were depending too much on our own resources instead of seeking the help we needed. There was only one place we were likely to find it.

I sat on the bench closest to the fountain where the occasional spray could reach me. I needed the sound and feel of my element to concentrate. When I was settled with my hands turned upward on my knees, I closed my eyes and attempted to clear my mind. One by one, I erased the jumble of symbols from my cluttered brain until only one remained. It steadfastly refused any attempt to remove it. A small voice in my head kept repeating, "This is the key."

After a great deal of discussion and some disagreement over the more obscure symbols a consensus was reached. Discovering the key to the code brought clarity, but it still did not result in a definitive interpretation, only the Descendants' best guess. What if we were wrong? Something this important should not be left to chance, but wasn't that always the way it went? The deities never gave a clear answer, only hints. The gods seemed to be of the opinion they had already given their people everything needed to make the right decisions without further assistance. We lesser beings had our doubts.

"What are we going to do with this knowledge or lack thereof?" asked the representative from the West. "If we use what we guess is a very powerful spell, we could vanquish Pyotr's army but unleash a greater horror on the world."

"I understand the rune of warning," offered the representative from the South, "but I think it refers to someone using the spell – and yes I agree we have to call it what it is – as an act of aggression not protection. It seems that the spell can only be used for defense and will not respond for any other purpose. The way I read it, the Guardian and Sleepers will return to their rest once their purpose is fulfilled."

West responded, "I still think there could be unintended consequences."

Gabriel had rejoined the group to check on our progress. He looked pointedly at the Council representative from the North.

"Has anyone from your kingdom seen your runes?"

North looked chastised and responded, "Pyotr is aware. I showed him when they first appeared. He is my king, after all, and I didn't understand the implications. However, he was dismissive and seemed to be unconcerned."

"Are there others?" he asked. "After all, it would make sense that the North Kingdom would have a larger proportion of Terran descendants than anywhere else."

"Yes," North admitted. "I heard rumors there were others. Since people were reluctant to reveal their secret, it is difficult to know how many there might be. We may have a larger proportion of descendants, but the North is no less prejudiced against anyone who carries that blood. Fear kept us from acknowledging what we were given and the ability to understand was withheld from us. Pyotr saw no reason to pursue the unusual occurrence."

"Well, that is good news," Gabriel responded. "It is my hope that it will not be necessary to use what we think we have learned, but I would rather not have someone on the other side uttering counter-spells against us. North, are you in contact with your King at this time? He left here in a rush, and no one seems to have heard from him since. Could you find a way to let him know that we are able to open the tunnels and release the Guardian and Sleepers against him?"

"But we're not there yet, are we?" West asked.

"He won't know that," Gabriel then looked pointedly at North, "unless we are betrayed."

North was indignant.

"It appears we have been given the means for our salvation and the seeds for our destruction. I for one do not intend to put that information into the hands of someone who would use it against any of us. I may be from Pyotr's kingdom, but my allegiance is to the Council and the Known World. It is my job to protect the entire immortal population. Council members are to have no political obligation to any one region. You should know that better than anyone, Gabriel, since you are Warden of the Middle Kingdom."

There was a loud gasp in the room.

"That is a closely guarded secret which you have ill-advisedly revealed to individuals who are not members of the Council. Who else have you told?" Gabriel hissed.

"I apologize. I thought this was a group who deserved know who you are and where your allegiance lies. It was meant to reinforce your position, not diminish it. I have told no one outside of this group, and I will not. You know it would mean my death."

I responded sadly, "It is one more of the many secrets we must keep. When will it ever end? But we must terminate this discussion and decide what we will recommend as a plan of action. North, as a Council member, I think you should present our position."

"Then I must get it straight. This group and any others who come forward will continue to work to completely understand the runes. At present, I will inform the emissary to King Pyotr that we have the means to raise the Guardian and Sleepers against his army if he continues to pursue his current course of aggression. Does that sum it up?"

"How will we deal with the animosity against the Terran race? Now that we have revealed ourselves as Descendants, we will be targeted. We took a great risk when we spoke out. Who will protect us?" asked East. "My country is more tolerant than most, but even there, the stories do not paint us in a flattering light."

I stood.

"That is not a battle we can fight right now. We have a bigger problem, and prejudice cannot be overcome overnight. I think that proving our worth in the current crisis will go a long way toward ensuring our acceptance. When the time comes, I will speak on behalf of the first children of the Earth Mother. I believe She has entrusted this task to me."

North moved to stand before me. Putting her hands on my shoulders in a gesture of support she said, "This cannot be your battle alone, Grace. We will all speak for the Descendants."

East held up his hand.

"Let's not get ahead of ourselves. I believe I have found something we should look at before we speak with the Council. There is a single rune that does not appear to be connected to anything else, and its position among the others is suspicious. It could be a further warning."

He pointed to the obscure symbol in question.

"It is one which has several different interpretations depending on the cultural context, but the meanings seem to point to danger and suffering, something to be avoided at all costs. At first, I thought it had something to do with the Guardian, but when I touched it as you taught us, Grace, the image separated into two distinct symbols, one meaning gateway and the other meaning unknown. Do you have any idea what this might mean?"

I looked at the rune and then touched it also. I sat for a moment in silence listening to the quiet voice of the Earth Mother then responded, "I agree with your interpretation, and that this symbol does not pertain to the release of the Guardian. Many cultures have a cautionary tale in their mythologies that refers to the destruction of their world and its inhabitants. In most cases, their deity also created a way for a chosen few to escape and avoid extinction of the species. This "gateway" is to be used only in that event. Our current situation does not qualify, and we cannot afford to get distracted. There must be a good reason this knowledge has been hidden and the message obscured by danger and suffering. Hopefully, we can spend time unraveling that mystery later. If we fail to stop Pyotr's army, none of this will matter."

However, I knew this was not entirely true. This message was for me. I now knew the location and purpose of the portal that was secreted in the tunnels under Hightower.

Chapter 74

The Presider cleared all spectators from the chamber so that only the Council members remained. North resumed her place with the rest of the Council, and Gabriel went to the chair designated for the Warden. He assumed his place only during closed Council meetings. It remained vacant on all other occasions. The remaining Descendants were given seats facing the Council.

North was first to speak.

"I have been asked to present our recommendations to the Council for your approval. We are all agreed that the meaning of the message is not completely understood. As such, trying to use the information without further study would be imprudent and could result in disaster. However, we agree that a course of disinformation aimed at the North Kingdom might be a deterrent to further aggression. If Pyotr or his generals believe that we have the means to protect ourselves, they might abandon their plans. An even better outcome is that his generals would realize the folly of Pyotr's intentions and turn him over to us."

The Council members nodded thoughtfully at the suggestion. No one really wanted to take action against another immortal, but it was clear that Pyotr had outstayed his welcome.

Lord Owen was the one who pointed out the elephant in the room.

"I agree with the suggestions proposed, but we have another problem. There were many others in the room when it was revealed that the Terran bloodline was alive and well in our midst. There is a great deal of animosity against that race, even after centuries of believing it extinct. Terrans have been the scapegoat for all kinds of atrocities because of their practice of human sacrifice. How will we explain that they have been part of our society at the highest levels of government hiding in

279

plain sight? We have been dedicated to eradicating all traces for centuries. This is a hard thing for me to swallow. I'm sure rumors are already rampant, and there will be calls for executions by the more intolerant factions."

Gabriel nodded encouragingly to Grace, and she began.

"As far as hiding in plain sight, there was never a way to detect Terran blood. I was not aware of my own link to the first children until the Earth Mother saw fit to intervene in this threat. For some reason, She has chosen this time to reveal Herself to the world. By doing so, She also revealed the presence of Her children. The Terrans were never an evil race. As the first children of the Earth Mother, they deserve respect not derision. Our society points a finger at them for the practice of sacrificing one of their own each year, but turns a blind eye to sacrificing thousands in every war that is waged. One versus a thousand – it seems a little hypocritical to me."

"Much of the animosity toward the Terrans is based on the beliefs and practices of a primitive people. Our culture no longer believes that we need to make sacrifices of any kind to appease gods, and there is nothing in the blood of the Descendants which compels us to do so. What we do have is access to the lore, which could very well save us all. It is that fact that must be made clear to anyone who wishes to condemn us. If we are not permitted to use that knowledge, we could all be sacrificed in a bloody, senseless war."

"Perhaps the Mother's plan all along was to show that sometimes the despised and rejected can be the salvation of us all. I encourage the Council to adopt a policy of active acceptance of those of us who carry the blood of the first children. If you cannot give us your support, you might as well execute us all where we stand and take your chances fighting a war you cannot win."

All eyes turned to the door as a loud banging interrupted Grace's appeal. A breathless messenger was admitted to the chamber. He bent over with his hands on his knees and slowed his breathing until he could manage to croak out, "Pyotr's army is on the move. They don't seem to be in any hurry, so it will take several weeks before they get to the pass but they are coming. It seems the time for discussion is over."

Gabriel looked at the Committee members and shouted, "We have to get our army mobilized and to the pass before they do." To Grace he added, "Then we will have to hope that the bluff works. If not, we might have to take our chances with what we know of the spell and face the consequences."

Chapter 75

Pyotr's army was taking its time. A forced march would lead to a tired army that would not fight as effectively. A part of Pyotr hoped that the size of the army marching against Hightower would intimidate their opponents to the point of immediate surrender. It would certainly make him look very good. The more blood-thirsty part of him though was spoiling for a fight. He hadn't had any real competition in a long time. His forces were large and growing with the promise of plunder to the victors. Humans were greedy, and it appeared Pyotr's large army was unbeatable. There was a downside to a leisurely march. It gave people time to reconsider.

General Ulrich sat his horse and looked over the amassed troops. He wondered once again why he was here. He had no dog in this fight of Pyotr's. He was here because of her, and now that the witch was dead, he could find no valid reason to stay.

She had to be a witch. Why else could he have been seduced by her? He had a wife and children, and he loved them all. His wife provided all the entertainment he desired, but still Lilith had gotten him into her bed and not just once. There was something about her that instilled lust, and he had found her irresistible. She had whispered in his ear about the lofty plans of the King of the North and how Ulrich could be an integral part of those plans. When Pyotr ruled the Known World, Ulrich might even be given one of the four kingdoms to rule. He did not think he was an ambitious man, but her promises were seductive. Then one day it all ended. Lilith informed him that she would expose his indiscretions and possibly destroy his marriage if he did not join Pyotr's cause and pledge his large military resources. She had him by the balls, and he knew it.

Ultimately, Ulrich was a rational man and a soldier. He didn't think Lilith's revelation would really do him any damage. After all, most men strayed. But he hadn't had a good fight in many years, and he needed to know he still had what it took, so he didn't need much encouragement to join the fight. It wasn't the promise of more riches or power. He didn't need any of that. But like many of the others here, he wanted to feel relevant again. In that, he could sympathize with Pyotr.

Now Lilith was dead, and Ulrich was free of her threats. He could take his men, turn around, and go home. Let the others fight Pyotr's insane war. He wondered how many of the other commanders were having similar thoughts. Would they leave also? All it would take was one brave soul to start the large-scale defections. Ulrich wondered if Pyotr and his small group of immortals would or could prevent them.

Then there were the rumors. Ulrich was an educated man, and he didn't give much credence to the stories of ancient civilizations that could control mythical monsters. Many of his more experienced fighters were older. They had homes and families, so they had resisted the call to arms. Their way of life was not threatened, so why would they leave? They would have been able to ignore the rumors. The men Ulrich was able to recruit had nothing to lose and much to gain if Pyotr won. They were also less educated and superstitious. They quailed under the news of the mysterious enemy they might have to battle. They were accustomed to fighting other humans, but the unknown made them anxious and jumpy. Several individuals had already disappeared the previous night, and Ulrich feared others would leave soon regardless of their leader's decision.

Ulrich's army was not the only one having second thoughts. There was whispering among the other troops which stopped abruptly whenever a commander was near. More than a few men could be seen checking out a quick means of escape should they decide to desert. It was difficult to fight a battle without a cohesive army and this one was quickly falling into disarray.

Pyotr seemed oblivious to the unrest. He was supremely confident that his cause would prevail. Yes, he had seen the evidence of strange runes showing up on a few of his subjects. His initial reaction was to destroy them, but there was always the possibility he could exploit their knowledge at some later date. Why destroy a potential weapon? One of his own representatives on the Council had them, but the king was not concerned. He had also heard that Gabriel Ross's newly sired vampire wife was heading a group of Descendants to analyze and determine how to use these runes to defend Hightower. Even that did not shake his confidence in the outcome. He, Pyotr, King of the North would rule the Known World.

Pyotr didn't understand how humans could be so gullible or maybe they were just cowards. The rank and file in his army was superstitious, and there was enough ambivalence on the part of some of the human generals that the rumors took on more importance than they should have. Some of these same generals had been enlisted by Lilith, and those men harbored suspicions about Pyotr's possible involvement in her death. He wondered how they would react if the Council threatened to unleash this mythical force. The unrest was beginning to erode some of his confidence and support his one doubt. Would they still follow if they knew the truth? There was only one who could reveal it, and that one would be standing on the other side of the battle lines opposing him. Although Gabriel Ross did not have first-hand knowledge of Pyotr's origins, Pyotr had revealed his beginnings when he tried to recruit Gabriel to his service. It happened centuries ago, but the sting of Gabriel's blunt refusal still rankled. Pyotr thought they could have been invincible together, but Gabriel had scruples. Imagine that! They had parted on uneasy terms, neither wanting to destroy the other. Gabriel had honored his promise to keep Pyotr's secret, and they kept out of each other's way – until now.

Pyotr was beginning to feel a sense of urgency. His plan to take things slowly and keep his fighters fresh was backfiring. The leisurely progress toward Hightower was supposed to show Pyotr's confidence in the outcome of the conflict and instill fear in his enemies. It was the people of Hightower who were supposed to be running for their lives, not his own men. Instead, Hightower stood firm and waited while Pyotr's men, unsettled by unsubstantiated rumors were the ones turning tail and running home. Two days from the pass, the king changed tactics and the forced march to Hightower began.

Chapter 76

The plan for defending Hightower was finally solidified. Hightower had soldiers, and they could make a serious dent in Pyotr's forces, but eventually, they would be overwhelmed. Lacking the manpower available to Pyotr, the Council chose to make the most of the assets they had. Their first line of defense would be the Descendants and their enigmatic tattoos, playing on the fears of the superstitious. The Council's spies reported that the rumors had made an impact on the already flagging morale of Pyotr's troops, and there had been defections, but there was nothing as compelling as confronting the proof. No one had to know that it was smoke and mirrors, but a convincing bluff was still better than a battle. If that did not prove an effective deterrent, Gabriel claimed to have an ace up his sleeve. If all else failed, they would invoke the spell and pray that they could survive the consequences.

Pyotr and his army arrived at the pass to find the battle lines already drawn, and Pyotr's old enemy, the immortal he had hoped centuries ago to make his ally, standing alone at the head of the group barring the way. A group of six unarmed people in white robes stood directly behind Gabriel followed by Hightower's pathetic little army. It was a unique formation for a battle. As Pyotr walked forward to confront Gabriel alone, he wondered what the immortal knew that he didn't.

"So you decided to go through with it," Gabriel said. "I'm sorry. I wonder though how many of these people will follow you when they know the truth. Are you going to tell them? I suggest you do. My version of your secret will not be nearly as benign as yours."

Pyotr shrugged, turned to face his army and in a loud voice recounted his story.

"The secret to which Gabriel refers concerns my origins. You see, I am not from your land." Pyotr could see shocked looks and shaking heads but no one confronted him so he assumed their acceptance and continued. "Most of the inhabitants of this land mass believe they are the only ones who exist. I am proof that they are wrong. I was a solder in my own land. I was one of the best and that was my undoing. When we ran out of wars to fight, the leaders of my country were left with a formidable fighting force, and no place to use them. They feared that in our leisure we might try to challenge them for control. To keep us occupied the leaders decided our next campaign should be exploration. We knew of the great waters which surrounded us and reasoned that there might be other places like ours if we could just get across the sea."

"Appealing to our egos, the leaders designated a group of the most accomplished of us to take on this task. We were aware that this was their way of getting rid of us, but we were bored and looking for a new challenge. There was no guarantee any of us would ever return. To ensure the elimination of a potential risk, we discovered that our leaders had a contingency plan. If we were to find land, a small group of loyalists were to burn all the ships but the one they would use to sail home. They were to condemn us to exile wherever we landed."

"Our former leaders (we no longer felt any allegiance to them) underestimated our will to survive or the presence of immortals in this new land – your land. We were not particularly eager to return to a place where we were not wanted, and your country suited us. Your indigenous people were scattered and did not pose a threat. In fact, they were more than happy to welcome new-comers who could teach them new skills and advance their society. We were treated like kings and we loved it."

"There were others in your country who were watching and waiting. The ancients who were here from the creation were anxious to return to their own beginnings. In me, they found a successor. When I was given the opportunity to be not just a king but a god, I jumped at the chance. It was the fulfillment of all my dreams. I chose two others to be sired along with me. As you know, blood-lust in newly sired vampires is impossible to control and in our resulting frenzy we killed the others who had accompanied us. We managed to refrain from completely decimating our food source and instead cultivated the remaining mortals like livestock offering them protection and security in exchange for their cooperation. Eventually, I came to believe there could be only one god, and I destroyed the other two immortals."

"For all my faults, it was I who created society in the North Kingdom. I gave you knowledge, culture, wealth, and a sustainable form of government. For many centuries, you accepted me as your god. You worshipped and adored me as you should. I reveled in the ceremonies and festivals in my honor. I finally had the love and respect I would never achieve in my own land. However, as your sophistication grew, you forgot the source of all your good things and believed you had done it on your own. You began to question my deity, and I became irrelevant. Such ungrateful children! Occasionally, I would embark on a well-deserved reign of terror, but even that was not enough to reestablish my sovereignty. Besides, it was not your fear I wanted, even though it was useful at times. I wanted your adoration."

"I went into seclusion for many years until, at last, I decided to reinsert myself and become the King of the North." Then Pyotr spread his arms in a gesture of inclusion and humbly, in his opinion, stated, "My people love and follow me and now here we are."

Following Pyotr's revelation Gabriel walked confidently toward the battle line.

"I don't suppose you have told them about the first children and what they can unleash."

Pyotr scoffed.

"That is just a silly myth. How is that relevant? The first children no longer have any power, and all their lore has been lost."

"That's not what your people believe. Perhaps you would like to meet some others who disagree," Gabriel replied and then shouted over Pyotr's head to his amassed troops. "Perhaps you all would."

The men from the North Kingdom looked at one another and began to grumble. Pyotr's revelation along with his obvious disdain for all human life had turned many against him. Now there was another reason to leave well enough alone and go home. They could be facing a more formidable army than they were led to believe. This would not be the easy conquest Pyotr promised. Several men turned and began to flee, the rumors having done their work with the more easily frightened among them. Now it was time to see if others could be swayed with proof.

"If you will indulge me, I will explain what you are about to see," Gabriel began. "First, the bloodline of the first children is not dead. We discovered this when runes began to appear on the bodies of their descendants. These runes when combined reveal the spell to release forces which were put in place by the Earth Mother at creation. I will admit that we do not know what the result of unleashing these forces will be. It could be catastrophic for all of us – or merely for our enemies. We have not been able to get far enough to understand the consequences. But you have forced our hand, and we do know enough to release them and will do so if you will not abandon this foolish act of aggression. We are willing to take our chances – are you? Is supporting this exile who has set himself up as your king worth the risk?"

Then Gabriel called the six others forward, and they exposed their tattooed backs to the opposing army.

One of the more belligerent generals yelled, "How do we know this is not some sort of trick? Maybe you just painted them on. This doesn't prove anything!"

The Council member from the North turned and replied, "I am one of you and I assure you that these symbols on my back are not man-made. I did not seek out this distinction, but I can no longer deny my heritage and the knowledge I possess. If you will not believe Gabriel, I hope you can believe one of your own. But this is all the proof you will receive unless we are forced to act."

The seven returned to the protection of their army to wait the reaction of Pyotr's men. It was clear that there was a great deal of heated discussion going on. With an odd expression no one could comprehend, Pyotr removed himself from the group and stood aside to let his men debate on their own. There was nothing more he could do. It was out of his hands.

Although the better educated generals remained skeptical about this development, their less educated, superstitious troops were sure the tattoos were a sign from the gods. The desertions were increasing the longer their generals debated the wisdom of continuing. The leaders realized they would soon lose a great deal of their fighting forces through fear of the unknown. Fear was something no rational argument would dispel. In addition, the revelation of Pyotr's origins had shaken them. Did they really want to follow someone who had deceived them all this time? It would be much easier to return to their homes and resume their lives. Many had forgotten why they agreed to come in the first place or were too embarrassed by their greed to admit it.

The bigger question was what to do about Pyotr if his army defied him and refused to continue. Pyotr was a powerful immortal and would not surrender himself to his mortal generals. The task would then fall to Pyotr's inner circle of immortals, who now viewed him as a traitor who would have to suffer the consequences of his treachery. As a group, they knew they could subdue him, but it would not be without bloodshed. They were not willing to risk their lives to bring him to task.

Pyotr

I could see it all slipping away. My generals kept glancing in my direction, and I could see the doubt and growing animosity in their expressions. On some level, they had known I was not one of them, and they ignored it as long as I continued to line their pockets. Now they were coming to face the reality of their predicament. Could they continue to follow me? My promise of an easy victory, which would reap them even greater wealth and power, was losing its certainty. Were they willing to pay the price? I could see the questions in their eyes, and their conclusions were not encouraging.

I suddenly realized I was tired – tired of this land, and my existence in it. I was tired of responsibility and politics. The weight of centuries rested heavily on my shoulders, and it had finally worn me down. I now understood why there were so few truly ancient immortals. Without a higher purpose that took one out of oneself, life was a meaningless progression of days, years, and possibly centuries. My feeble attempt to reinvigorate myself through self-serving means had failed miserably.

The adherents of many religious groups believe there is something beyond this existence. I had never embraced any of that nonsense. After all, I was a god, and I would exist forever. Then again, what if it was true? I wondered for the first time if there was a state in which I could just BE. Many certainly believed it. Some even longed for it. There was a catch however. Some kind of repentance or atonement was required. What would that mean for me? I guess I would find out soon. I was finished.

Chapter 77

Pyotr stood before the executioner.

When the Presider asked if he had any last words before he met his end, Pyotr stood tall and spoke:

"After all these millennia it is time. I die with the hope that there is something beyond ruled by an entity that is truly forgiving. When I became 'a god,' I lost faith in anything beyond the land I now ruled. I did not believe there could be anything better than this life. After the hard work of establishing a functional society among the human tribes I found here, I was still hungry for power and control. I loved the awe I saw in the faces of my subjects. I reveled in their fear at my displeasure. I even enjoyed the groveling of my retainers as they jockeyed for my favor and elevated position. It was exhilarating for a while. But I needed more."

"I realized no one loved me. They all wanted something from me that would make their lives better. I enjoyed the adoration of the women I bedded, but I knew it was temporary. They too just wanted to be in the presence of power. My favor elevated their status among the other women and made them more desirable to men who could give them a future. I never enjoyed a love like the one Gabriel and Grace share. That is one more reason to envy you Gabriel."

"I thought that starting this conflict would make me feel relevant once more. It would give me a sense of purpose. It did not. When it was too late to stop the momentum I created, I realized this was not the cure for my ennui. I express my regret, but I refuse to apologize. Gods do not apologize."

"So this is where it ends. The appeal of this world has dulled. It no longer has the ability to delight and surprise me. I go willingly. I ask only one favor. I want my long-time rival but the immortal I most respect to end my existence here. I want

Gabriel Ross to conduct my execution. After my beheading I wish my shell to be consumed by fire until I am nothing but ash."

There was a collective gasp from the assembled immortals. Gabriel and Grace looked at each other.

"Can you do this?" Grace whispered.

The Presider of the Council looked at Gabriel and asked a similar question, "Will you accommodate the final request of the condemned?"

Gabriel stood tall and faced Pyotr.

"I will grant this request not because you deserve it for the crimes you have committed but because you deserve, as we all do, to die with dignity. You are one of the immortals, and when our time comes, we can only hope to receive the same treatment from our peers."

Gabriel took the sword from the executioner. He did not cover his head with a hood as was the custom. He would do this not as an anonymous tool but as himself. He swung the sword and severed Pyotr's head in one swift, sure stroke. He then summoned the fire and directed it to the shell of Pyotr's body. It ignited and became a caution to all who aspire to be gods.

Grace looked at Gabriel's blood-spattered body.

"How are you able to do that and live with yourself? Doesn't it take its toll on your soul?"

"I know you will never be able to truly understand the atrocities I was compelled to commit in my younger days as a vampire and how I can reconcile them to the man I am today. I have learned to separate myself from that time. I will admit that even though I did these things at the command of others, I reveled in the power. I had to be feared to be effective. Because of that fear, I was able to convince many to change their behavior to avoid execution. Those who refused, I was more than happy to dispatch. My reputation has allowed me to be a negotiator more often than an executioner. As for taking its toll, I am haunted by every death in which I had a part."

"Because of my past, I understand Pyotr. I too need to atone for some aspects of my life. I did not comply with his request because I hated him, I saw it as an act of compassion – one I hope will be extended to me when I tire of this existence."

Grace had tears in her eyes when she addressed him.

"I do not condemn you. I understand the overwhelming appetites of a newly created immortal. I share them now. I fear what Pyotr confessed about his disillusionment with life. Will that happen to us? Will we create inappropriate diversions, just to enjoy living again? I have discovered a rare power resides within me. Will I be tempted to misuse it?"

Gabriel brushed a tear from Grace's cheek and held her closely.

"I will never lose my joy in living as long as I have you. I believe we can provide the balance we both need to avoid Pyotr's temptation to 'be a god.' But when we tire of this existence, and we eventually will, I hope we will choose to leave it and move on to the next chapter together."

Epilogue

The Earth Mother breathed a sigh of relief – figuratively speaking. Once again, sanity had prevailed. Her beloved first children had made the right decision and averted a catastrophe. Not only had they refused to take a chance and use the limited information they had, but they had chosen to keep the greater secret safe from the rest of the Known World. Grace now knew the existence of the portal – the failsafe She had created if the extinction of her chosen was threatened. But the portal had another purpose, which only Grace knew.

Her people would never know that the Earth Mother was the Guardian. She had provided them with enough information to act on the hope of intervention by a higher power. She would never allow them certainty. Hope was all they needed. Had they called Her forth, She would have destroyed Her creation. It would have been a shame, but She had birthed one world, She could create another. Her song was never ending.

If She wanted, She could have seen this outcome. She chose to watch the drama unfold instead. There were infinite possibilities and unforeseen consequences for every decision. That was the joy of free will. Anticipation. Not all outcomes were good. Not all choices prudent. But that was Her plan. How boring eternity would be if there were no surprises. Watching Her creation mature and flourish had been the joy of the Earth Mother's existence. She refused to see how it would end. Fortunately, it was not going to be today.

The Earth Mother mourned the loss of mystery in the lives of Her people. Many believed that the pursuit of knowledge would be their salvation, not realizing that they already had everything they needed to thrive. The old stories and ancient lore contained the clues. Still, they had abandoned mystery for answers and provable outcomes. Only She knew they would eventually require Her knowledge, so She entrusted Her first children with the lore and the ability to understand it. She did not give them the full story, however, and complete understanding would be withheld until there was need of it.

But for now, the Earth Mother could return to Her eternal song knowing that there were still those who heard and cherished it.